WHO KILLED ALEX SCOTT?

SERENA SCOTT

The actor's screenwriter wife who readily admits to hating her husband?

DARIO MAURIN

The dashing Alex Scott look-alike who is scheduled for a minor role in Scott's next film?

LINETTE MURZEAU

The beautiful French girl who had a date with Scott shortly before his death?

TRISTAN MURZEAU

Linette's powerful, protective father?

JENNY CARSTAIRS

The mysterious woman who sent letters to Scott in California?

The PARIS PUZZLE

Vincent McConnor

An Inspector Damiot Mystery

BALLANTINE BOOKS • NEW YORK

The characters in this novel have not been derived from or suggested by any actual persons, living or dead, but are personal conceptions of the author.

The city of Paris is also a personal concept in the minds of millions.

Millions who were born there, have lived there, or have only visited, as well as countless others who have never seen Paris.

There is no one city of Paris, and each concept is different.

This puzzle contains some pieces of my Paris.

Published in the United States by Ballantine Books, a division of Random House, Inc., New York, and simultaneously in Canada by Random House of Canada Limited, Toronto.

Library of Congress Catalog Card Number: 81-14257

ISBN 0-345-30811-5

This edition published by arrangement with Macmillan Publishing Co., Inc.

Printed in Canada

First Ballantine Books Edition: March 1984

To the memory of
Nicholas Joy—
actor, gourmet, and dear friend—
who also loved Paris in the rain,
when he could find a taxi . . .

The PARIS PUZZLE

CHAPTER 1

PARIS WAS COLD AND UNINVITING.

Autumn rains had drenched the streets for two days, and the ancient buildings gave off a dank smell of wet stone and decay.

No traffic moved through rue de Caumartin, but cars had been parked for the night along the curbs on both sides.

Shop windows were iron-shuttered for the weekend, the apartments overhead curtained and dark. This was Sunday night and their occupants had retired early in anticipation of the week ahead.

One streetlamp glimmered faintly at a far corner, where headlights from an occasional car flashed past on the boulevards, its globe circled by a nimbus of haze.

A gray cat soggy with moisture crouched in a shallow entrance, out of the rain, its body a dark blur against the lighter gray of a marble doorstep. Only its eyes moved, turning in reaction to the sound of footsteps.

The figure of a man loomed out of the night, coming down the street past the dark theater, leather heels echoing on the pavement. He wore a hat, pulled down to keep the drizzle away from his eyes, his face a featureless blank under the brim. Both trouser legs were splashed with rain, and a light-colored raincoat was buttoned to the throat.

His breath shot out in ghostly spurts, exhaled in sudden gulps, as though he might be having difficulty breathing.

He held his body curiously straight, his legs moving swiftly and feet stepping cautiously, although there was no ice on the pavement.

The cat's eyes turned slowly as the stranger passed, observing him, then it lowered its damp head and settled down for the night.

No one else watched as the man swayed slightly, then straightened again and went on, even more carefully, toward the distant streetlamp.

Another few steps, then he wavered and changed direction, moving abruptly toward one of the dark shops.

Something was wrong with his legs.

He swayed again but reached out and steadied himself against the wooden door. He rested for a moment before pushing his body erect and continuing down the street.

Now he was hesitating unsteadily, every few steps, before lurching on. Still some distance from the lighted corner.

His knees buckled suddenly, but he managed to straighten and stumble on his way.

Each time this happened he appeared to freeze, mustering his strength, before lunging a few more steps.

His breath, coming from under the hat brim, was less visible, the spurts of gray fainter.

The man's right hand reached up and pressed the wet surface of the raincoat over his chest as though he might be having a heart attack.

His body stiffened, in reaction to the pain, and his left hand reached out blindly for support from something—anything—but found nothing.

He moaned softly, his voice muffled by the storm.

The rain was clattering on some metal object overhead, and a cold wind from the north knifed through the street.

The man stumbled again, hands groping desperately for support.

He managed to find the hood of a car and leaned against it, body shuddering, his palms flat on the cold metallic surface.

Gasping for breath now. A cloud of vapor shooting out from his open mouth and masking his face.

His hands began to slide, slowly, down the wet metal.

He realized that he was falling and made a frantic effort to straighten, but only slipped farther.

His body suddenly collapsed and he pitched forward between two parked cars.

Nobody saw him fall.

The cat was asleep.

CHAPTER 2

FRIC-FRAC, AS ALWAYS, ENJOYED THE RAIN.

Damiot was not so happy.

His second-best hat, which hadn't dried from an earlier walk across the Pont Neuf for dinner at the Périgourdine, was getting soaked again, his raincoat glazed with rain.

The damp weather made his hip send out sharp twinges of pain. He wondered if the pin those surgeons had inserted more than two years ago could be rusting.

Fric-Frac's black curls were limp and bedraggled. When they returned to the hotel he would towel her dry. Nose to tail.

Meanwhile, she was enjoying her final stroll of the day. Stepping into every puddle. Pausing to piss at each favored spot—there were nine of them—her final effort, as usual, was on Quai du Marché-Neuf directly opposite the main entrance to the Préfecture.

Her performances had been observed from time to time by his associates and caused talk. All favorable.

They had followed this same route, morning and night, since he had moved into the Hôtel Dauphin. She had selected it that first day and never permitted him to vary, rain or shine, winter or summer.

They walked twice every day. Early in the morning after he finished a breakfast of croissant and black coffee—Fric-Frac accepting both crunchy ends of his fresh croissant—and last thing at night before they retired.

He gave the concierge a weekly pourboire to take her out, at the old man's convenience, in the middle of the day and early evening. Never asking where they went, certain that she would have introduced him, on their first walk together, to this same route.

When they left the hotel tonight, Fric-Frac pulling on her leash, she had led Damiot through Place Dauphine between the rows of bare chestnut trees—the grilles around the base of each tree overflowing with rain—straight across Place du Pont Neuf and past the statue of Henri IV on his gleaming wet bronze horse to the worn stone steps leading down to the Square du Vert Galant.

In good weather she ran down the steps and paid her respects to a huge poplar—rumored to have been planted when Henri himself had promenaded here with his mistresses—then along the narrow paths past the benches that in warm weather were occupied by young lovers or sleeping vagrants, then back up the steps, across Place du Pont Neuf again to the Quai des Orfèvres.

Tonight she hadn't cared to venture down into the empty park. Smart dog! She knew that whenever it rained, pebbles from the gravel paths would stick between the pads of her feet.

No one else was walking. Only people with dogs came out in such weather. Except, of course, criminal types. For them there would be business as usual. He hoped nobody was planning a murder tonight. . . .

After dinner he had read two of the magazines that had piled up during the Bertrand investigation, then dozed off until Fric-Frac wakened him, pawing at his dressing gown, telling him it was past time for her final walk of the day.

Damiot was depressed. It wasn't only the weather. Paris was like this most years in early November.

As he followed Fric-Frac along the quai, rain slanting under his hat brim from the north and wetting the left side of his face, he saw that the Rôtisserie Périgourdine on Place Saint-Michel had closed early. The restaurant had been pleasantly empty when he ate dinner. No tourists at this time of year, and most Parisians dined at home in such weather.

His dinner had cheered him up briefly, as he sat beside a window facing Nôtre-Dame. Curtains of rain gave the cathedral an eerie look, as though it were floating in the air.

He had ordered each course with extra care for his lonely celebration.

Today he was forty-six years old! Forty-six . . .

That was one of several things that had caused his depression.

Dinner had relaxed him—a good meal always did—helped him to forget this was his birthday and briefly pushed the Bertrand investigation out of his mind.

It had started with an order of portugaises and a glass of the house Chablis, followed by half a grilled chicken, crisp-skinned and sweet with herbs, accompanied by his birthday gift to himself, a bottle of Chambertin. He polished off the wine with a slice of Pont l'Évêque, avoiding dessert and finishing with black coffee and a glass of marc.

The Burgundy cost more than his dinner but had given him great pleasure.

He savored the entire meal again, start to finish, as they crossed Boulevard du Palais to the Quai de Marché-Neuf, continuing along the embankment.

Nobody had remembered his birthday. No one!

Last year Sophie had telephoned from Cannes to say that she'd been thinking about him all day. This year she hadn't bothered.

Probably because he didn't answer her last letter. So full of complaints—repeating old grievances and forgotten quarrels—there had been no point in replying. Her only good news was that she'd taken a job as vendeuse with some fancy boutique on the Croisette, earning her own living again, quickly adding that he should continue to send her monthly check because prices were getting higher every day. She was probably giving most of what he sent to her bitch of a mother.

They had been separated more than two years, and he was completely happy living alone in a hotel, with an occasional visit to one of the prostitutes he'd known before his marriage. They were older now and even more agreeable.

Fric-Frac yanked on her leash, and he saw that they had reached rue de la Cité, where they always crossed to the other side.

"All right, Madame. No traffic tonight. Go ahead." He followed her to the opposite corner and turned, past the heavy stone mass of the Préfecture, back toward their hotel.

Had Olympe thought about him today? She was the only

other person who knew this was his birthday. More than six months since he received a note, in her familiar childish handwriting, from his former mistress. Chère Olympe! She'd been singing *La Belle Hélène* with some second-rate opera company in the provinces and was motoring up to Paris for an audition at the Théâtre Mogador. He'd been in the middle of some investigation, working endless hours as usual, and once again hadn't bothered to answer. There was nothing about Olympe in the newspapers when that new opérette opened at the Mogador. She was always doing auditions, then screaming like a coloratura when she didn't get the job. Singers' lives were as desperate as the roles they sang on stage.

Sophie and Olympe!

He didn't miss either of them, not anymore.

Only today. His birthday . . .

Damiot glanced up at the main entrance to the Préfecture, its heavy wooden doors closed against the weather, as he followed Fric-Frac past. Sunday night was usually quiet here. The guard on duty inside would be snoring at this hour.

He always wondered if the Préfecture looked like this when Vidocq created the Brigade de la Sûreté. More than a hundred and fifty years ago.

Checking the window of his office, he saw that the curtain had been closed by the cleaners. Heat would be turned off for the weekend and his office would be as cold as the prisoners' cells at the far side of the ancient building.

Fric-Frac was trotting now, heading toward their hotel.

His inability to find the Bertrand murderer also contributed to his feeling of malaise tonight. Part of the reason for his failure was that nobody gave a damn about that old man. No one had cared while Bertrand was alive and nobody was interested in Bertrand dead.

Apparently he had no relatives, friends, or enemies.

Jacques Bertrand had for many years worked as an accountant for a manufacturer of cardboard boxes on Boulevard de Magenta.

When Damiot questioned his fellow employees he had met blank walls of indifference.

Bertrand's body was found in a side street between the small café where he ate dinner every night and the shabby building where he had lived. His home was one miserable room in the cramped apartment of an aged couple who occupied the kitchen and rented out their other rooms to anonymous people with no past and no foreseeable future.

Damiot hadn't been assigned to the case until several weeks after the murder, when his chief asked him to take over from the young detective who had been working on it without success.

He had known immediately that he would do no better because the case was hopeless. One of those that you realize from the start is doomed to remain unsolved.

When he showed a photograph of Bertrand to his neighbors they didn't recall ever having seen the old man.

His body in the picture taken by the police photographer looked as though he had curled up on the wet pavement for a nap, but there was a neat bullet hole in his head.

Bertrand had been a methodical type, even in death. His small room immaculate, everything in order. A few faded documents revealed nothing. No personal letters and not a single family photograph.

There must have been some tragedy, possibly during the Occupation years, which had turned this human being into a cipher. His family lost or killed. No one would ever know.

The old man's wallet had been missing, which suggested that the only motive for his killing had been robbery.

His murderer had to be one of those casual killers, unknown even to their victims, who had attacked Bertrand in the dark street and shot him when he attempted to resist.

Damiot's only other theory was that the dead man might have changed his name for some reason during the war years. Taken Bertrand's identity—whoever the original Bertrand might have been. Perhaps he'd been killed during the Occupation and this man had somehow found his papers. Maybe he had murdered Bertrand himself, and someone from the past had recognized him on the street, followed and shot him.

So many senseless murders in Paris these days! Too many guns passing from hand to hand . . .

The only way the Bertrand case might ever be solved would be if his killer boasted to some copain of girlfriend, who would repeat what he said to the police. Most criminals, fortunately, talked too much.

Or the killer would use his gun again and the bullet would be traced to the one removed from Bertrand's skull.

The chief had thanked him personally for trying to solve another hopeless puzzle, but too much time had been wasted on this one.

A thin dossier marked Jacques Bertrand was all that remained of the dead man, filed away in the depths of the Préfecture. It would remain there, forgotten, probably never to be opened again. Along with hundreds of others.

He wasn't sorry that the chief had halted the investigation.

There had been many such incompleted cases during his years with the police, and he resented his inability to solve every one of them.

He remembered some of the victims' names. Jean Chagot, Pierre Vallon, Dora Brunard . . .

At least he hadn't forgotten them.

Fric-Frac was moving faster now, tugging at her leash, as they came closer to Place Dauphine.

He followed her around the corner and across the wide end of the small triangular square toward his hotel.

As he peered through the rain he visualized François Villon running through here to escape the police. This had been the heart of Paris for centuries. Villon had lived here, on Île de la Cité, walked every street and alley. He imagined Vidocq pursuing the poet even though they had lived centuries apart. The most incredible criminal and the greatest detective! Rascals, both of them! They would surely have respected and even admired each other.

Damiot paused beneath the small glass and wrought-iron canopy, above the entrance—which offered no protection from the storm—as he pulled out his keys. Unlocked the glass-paneled door and pushed it open, dropping the leash so that Fric-Frac could run ahead. Swept off his hat and shook it to scatter some of the raindrops before following her inside, checking that the lock had caught before continuing toward the elevator.

The Hôtel Dauphin had no lobby, only a narrow marble-floored passage leading to an almost invisible registration desk.

To his left was the manager's office, closed at this hour, and on his right a waist-high wooden partition, topped by panels of etched glass that separated the entrance from a small public lounge.

Fric-Frac had vanished.

When Damiot turned the corner, past the desk where a shaded bulb cast a circle of light, he saw her seated facing the elevator.

"Good girl."

She wagged her tail in agreement.

Checking the mailboxes above the miniature switchboard, behind the desk, he saw tht his box was empty. Grâce à Dieu!

Continuing on, past the cul-de-sac of a hall that led to a narrow red-carpeted staircase behind the elevator, he pressed the button and heard the ancient machine clank in reluctant response before it started to descend.

He glanced into the dark lounge with its squat armchairs and clumsy sofas upholstered in brown plush. A carpet that might, long ago, have been tan and orange. It was possible to see traces of a pattern that had worn to a dirty brown. A few ugly prints on the walls, their colors faded, in cheap wooden frames.

The first time he came here was when a fellow detective had brought him into the lounge to discuss some long-forgotten case they were investigating. Years ago! It had always been a quiet haven for the overflow from the corridors of the Palais de Justice when attorneys needed to plan a new attack on some witness. They could talk here without fear of being overheard before adjourning to a nearby restaurant for lunch.

Damiot was aware of the protesting creaks from the approaching elevator.

Before the departure of his wife he had stayed here many times while working on important investigations. Instead of going home to their apartment, late at night, he would enjoy a hot tub and catch a few hours' sleep before hurrying back to his office. There were times when he had stayed for more than a week. Sophie never complained, although he knew she didn't approve of his absences. He always warned the hotel's téléphoniste and the night concierge to inform his wife whenever she phoned that he had just returned to the Préfecture, knowing she wouldn't call his office. Evenings when he was with his mistress he had always told Sophie he was spending the night here.

The elevator reached the ground floor with a final thud and series of rattles.

Fric-Frac stood on her hind legs, pawing the air.

"All right, Madame la Duchesse. We go upstairs." He swung the elevator door open and shoved back the metal grille with as faint a clatter as possible, in order not to rouse old Pierauld, who slept on a cot behind the switchboard.

Fric-Frac darted inside and sat, facing the door, as Damiot followed.

He closed the door and grille, then pushed the button for the fifth floor. The elevator gave an abrupt jerk, groaned, and started to rise. As the cage lifted, its creaking echoing through the silent corridors, Damiot considered the week ahead.

Pray God there would be a quiet period at the Préfecture. No new investigations for a while.

There were stacks of paper work waiting to be done—official forms to fill out, papers to be sorted, documents that must be studied and passed on to other departments—enough to keep him occupied for much more than a week. Officials to be consulted—he was involved in two murder trials that should get under way in another few months—endless typed pages of confessions to be read again, evidence that must be reexamined before he was called to give testimony in court.

He disliked those long days in crowded courtrooms, answering questions and testifying. His court appearances made him sweat like a second-rate actor.

Much rather work in the quiet of his office with its peaceful view of the Seine.

He hadn't spent a full day at his desk in months!

If this rain continued, he would be happy not to work outside.

In good weather those were his favorite times. Tracking clues through the Paris streets. Searching day and night for some elusive suspect.

But the city had changed. It wasn't only the new skyscrapers, which he loathed. Even the people seemed to be different. Parisians looked worried and unhappy. Everyone these days looked guilty.

The night streets were becoming more and more dangerous. Unsafe, even for a policeman. Too many people on drugs.

Or were his feelings a part of getting older? Forty-six!

He glanced down at Fric-Frac as the elevator cage gave one final lurch and clanked to a halt at the top floor.

She was standing up again, pawing to get out.

Damiot eased the metal grille back, then opened the wooden door.

Fric-Frac scampered down the long corridor, toward their room, trailing her leash on the worn strip of carpet.

He closed the grille as silently as possible and shut the heavy door before he followed, pulling his key ring out again and fumbling in the dim light from a single ceiling bulb to find his room key.

He wondered if Madame Lambord was alone in her suite at the other end of the corridor. Attractive woman. Much younger than her late husband, who had worn himself out restoring this hotel to the way it had been before the war. Yvonne Lambord was still a beauty and, like most young widows, eagerly available. One night he would invite her to dine with him at some restaurant. He would have done so long ago if she hadn't reminded him of his wife.

Fric-Frac was dancing in front of the last door, growling softly to make him hurry.

"Quiet, Madame. Consider our neighbors." He slipped his key into the lock and opened the door.

Fric-Frac bounced into the lighted room, shaking herself, sending drops of water spraying.

"Into the bath! Immédiatement! And sit there. Vite! Vite!"

She slunk into the dark bathroom and crouched forlornly on the white-tiled floor.

He followed, snapping the wall switch, resting his soaked hat on the edge of the porcelain tub, then removing his raincoat and easing it onto a plastic hanger in the shower.

Selecting a towel, he wrapped it around Fric-Frac and carried her back to the bed. He sat beside the squirming body and began to rub her dry.

She accepted this with mixed emotions, enjoying the brisk motion of the towel but protesting and kicking when it reached the intimate parts of her anatomy.

Damiot glanced around the room as he dried her soaked black curls.

Central heating was turned off at nine, but enough heat remained to keep the air warm until he could get into bed.

Rainy Sundays always made him drowsy, and tonight there would be no tossing and turning while he sorted through every detail of his current assignment. He had no assignment.

This hotel room wasn't too bad, or was he becoming accustomed to living here? Daily maid service, but he managed to keep everything nicely cluttered. The maid, unlike his wife, never complained.

His room was large and high-ceilinged, with a pair of windows overlooking Place Dauphine, dominated by an old-fashioned wooden bed that had a towering carved headboard.

Not much here from his old apartment.

Sophie had taken most of their possessions—all the valuable ones—when she moved back to live with her mother, Madame Fromont, in Cannes. The pair of antique rosewood chairs they had discovered before their marriage and bought for their small salon; the new white and gold double bed from Au Printemps, along with that antique bookcase that had been a wedding present from his mother-in-law. Sophie had taken all of those to Cannes, where they would have long since become a part of the old woman's apartment. Assimilated and forgotten.

He had brought one comfortable chair from their apartment. His favorite chair. Sophie hadn't wanted that, and now it was Fric-Frac's chair. His small black-and-white television set, on top of his record player. His collection of discs, mostly Bach, Offenbach, and Yves Montand.

As he continued to towel Fric-Frac, he glanced toward the shelves of books. Dozens of volumes on his native Provence, which he had picked up in secondhand shops. Two shelves held a collection of books on crime and criminal psychology—several about his idol, Vidocq, the world's first detective—another three shelves of romans policiers, at least half of them by Simenon. His books filled a pair of old bookcases the hotel had produced from its cellars when his friend, the manager, saw the cardboard boxes overflowing with books as he moved in.

The pictures on the walls, with two exceptions, had come

from his apartment. Old prints of Paris streets he had picked up from stalls on the Left Bank. Sophie hadn't wanted those, only the hideous oil painting of roses that had hung in their dining room and the flower prints she had bought for her kitchen. She was welcome to all of them.

Since moving here he had added two new pictures. Large and handsomely framed reproductions from that print shop near the Opéra. A Lautrec lithograph of whores in a café and a large Cézanne landscape. They recalled two of his most important investigations. People he had known. Living and dead.

The Cézanne with its golden greens also reminded him of Provence.

He realized that Fric-Frac was almost dry and, after one final flourish of the towel, he released her.

She immediately scampered around him on the bedspread, jumped to the floor, and dashed back and forth across the room. Underneath the bed, onto a chair, into the bath and out again. Happy to be dry. Although, if this rain continued, she would get soaked again tomorrow.

He carried his damp towel into the bath, leaning down to mop the puddle she had left on the tiles, before draping it over the tub to dry.

Fric-Frac continued to race around him in circles, barking and nipping at his ankles, while he prepared for bed.

"Settle down, Madame. Time to sleep." He pointed toward the big yellow pillow on the floor, in a corner where no drafts could reach her from door or window. "Get to bed!"

She stepped onto her pillow, circling several times, digging into it as though arranging a nest for the night, before settling down, both paws tucked beneath her small body.

Damiot covered her with an old sweater and watched her adjust it, more to her liking, pulling it into place with her teeth as he undressed.

When he took off his wet shoes he discovered that his socks were damp and there was a large hole exposing his left big toe. He pulled off both socks and tossed them into the wastebasket as he went into the bath. Sophie would have screamed and rescued them, but he hated to wear darned socks and never did anymore.

Fric-Frac stayed on her pillow when he got into bed and wouldn't move while he read. Before he turned off the light she would be asleep, but in the morning he would find her snuggled against his bare chest and snoring. She always managed to slip under the covers during the night without waking him. In mid-winter her warm body would be pressed against his cold feet in the morning. Something his wife had never done.

He noticed the scales on the floor in the bath as he brushed his teeth and glared at them. He hadn't eaten anything rich for dinner. No dessert.

Maybe he'd weigh himself this week. Hadn't done that in more than a month. Must watch his weight now that he wasn't walking the streets every day investigating a murder.

Finished in the bath, he turned off the light but left the door open. He lighted his reading lamp on the bedside table before crossing to the corridor door, where he switched off the plastic-shaded bulb in the center of the ceiling. Circling the foot of his bed, he pulled back the heavy quilt. Climbed into the high bed, hip protesting, and stretched his legs out between the fresh sheets. Relaxed on his back, staring at the ceiling.

This rainy weather was depressing him more than usual.

No! That was because of his birthday. Forty-six! That's what was bothering him. Half his life gone. Quelle folie! He would never live to be ninety-two. Lucky, in his profession, to reach seventy. Or even sixty.

More than two-thirds of his life already over.

Mustn't think of that or he would never get to sleep.

Glancing at the bed table, he noticed the portable radio and pile of magazines next to his electric clock. No radio or magazine tonight. Much too tired.

Reaching out, he snapped off the reading lamp.

Punched the bolster under his head and, as was his habit, turned onto his right side before settling down for the night.

In the dark he heard the rain rattling against his windows.

No sounds from the adjoining room. The manager never put anyone in there unless the hotel was crowded. This was a corner of the building, with only one room adjoining his. The fourth wall, facing the Palais de Justice, had no windows.

Most of the guests on this floor were permanent. Some had

lived here for years. Middle-aged—department heads and executives of small companies within walking distance of their offices—mostly widows and widowers with a few who had never married, whose salaries made it possible for them to live in a hotel. Of course, like him, they were given a monthly rate.

During the week the lower floor had transients, in and out, especially when the courts were in session. Witnesses who came from the suburbs or the provinces. Lawyers and detectives in Paris to defend a client or give evidence. As well as some who lived in the city but required a room for the night, as he had done many times in the past.

Tourists rarely discovered the Hôtel Dauphin. For that matter you only saw foreign visitors in Place Dauphine during the summer.

He realized that he was getting drowsy. Tonight he would sleep. Another few minutes and . . .

The telephone shrilled near his head on the bedside table.

"Merde!"

Fric-Frac growled.

Damiot reached out, wide awake, and snatched up the phone before it rang again. "Damiot speaking."

"Hope I didn't wake you, M'sieur l'Inspecteur."

He recognized Chamard's voice; he was one of the night operators at the Préfecture. "I wasn't asleep."

"Sorry I had to call, but the chief gave orders that—"

"Just tell me what it is."

"Report came in ten minutes ago. Policeman found a body. Could be murder."

Damiot remained silent as the familiar word vibrated in his ear.

". . . cause of death unknown."

"Sex?"

"Male."

"Where was the body found?"

"In the street."

"This street has a name?" Damiot snapped.

"Rue de Caumartin. Near Boulevard des Capucines where it joins Boulevard de la Madeleine."

"I know the corner. Call Graudin. Tell him to meet me there."

"Right away, M'sieur l'Inspecteur."

"And send a car for me. Ten minutes." He fumbled the phone back onto its cradle, reluctant to switch on the light.

One word continued to echo in the darkness.

Murder.

THE POLICEMAN STANDING NEAR THE CORNER STREETLAMP, his water-proof cape glistening with rain, recognized Damiot and waved his car into the side street.

Damiot saw a bright glare of light as his driver, Risard, turned up rue de Caumartin. Several other police cars blocked the street, and a windowless van from the Institut Médico-Légal was waiting, as usual, to remove the body.

As the car slowed to a stop, Damiot saw that his assistant, Graudin, was already on the scene. The young detective's skinny figure towered above a dark clot of men silhouetted against the headlights of the parked cars.

Damiot got out into driving rain and walked toward them. He recognized the familiar cast of police officials. Sauger, an old acquaintance from the public prosecutor's office, beside a heavy-set man holding an umbrella whom he remembered as a local superintendent from this, the 9th arrondissement. Dr. Allanic, with his black leather satchel, talking to Paupardin, the examining magistrate's clerk. Two ambulance men in hooded white raincoats, one grasping the upright poles of a rubber stretcher. A police photographer, shielding a camera under his duffle coat. Several faces he didn't know.

Graudin, sensing Damiot's presence, as frequently happened at such moments, looked around and grinned. "M'sieur l'Inspecteur! Only just got here myself."

Some of the others turned.

"Ah, Damiot!" Dr. Allanic exclaimed, his voice hoarse. "Been waiting for you. Suggested they call you when I saw the cadaver."

"What do we have here?"

The group of figures moved back, away from the rubber-sheeted thing on the pavement, which, wet with rain, gleamed like silver in the glare from the headlights.

One ambulance attendant, whose hands were free, stepped forward and whipped the rubber sheet away with a hollow crack of sound, sending a cascade of drops flying. Some of the group cursed and retreated.

As Damiot moved closer to view the body he was conscious of Graudin at his side.

The dead man was young and unexpectedly handsome. Not the sort usually found in a gutter. Lying on his back, between two parked cars, blue eyes staring into the rain, hat resting beside his head. As so many faces in death, this one appeared to be smiling.

"The idiot of a policeman who found him," Graudin was saying, keeping his voice low, "unfortunately turned the body over."

"The body was facedown?"

"That's correct, M'sieur l'Inspecteur," Sauger responded, crowding in with the others.

"Identification papers?"

"No papers and no wallet," Graudin answered. "His pockets were too soggy to check. The lab will have to dry them out."

"How long has he been lying here?"

"An hour, perhaps." Dr. Allanic edged closer, clutching his black valise, rain dripping from the brim of his hat. "More or less."

Damiot circled the body slowly in the narrow space between the cars, followed by Graudin. "Any sign of violence?"

"None," Allanic rasped. "When I arrived there was a trace of blood on the left side of his cheek, but the rain has washed it away."

Damiot stooped to peer at the face. "I see a little blood in the left corner of his mouth."

Allanic leaned down and pushed the upper lip back with a leather-gloved forefinger. "Probably from concussion. Although there's no sign of a blow on the head. No flesh wound of any kind. Even so, I've a strong feeling it's murder. That's why I had them send for you."

The photographer was taking pictures of the dead man's face.

Damiot saw perfect white teeth outlined by blood as a bright red thread moved down the cheek and was immediately washed away by the rain. The effect was startling.

"Good teeth," Graudin muttered.

"They're fake," Allanic wheezed, releasing the lip and straightening. "He's had expensive dental work."

The lip slowly covered the teeth again.

"You've examined him, Doctor?" Damiot asked.

"In this rain? Even more superficially than usual. I'm about to catch pneumonia standing here!"

"You think death was caused by a blow on the head?"

"Can't know cause of death until I perform an autopsy."

"Any chance of doing that tonight?"

Allanic looked horrified. "Sunday night?"

"Tomorrow then." Damiot studied the dead man's face, under its film of rain. His skin was deeply tanned, as though he had spent much time out of doors, but his clothes were not those of a workman. Curly black hair matted and clinging to the skull. "Looks young."

"Middle thirties, I'd say." Allanic sneezed, producing a crumpled handkerchief and blowing his nose.

Graudin moved closer. "Checked the label in his hat, another on the inside pocket of his raincoat. Both came from London."

Damiot saw that the hat, resting on the wet pavement, was soggy with rain. His eyes noted the open raincoat, tweed jacket, wet cravat, white shirt clinging to the muscular chest, sodden trousers, and heavy brown walking shoes. "His shoes also were bought in London. Can't mistake them. British and expensive."

"If he's English, and somebody important," Allanic rasped, the handkerchief still clutched in his black-gloved hand, "Monsieur le Directeur will be on the phone first thing tomorrow. And the British consulate!"

Damiot sighed. He saw the quiet week he had anticipated, working at his desk, ending before it started.

"Have you finished with the remains?" Allanic asked.

He nodded. "Nothing more I can do here. Let Graudin have the clothes when they're dried out. I'd like to look over them before they go to the lab. And give me a call, after you complete your autopsy."

"That'll be late morning." Allanic raised his voice to a harsh croak as he motioned for the attendants to remove the body. "You can have him, mes enfants. I'm going home to bed."

Damiot turned to Graudin. "Where's that policeman who found the body?"

"Somewhere out of the rain, probably waiting in a doorway. His name's Rispol. I'll find him." Graudin moved through the crowd, which had begun to break up.

Most of them were going toward their cars, but a few remained to watch the attendants arrange their stretcher on the pavement, heave the dead weight of the body onto the dark rectangle of wet rubber, and cover it again with the slippery rubber sheet.

Damiot wondered, as he always did at such moments, who this human being was and what could have led him to his death on this particular street. Had he arrived earlier today, by plane from London, to meet someone in Paris? Some criminal? Pray God this wouldn't be another murder involving narcotics.

What possible reason could have brought this young man here at this late hour? Had he lost his way, confused by the rain, turned off Boulevard de la Madeleine? Followed, perhaps, by a dark figure from the Paris night world? There might have been a large sum of money in the Englishman's missing wallet. Could it be as simple as that? Not likely.

He watched the attendants shove their covered stretcher into the van and slam the doors.

This man should have friends and relatives. People who would demand to know who had killed him. Not like Jacques Bertrand, who had no one to mourn for him or care that he had been murdered.

All the others were getting into cars now, eager to escape from the rain and return to their warm beds. The photographer rolled his motorcycle down the street, ahead of the black police cars. They moved silently, no sirens sounding to rouse people in their apartments above the dark shops.

Damiot nodded to Allanic as the police chauffeur backed the doctor's car down the street, followed, last of all, by the clumsy van. Now the only light came from the headlights of the two police cars that had brought him and Graudin here.

He waited until the dark bulk of the van turned the corner into Boulevard des Capucines before glancing around again.

Graudin waited on the sidewalk with a uniformed policeman.

As Damiot walked toward them he observed that the policeman was short and stocky, or did his rain cape make him appear small next to Graudin's lean height? He looked to be in his twenties—they were accepting them younger these days—with black eyebrows that seemed too large for his thin face. Shrewd eyes. At the moment they were impressed at meeting the famous Chief Inspector Damiot. "Rispol?"

He saluted awkwardly.

"You found the body?"

"Yes, M'sieur l'Inspecteur."

"Was he wearing his hat?"

"It had fallen off in the street."

"Probably as he collapsed between the cars. You turned him over?"

"I'm sorry, M'sieur l'Inspecteur. I—I thought . . ."

"That he was a Sunday-night drunk? I would've thought the same thing."

The policeman's face brightened, and he looked even younger.

"Impossible to examine him—find out if he was drunk or dead—unless you did. Was it you unbuttoned his raincoat?"

The policeman hesitated. "Yes, M'sieur l'Inspecteur."

"Check his heart?"

"Couldn't find it. That's when I knew."

"And his pockets?"

"Both pockets of the raincoat and all his jacket pockets. There was nothing. Except a pair of brown leather gloves."

"What did you do then?"

"None of the shops along here was open. So I ran back to Boulevard de la Madeleine where there's a public phone near the taxi stand. I called in and reported I'd found a dead man in rue de Caumartin. They instructed me to return and wait here until someone came."

"Did you notice anything unusual when you discovered the body or when you came back from your phone call?"

"Nothing, M'sieur l'Inspecteur."

"No cars through here? No pedestrians?"

"None. This street doesn't get much traffic after the theaters close. In good weather you'll have a few people hurrying home from work—waiters, mostly, who live near Gare Saint-Lazare—but in weather like this they take a bus. There was nobody tonight."

"Thank you, Rispol."

Rispol saluted again, this time with more confidence.

"Sergeant Graudin will contact you tomorrow, if you're needed."

"Yes, M'sieur l'Inspecteur. I'll be going off duty now."

"Wait in my car." Graudin pointed toward the waiting police cars. "I'll drop you off."

"Tell both drivers to switch off their headlights," Damiot ordered. "I want to see this street as the Englishman saw it."

"I'll tell them." Graudin led Rispol toward the cars.

Damiot waited until the four headlights went dark.

The street vanished behind a heavy black curtain. Impossible to see anything, parked cars or buildings.

He squeezed his eyes shut.

Heard the rain again. For the past few minutes he hadn't been aware of whether it was falling or not. Now there was a surge of sound. Heavy drops thudding on his hat. Striking like sharp pebbles against something metallic overhead. Waterspouts gurgling. Felt it on his chin and realized that the lower part of his jaw was wet and cold.

He opened his eyes and saw the weak glow of the streetlamp at the distant corner. Had the Englishman come from there or from the opposite end of the street? He looked up rue de Caumartin, past the dark theater, toward rue des Mathurins. Perhaps the dead man had been visiting someone in an apartment or hotel in that area.

But why was the Englishman walking? Most wealthy visitors owned cars. Or rented them.

Of course, he didn't know for a fact that he was English or wealthy! Jumping to conclusions again.

There had been no money in his pockets, but the dead man looked as though he would carry a large amount of cash. Rich people somehow always seemed different. They looked rich.

Englishmen usually carried fine leather wallets. If this man had one, it was probably already sold to someone in Pigalle.

Damiot noticed that the upstairs windows on both sides of the street, above the closed shops, were dark or curtained. The small apartments would be occupied by people who worked nearby.

This empty street was the last thing that Englishman had seen before he died.

Perhaps he'd been drinking. Stumbled in the rain. Turned an ankle on a loose stone and struck his head on a car as he went down.

But Dr. Allanic had found no evidence of a blow on the head. No flesh wound.

Tomorrow's autopsy would establish cause of death.

As Damiot walked toward the dark police cars, his hip throbbing again, he sensed a whisper of movement in the doorway of a shop.

Turning instantly, he saw a gray cat walking beside him, along the edge of a marble doorstep. The sinuous motion of the rain-soaked animal was unpleasantly like that of a rat.

Continuing on, he wondered if the cat had been here earlier? Had it watched the stranger die? Did it see a dark figure, stooping in the rain, emptying the dead man's pockets?

Many questions to be asked.

His work would begin tomorrow.

CHAPTER 4

MONDAY MORNING DAMIOT TRIED TO STUDY SOME OF THE documents stacked on his desk while waiting for the autopsy report from Dr. Allanic.

As he read the typed words, his mind kept returning to that body, last night, in rue de Caumartin.

Something curious there. Only a trickle of blood from a corner of the mouth. Yet the Englishman was dead.

There had been no urgent morning summons from the old man upstairs, which meant the British consulate hadn't been heard from. Of course, they knew nothing as yet about the death of one of their subjects. For that matter, Damiot didn't know for a fact that the dead man was English.

He felt irritable and out of sorts. This always happened when he had to wait for an autopsy report. His inability to get started promptly on an investigation—if this turned out to be murder—annoyed and frustrated him, gave him a feeling that evidence was vanishing or being destroyed. Important facts slipping away, never to be found.

And he was still recovering from the unpleasant trauma of his forty-sixth birthday.

Mon Dieu! He was in his forty-seventh year now.

He kept checking his wristwatch and, finally, just after ten-thirty, stamped twice on the button under his desk and returned the sheaf of documents to their proper piles. Have to read them again, more carefully.

There was a faint knock and Graudin came in, his carrot hair the only color in the room. "Better call Dr. Allanic. Find out when he expects to be finished."

"Yes, M'sieur l'Inspecteur."

"But, as usual, don't say anything to antagonize him." Damiot swiveled his chair as the door closed and glanced toward the rain-spattered window. The river was a ghostly smudge, and the buildings on the Left Bank were the same color as the sky, a dirty, smoky gray. He noticed that the cars crossing Pont Saint-Michel had turned on their headlights. They moved like disembodied yellow eyes.

Thank God none of the newspapers had been notified that an unidentified foreigner was found dead last night in a Paris street.

Another knock, sharper this time, made him turn his worn leather chair as Graudin hurried in, his long face even longer than usual.

"They've only just started the autopsy."

"What?"

"Dr. Allanic didn't come to work this morning. He's ill."

"He had a cold last night."

"His wife didn't notify anyone until after ten o'clock. Two of his assistants are performing the autopsy."

"One of them, I trust, will be young Bretty. How long will it take?"

"They didn't know. I said to call when they finish. Told them you're waiting."

"See if you can reach Madame Allanic for me." He sank back in his chair as Graudin withdrew.

Something always went wrong when Allanic was unable to do an autopsy.

He stared at the two framed pictures on the wall, above the hissing radiator. An engraving he had found in the flea market showing the Pont Saint-Michel from the other side of the river. The Seine was much wider in those days, and you could see the distant hills surrounding Paris. Near that was an old lithograph of his idol, Vidocq, which used to be hung in an upstairs corridor. He had lifted it from the wall and brought it down to his own office. Nobody had ever noticed or, probably, knew who it was, although the name—François Eugene Vidocq—was visible across the bottom.

The buzzer whirred under his desk.

Damiot snatched up the phone. "Yes, Graudin?"

"Madame Allanic's on line one. Says Dr. Allanic's asleep."

"Let me talk to her." He jabbed a button. "Bonjour, Madame."

"Ah, Inspector Damiot!"

"Sorry to hear about your husband."

"Unfortunately, Monsieur, he can't even come to the phone."

"I understand."

"The doctor had to be summoned in the night. He gave Honoré a powder for his fever and an injection to make him sleep."

"Even doctors have doctors, do they?"

"Honoré's a baby when he's ill. But don't tell him I said so!"

"No, Madame."

"Never treats himself. Always has me phone some specialist."

"I hope he'll be feeling much better."

"He shouldn't have gone out last night in all that rain. His cold was much worse when he returned home. I made him a hot toddy and tucked him into bed. Sorry I couldn't call in earlier this morning. Honoré slept until ten o'clock. When he woke he asked me at once to inform his office that somebody else would have to perform that autopsy he had scheduled."

"It's been taken care of."

"Honoré ate some breakfast and went right back to sleep."

"Please tell him when he wakes that I called. And everything's under control."

"I will, Monsieur Inspecteur."

"Au 'voir, Madame."

"Au 'voir."

He set the phone down and turned toward the window.

This weather would give anyone a cold. He was glad he didn't have to be out in it. Although, at the moment, his hip wasn't bothering him.

He observed a group of nuns carrying open black umbrellas, scurrying along the quai. Probably up from the country and on their way to Nôtre-Dame. He wondered if the wings of their headdresses would keep stiff in this weather and smiled, for the first time this morning, at the thought of those great white wings collapsing around their surprised pink faces before they reached the cathedral.

Maybe he should phone his hotel and tell the concierge not to bother walking Fric-Frac today. Always danger of her catching a cold or even pneumonia. Fortunately the heat would be on in their room, at least part of the day.

Nothing would happen here for another half hour. It would take them at least that long to complete their autopsy.

The morning was going to be a total waste.

He hoped the autopsy would show that the Englishman had died of natural causes. Then the dead man wouldn't be his problem.

Another knock. More urgent than the last.

He glanced around as Graudin appeared.

"Policeman Rispol's here."

"Rispol? Oh, yes! Last night. . . . Who sent for him?"

"Nobody. Says he knows the identity of that dead man on rue de Caumartin."

"Knows his name?"

"Didn't say. He wants to talk to you."

"All right." Damiot swiveled his chair as Rispol stepped into the muted gray light seeping from the window.

"Bonjour, M'sieur l'Inspecteur."

"Bonjour." This skinny youth bore little resemblance to the policeman he had met last night. "Come in!" He reached out and snapped on his desk lamp.

Rispol seemed even smaller out of uniform. Shorter and thinner. Wearing an old black leather jacket with dungarees tucked into worn boots. His black hair was long and glistened with rain.

"Sit down, sit down." Damiot motioned to a chair, aware that Graudin had closed the door but hadn't left. "You've identified that man you found last night?"

"I think so, M'sieur l'Inspecteur. In fact, I'm sure I have." He sat on the edge of the chair, fumbling inside his leather jacket. "I had a hunch last night I'd seen the guy somewhere."

"Why the devil didn't you say so?"

"Because I wasn't positive. And I couldn't remember where." He pulled out a crumpled newspaper clipping. "I've been told never to report anything to a superior unless I'm absolutely certain. And have some proof."

"That's wise most of the time, but there are other times when a small suspicion may lead to an important fact."

"I wasn't absolutely sure until this morning." He smoothed out the torn piece of newsprint as he explained. "My girlfriend always wakes ahead of me."

"Your mistress?"

"We've been together more than a year. She goes out, even in the rain, to get fresh croissants for breakfast and buy a morning paper. I didn't look at the paper today until I'd finished eating, and there was his picture! Not on the front page, but inside."

Damiot reached across his desk and took the clipping from Rispol's trembling fingers.

"That's when I remembered where I'd seen the guy before. Another picture in a newspaper. Last week."

The photograph showed a man and woman, half nude and kissing passionately, on a sandy beach. Photographed with both their faces turned toward the camera. No one ever kissed like that! Only in a Hollywood film.

He peered at the man's handsome face. Curly black hair. Muscular shoulders. The print was gray and smudged, but this was unmistakably the face of the dead man.

There was a caption underneath: "The young American stars, Alex Scott and Mara Varna, in a scene from the new film *Guessing Game*, at the Marignan."

". . . upset my coffee," Rispol was saying, "when I turned a page and there was his picture."

Damiot read the name aloud. "Alex Scott? Never heard of him."

"He's been in other American films. I haven't seen any of them, but I had a feeling last night that I'd seen his face somewhere recently and I was right! The other photograph last week showed him getting off a plane. Said he was here to make a film."

"But this man last night was British. The labels in his hat and raincoat came from London shops." Damiot picked up a small magnifying glass and held it over the actor's face, which only turned the picture into a blur of dots. "I can't be certain this is the same man."

"That's his face, M'sieur l'Inspecteur. I know it is!"

He handed the clipping to Graudin.

Graudin squinted at the picture and shrugged. "All Hollywood actors look alike to me."

Damiot scowled. "Film stars do travel all the time. He could have bought that hat and raincoat in London."

The phone rang on his desk.

Graudin handed the clipping back.

"Take that call here," Damiot ordered, glancing at the photograph again. "It may be the autopsy report."

Graudin pushed a button and picked up the phone. "Chief Inspector Damiot's office. Sergeant Graudin speaking."

Damiot stared at the young policeman. Was it possible that, by sheer luck, he had identified the dead man so quickly?

"It's Joffo in the lab," Graudin explained. "They just received a parcel from Médico-Légal."

"Parcel?"

"The dead man's belongings."

"But Dr. Allanic was to send that to me first." Damiot sighed. "Of course he wasn't in his office this morning to tell anyone. I wanted to look at that stuff myself, before anyone else. Eh bien! Tell Joffo to go over everything and let me know what he finds."

Graudin spoke into the phone again. "The inspector says to check everything. . . . No. There's no indication of murder, so this may not be a case for Chief Inspector Damiot, but even so, let him know if you turn up anything unusual. . . . What?" He looked at Damiot, then glanced at the young policeman as he continued to listen. "I'll tell him." He set the phone down. "Joffo called because he noticed something as they opened the parcel. The hat, shoes, and raincoat have London labels, but all the other items came from Beverly Hills in California."

"He is American!" Rispol jumped to his feet.

"So it would seem." Damiot rose from the desk. "You've done an excellent piece of work, young man. I'll see that your superiors in the 9th arrondissement hear about it. That's if your suspicions are confirmed and the dead man is actually this actor."

"Merci, M'sieur l'Inspecteur!" Rispol straightened, smiling.

Damiot thought for a moment that Rispol was about to salute. "But I must warn you . . ."

"Yes, M'sieur l'Inspecteur?"

"Repeat nothing that was said here this morning."

"Of course."

"Especially that the deceased may be this American actor."

"I understand."

"We must have positive identification before we can be certain. And if, as I hope, he died of natural causes, there will of course be no murder investigation. Meanwhile, the newspapers mustn't get wind of this. We'll be besieged by reporters when they learn an American film star has died in a Paris street. That must be avoided until cause of death is determined and the American authorities have been informed." He held out his hand. "You've done a good job. Coming here and telling me this."

"Merci, M'sieur l'Inspecteur." Rispol reached across the desk and shook hands as Graudin went toward the door.

"We'll meet again, I suspect."

"Yes, sir. I certainly hope so."

Graudin opened the door and led him out.

Damiot smiled. Better keep an eye on Rispol. With his sharp memory he might one day make a detective.

The phone rang on his desk, but he didn't move to answer it.

He'd never heard of this American actor, Alex Scott. But he hadn't seen many foreign films since his wife left him. Sophie was the one who liked Hollywood stars.

A sharp knock on the door and Graudin returned. "Dr. Allanic's assistant calling back."

Damiot snatched up the phone. "Damiot speaking."

"This is Bretty, M'sieur Inspecteur."

"Yes, Dr. Bretty?"

"We haven't completed that autopsy yet. May take another hour."

"What's holding you up?"

"We've found a knife wound in the back."

"One wound?" Damiot looked at Graudin as he listened to the precise voice in his ear.

"Didn't notice it at first because there was no blood on his clothing. The mouth of the wound had closed."

"What sort of knife?"

"Narrow blade, with a sharp point. I would guess a small stiletto or dagger. The wound's deep enough to reach an artery. That alone would be sufficient to cause massive internal bleeding. Our autopsy must now be much more extensive."

"Get back to me when you finish."

"I'll phone you before I make out the report."

"This one wound's enough to call it murder?"

"Absolutely. Even if we don't find anything else."

"I'll be waiting for your call." He put the phone down.

Graudin smiled. "So it's murder?"

"Why are you smiling?"

"Because you'll be in a better mood now. With a murder on our hands."

"Merde!" But he knew, of course, that Graudin was right.

CHAPTER 5

"YOU HAVE A GUEST HERE NAMED SCOTT?" DAMIOT asked. "An American actor, Alex Scott?"

"Scott?" The eyes of the sleek young desk clerk, recognizing trouble, darted from Damiot to Graudin as he grasped the edge of the reception desk, then back to Damiot. "Your name, Monsieur?"

"Damiot."

The eyes widened. "Damiot? Not . . ."

Damiot sighed. "Yes." His name was getting much too familiar.

"If this is a police matter . . ."

"It is."

". . . you'll have to speak with the manager." He escaped through an open door, partially hidden behind an enormous potted plant.

"Fancy place," Graudin whispered, peering around.

"Not so fancy as it used to be. This hotel was one of the best when I first came to Paris." Damiot's eyes swept across the spacious lobby. "Still expensive, I suppose, but not as modern as those new ones on the Right Bank. Always catered to rich foreigners."

"You've been here before?"

"Once. Looking for a rascal who preyed on rich American widows. Stole their jewels and took money from them. Unfortunately, he killed one. Pushed her off a hotel terrace in Monte Carlo. I still think it may have been an accident and he never meant to harm her. He had no previous record of violence."

"You caught him?"

"Upstairs. Living with his mistress in a suite of rooms on money he'd stolen from other women."

"Was he American?"

"He'd been using a Swiss passport, but it turned out he was British." His eyes continued to inspect the lobby. "This lobby hasn't changed since that other time I was here."

The mirrored lobby stretched away from the reception desk, between white marble columns supporting a ceiling of many-paned skylights. At the moment only a suspicion of daylight filtered from overhead, but there was a glow of shaded lamps on tables placed between comfortable sofas and chairs. Antique vitrines displayed bottles of perfume, scarves, and jewelry. Fresh flowers on each table with tall green plants in every nook and corner.

The chairs and sofas were unoccupied at this late morning hour.

"Chief Inspector Damiot?"

Turning, he faced a plump man with gray hair, standing behind the reception desk, wearing a dark gray suit, white shirt, carefully tied silver and gray cravat. "I'm Damiot. This is Sergeant Graudin."

"Sorry to keep you waiting. I was having a late breakfast." He extended his hand. "Claude Valentin, manager of the Hôtel du Pont."

Damiot grasped the soft hand briefly, found it slightly moist to his touch.

"My assistant mentioned something about the American, Monsieur Scott."

"Staying here, wasn't he? Alex Scott, the actor."

"Monsieur Scott arrived last Friday from Beverly Hills. He has been a guest with us three times before in the past year." Hesitating, as though anticipating unpleasant news. "I believe you just said he *was* staying here? Has something happened to Monsieur Scott?"

"He's dead."

"Mon Dieu!" The pink hands clutched each other, as though for mutual protection, on the rim of the desk. "You can't mean—he was . . ."

"Murdered." Damiot thought from the way Valentin's

eyelids flickered that he was about to collapse. "I learned from the American consulate he'd been staying here."

"How did he . . . die?"

"I can only tell you that his body was found last night in rue de Caumartin."

"At least it didn't happen in our hotel!"

"I wish to see his room. Examine any belongings."

"We're always happy to assist the police. I will personally take you up to Monsieur Scott's suite. Let me get a key." He turned to the rows of keys hanging on a rack and lifted one from its hook.

"While I'm upstairs, Sergeant Graudin will question your staff—those who came in contact with the deceased."

"My assistant will arrange for him to interview everyone." He snapped his fingers. "Paul?"

The desk clerk appeared, too quickly, from the inner office where he had obviously been listening.

"You heard? Monsieur Scott has been murdered! I'm going upstairs with Inspector Damiot, and you can assist Sergeant Graudin. Let him question anyone he wishes." Waving his hand, causing a copper disc with its embossed numeral to clink against the key. "This is my assistant, Paul Renant." He lifted a hinged section of the reception desk and edged through the narrow space to join Damiot. "And, Paul, I don't wish to be disturbed while I'm in Monsieur Scott's suite, unless it's urgent."

"I understand, Monsieur Valentin. If you'll step in here, Sergeant. You may wish to start with our téléphoniste."

Graudin went behind the reception desk and followed the assistant toward an inner door partially hidden behind an immense old-fashioned safe.

Damiot walked beside Valentin, past an impressive marble staircase toward an elevator that resembled a gilded birdcage.

"Have the newspapers been notified of Monsieur Scott's death?"

"That's being handled by the American consulate."

"Would it be possible, Monsieur Inspecteur, to avoid telling the press that Monsieur Scott was staying here?"

"I see no reason for the police to give out the name of this hotel, since he died in another arrondissement."

"Excellent! We've never had a scandal. Certainly no murder."

"Unfortunately, the reporters will learn where Monsieur Scott was staying from his consulate."

"Then we're in for it! Reporters!" He spat the word like an obscenity. "This lobby will swarm with them. I must alert my entire staff. Place guards at every entrance." He swung open the polished mahogany door of the elevator. "Permit me." He pushed the elaborate grille back and motioned for Damiot to precede him.

Damiot stepped inside, noticing the mirrored interior.

"Monsieur Scott is—was—on the top floor." Valentin closed the door and slid the grille shut. "Such a pleasant young man! Not at all like some of the types we get these days from Hollywood."

The massive elevator rose with a silken hum, as though it had been warned not to disturb the guests.

"This is the first time," Valentin continued, "the Hôtel du Pont has been involved with murder—even one that happened elsewhere."

"I believe there's been at least one other."

The manager looked startled. "What?"

"Happened in Monte Carlo, but I caught the murderer here."

"Did you? I had no idea! But then I've only been manager for three years. I certainly hope the newspapers won't dig that one up."

"No reason why they should."

"Reporters will do anything to make a story sensational. I most certainly wouldn't want us to be identified with two murders. Even if they didn't happen on the premises. Here we are!"

Damiot realized that the elevator had stopped.

The manager thrust back the grille and pushed the door open. "After you, Monsieur Inspecteur."

Damiot stepped out into a wide corridor extending through the heart of the hotel. Cream-colored walls and an immaculate carpet patterned with large red and white roses. He was aware of the manager, behind him, closing the elevator door.

"We go this way." Valentin trotted beside him, toward a pair of windows at the end of the corridor. "Most of our California guests prefer a suite on the top floor. They like the view, the fresh air and sunshine. Although we haven't seen any sun for several days." He paused before the final pair of paneled doors, inserting his key into the lock.

Damiot glimpsed the distant Seine through the windows, beyond a gray confusion of church spires that must have been at least a block away. Impossible to judge distance because everything was flattened by the rain.

"Monsieur Inspecteur? Please . . ."

Damiot turned to see that the manager had opened one of the doors and was gesturing for him to enter.

Valentin led the way through a shallow foyer and, swinging open another pair of doors, into a spacious salon that had a row of windows in an alcove with a view across the street of endless rooftops gleaming black in the rain.

Crossing toward the windows, Damiot saw that the sky was churning with more clouds. Peering through the angled end window, facing the river, he glampsed a distant bridge—the old Pont Royal—but the other bank of the Seine was blotted out by the storm. Looking down, directly below, he recognized the corner where rue de Verneuil crossed rue du Bac. He moved away from the window, turning to inspect the salon.

Valentin snapped a wall switch, lighting several shaded lamps.

Damiot hesitated, glancing around, conscious of the warm air. These deluxe hotels kept their heat on all day.

The salon was like a window display for some expensive shop. Copies of antique furniture, the wood finished to make it appear old. Sofas with narrow yellow stripes on white satin, pillows carefully arranged so you would think twice before moving one. A large television set. No pictures on the walls, but drooping flowers in bowls and vases—yellow roses and some kind of white flower he didn't recognize. The heat had killed all of them. The only signs of occupancy were three shiny new magazines—*Time*, *Esquire*, and *Playboy*—someone had left spread out on a low table. He glanced at Valentin. "It's as though nobody's been staying here."

"It's always that way in these suites. Unless there's been a party the night before. Then you'll find glasses and remnants of food next morning. The bedroom, however, is a different story. Everything upside down!"

"I'll have a look." Damiot went toward an inner pair of doors, opened one, and entered the dark bedroom.

"Permit me." The manager clicked another switch.

Table lamps came alive, and a small chandelier above the center of the room cast splinters of light across a huge bed that had convenient shelves instead of a headboard.

Damiot saw that the bed had been turned down. The maid would have done that last night, but Scott had never come back. Hesitating at the foot of the bed, looking at everything, he was aware of the manager behind him.

Curtains in a bold pattern of purple and white leaves covered the windows. Heavy material that would keep out all light for late sleepers. Two comfortable bergères and a chaise upholstered in pale violet. A quilted white and purple spread on the bed. No pictures on the walls, but this room had certainly been occupied.

A sport shirt and two white dress shirts were flung across the back of the chaise. Two neckties draped over a bergère.

A small trunk, open and empty, its drawers pulled out. An enormous armoire, one door open, held jackets and topcoats on hangers. Trousers and slacks suspended from clip holders. Two hats on an overhead shelf. Four pieces of expensive luggage underneath, on the floor of the armoire, arranged in a neat row.

He had never seen such a wardrobe belonging to one man. Of course, this man was a Hollywood actor.

The top of a chest of drawers held an assortment of jewelry: two chains coiled like snakes, a bracelet, and several rings—all of heavy gold. Scattered as though they had meant nothing to their owner.

The shelves, at the head of the bed, held some American paperbacks and several bound manuscripts. Color photographs in two brown leather folders.

A crookneck reading lamp, chromium and white plastic, on the bedside table near a portable radio. White phone with a pad and slim gold pen.

Damiot went closer to read the words he glimpsed on the pad.

Scott's handwriting was more legible than most, bold and open with heavy downstrokes, revealing an extrovert.

> Call Serena—Saturday midnight
> Meet L after show Saturday
> Check with Tristan—time—Monday conference

Who were Serena and Tristan? Even more important, who was "L" and where did Scott meet "L" after a show Saturday night? Which show?

Better not mention any of this to the hotel manager.

"Something important?" Valentin asked, behind him.

He turned without answering. "This suite will have to be checked for prints."

"I understand, Monsieur Inspecteur."

Damiot removed his hat and raincoat, placing them on a glass-topped table as Valentin sank wearily onto a bergère near the bed table, as though he wanted to stay within reach of the phone.

Damiot moved around the other side of the bed, pulling out a clean handkerchief, folding it between thumb and fingers before reaching for one of the leather folders from the shelf.

It contained color photographs, one on each side, taken by an amateur photographer. Probably Scott himself.

Two small boys, posed together—one older than the other, handsome and well dressed—facing a picture of a young woman with brooding eyes and large mouth. Scott's wife and children? The boys resembled the dead actor. Black hair and blue eyes. The older one had his mother's mouth and chin. Something about the line of her jaw, as well as the firmly set lips, indicated that the lady had a will of her own. Her hair was auburn, and she wore an attractive pale green dress.

The phone shrilled in the silent room.

Damiot turned as Valentin reached to pick it up.

"This may be for you, Monsieur Inspecteur." He held the phone to his ear. "Yes? Valentin speaking."

Damiot replaced the leather folder on the shelf and picked up the other one.

It was a photograph of the actor with his wife on their wedding day, smiling as they posed in a sunny garden. The other half of the folder contained a photograph of a middle-aged man and woman in work clothes, standing in front of what appeared to be a farmhouse, shading their eyes from the sun and scowling. Could they be Scott's parents?

"Monsieur Inspecteur? Someone is asking for Monsieur Scott."

Damiot placed the leather folder back on the shelf and returned the handkerchief to his pocket. "Who is it?"

"A well-known film producer. Our téléphoniste tells me he has called twice this morning. It seems Monsieur Scott was to attend some sort of conference in his office."

"Name?"

"Murzeau—Tristan Murzeau."

"Where'd he get that name?" Damiot circled the bed to take the phone.

"I've read somewhere that he's Viennese."

"Put Monsieur Murzeau on." He handed the phone to Damiot.

"Yes, Monsieur?"

"Who is this?" The voice was a deep rumble, sharp with irritation.

"An associate of Monsieur Scott's."

"Where is that bastard? He was to contact me this morning to confirm what time he'd be available for a story conference."

"I'm afraid Monsieur Scott will not be available today."

"Not available! Lieber Gott! He's the one wanted changes in the script, not I! Both writers are waiting here in my office. When will that arrogant bastard condescend to see them, may I ask?"

"I couldn't say, Monsieur."

"We're in trouble before we start filming, if this is how he keeps appointments. Wer bist du?"

"What?"

"What did you say your name is?"

Damiot set the phone down without answering.

It rang again immediately.

He snatched it up. "Yes?"

"It's Graudin, downstairs. I've finished. Didn't learn much from the hotel staff."

"Better come up here. But first have headquarters send a man to check for prints. And a photographer."

"Right away."

He put the phone down again. "Tell me, Monsieur Valentin, anything you can about this American actor."

The manager straightened against the back of the bergère, arranging his hands more comfortably in his lap. "I suppose you mean anything . . . unusual I've noticed about Monsieur Scott."

"Anything at all you've observed."

"Nothing really out of the way. This is the fourth time he's stayed with us. First was a holiday last summer with his wife and two small sons. The second and third times, in August and September, he arrived alone. Told me Madame Scott was working on a film in California."

"An actress?"

"Oh, no! She writes screenplays as Serena Scott."

"Serena?" So Scott had called his wife Saturday night.

"She's quite well known, I'm told. Monsieur Scott was here, those last two times, on business—to discuss filming in France. Probably this film he's supposed to be making with Monsieur Murzeau."

"What about friends? Were they mostly French or American?"

"I've no idea. We don't check on our guests' private lives, unless there's something suspicious about them. Which, fortunately, rarely happens. There was never anything of that sort with Monsieur Scott."

"Women?"

Valentin shrugged. "I never saw any. There were, of course, the usual autograph seekers in our lobby, after some newspaper unfortunately mentioned he was staying here. Those wretched teenagers who turn up whenever there's a Hollywood personality in residence. Monsieur Scott avoided them by using our side entrance on rue de Verneuil. I can tell you, like most actors, he slept late every morning. Usually left the hotel around noon and seldom returned before evening. He went out most nights for dinner. If you wish to find out about his personal habits, here in the privacy of his suite, you'd better question the maids. They always know more about our guests than I. How many bodies occupy each bed." He pushed himself up from the chair. "I'll be in my office, Monsieur Inspecteur."

"A word of warning. Don't tell anyone—even your staff—that Monsieur Scott has been murdered."

"I understand."

"Not until it's in the newspapers."

"Après ça le déluge! I will prepare for the defense of the Hôtel du Pont." He headed toward the open door. "It will be chaos for our other guests. Total chaos!"

With the manager's departure, Damiot pulled a pair of gray silk gloves from a hip pocket, slipped them over his hands, and began a more thorough examination of the armoire. It always inhibited him when someone watched him at work. Even his assistants.

Opening the second door of the armoire he saw shelves holding neat piles of shirts, underwear, socks, and handkerchiefs. One shelf was stacked with folded sweaters. So the actor had come to Paris for a lengthy stay.

Turning his attention to the suits, checking each pocket, Damiot quickly discovered that Scott didn't smoke. No cigarettes, lighter, or matches, and his clothes held no scent of tobacco.

The pockets contained a small tin of French throat pastilles, some American coins, and several other meaningless objects, all of which he left where he had found them.

The luggage was unlocked and empty.

Behind the row of luggage, propped against the back of the armoire, was a slim attaché case. Brown leather with gold fittings and a steel lock.

He lifted it out and, resting it on a chair, snapped the catch. The attaché case fell open but, to his surprise, contained nothing.

Why would Scott hide this behind his other luggage? An attaché case was supposed to hold documents and papers. One usually left it on a convenient table. Unless, of course, it contained something of value.

He picked it up again, in both hands, jiggling it and judging the weight. Slightly heavier than he would have thought, and something seemed to be moving inside.

Holding it to his ear, he realized that the sound came from within the lid. He quickly discovered that one gold corner had a tiny steel hasp. He flipped it out with a fingernail, freeing some hidden mechanism that released the inner lining of the lid.

He spread the attaché case open again and found a zipper running along the edge of the lid under a leather flap. Zipped it open carefully, around three sides, and saw what was in the shallow hiding place.

Packages of new American money.

Damiot picked one up and counted ten hundred-dollar bills. One thousand dollars. And there were nine identical packages. Scott had brought nine thousand dollars in American money to France. Probably without declaring it.

He returned the package of money to its hiding place, closed the zipper, and laid the attaché case on the bed before moving on to inspect the open trunk. Its drawers had been emptied, except for one filled with glossy photographs of Alex Scott.

He picked up one of the pictures and studied Scott's face. The actor smiling, flashing those perfect teeth Allanic had said were fakes. There were several poses, each in a separate pile. The sort of pictures actors hand out to admirers—usually autographed—even French actors. These had not been signed.

Damiot put the smiling photograph back on its pile and selected a more serious pose. He took five copies and placed them on the bed. They would be useful tonight when he and his assistants walked the streets, starting in rue de Caumartin, hoping to discover where Alex Scott had spent the hours immediately prior to his death.

Moving around the bed again to the shelves overhead, parallel to the bolster, he saw that the paperbacks were American romans policiers, with gaudy covers, by writers whose names were unfamiliar. So the actor liked to read detective stories.

The bound manuscripts were, as he had guessed, shooting scripts. Same title on all three covers—*Paris Pursuit*—a different numeral on each. Must be three versions of the same script.

Tristan Murzeau Productions was printed at the bottom of each one.

A buzzer sounded in the salon.

Damiot turned, pulling off his silk gloves, crossed the bedroom, and went through the salon toward the dark entrance foyer. He rolled the gloves and slipped them into his pocket before opening one of the corridor doors.

Graudin stood there.

"Come in." Damiot turned back into the salon as Graudin closed the corridor door and followed. "Learn anything from the téléphoniste?"

"She remembers you from that other investigation."

"Does she?"

Graudin grinned. "Sends you her best."

"Attractive girl. Blond, and what a figure! She'd been a dancer at the Casino de Paris until she tripped down a flight of steps in the Métro. Injured her spine, never danced again. I asked her why she hadn't married, and she told me there were so many men around when she was a dancer that she never considered marriage. How does she look?"

"Dyed red hair. Fat."

Damiot sighed as he sat on the sofa. "Better take that coat off. It's warm in here."

"I've made a list of all the phone calls Scott put through the switchboard." Graudin produced a small pad before removing his hat and overcoat. He rested them on a chair, then sat awkwardly on a fauteuil facing Damiot with the pad in his hand.

"Did she have any information? The fat téléphoniste with dyed red hair?"

Graudin glanced at his pad. "The American arrived last Friday morning, and his first phone call was to Monsieur Murzeau, the man you spoke to earlier."

"He's a film producer."

"Most of the calls, in and out, were to and from Murzeau's office. I have his address. Avenue Champs-Élysées."

"I'll see Murzeau after we leave here. What else?"

"Several phone calls from reporters. Monsieur Scott talked to all of them. If he happened to be in."

"Any calls from women?"

"A few. But none of them left a name or any message. Monsieur Scott called two restaurants to make reservations for dinner. Friday night it was"—checked his notes—"a place called Tour d'Argent."

"All rich Americans go there!"

"And Saturday night it was a restaurant called Lasserre."

"Another five forks! Check both places. Find out if Scott dined alone or with someone."

"The téléphoniste wondered what happened to that man who killed the American widow. You traced him to this hotel. I told her I would ask you."

"He was a British citizen and he killed an American in Monte Carlo. There was a question of jurisdiction. France didn't want him, so he was shipped off to London. They had a trial, but the British don't like to hang people. Last I heard he was doing time for manslaughter." He glanced at the objects on the bed. "I've found something here. Hidden behind Scott's luggage—an attaché case with a secret compartment containing nine thousand dollars in American money. New hundred-dollar bills."

Graudin whistled softly.

"Scott had a wife named Serena and two small sons. He made one phone call to his wife in California."

"Saturday night. I have that on my list."

"He also went to a show that night. There's a note on the phone pad. And he planned to meet someone afterward."

"Man or woman?"

"The note only says 'Meet L after show Saturday.'"

"I've talked to the maid who takes care of this suite and the floor waiter. They didn't notice anything out of the way or odd. They say Monsieur Scott was always pleasant, and he tipped well."

"Wait a minute! Where did Scott eat dinner last night?"

"I asked that but nobody knew. Monsieur Renant, the assistant manager, saw him go out. Talked to him, but Monsieur Scott didn't mention where he was going. The téléphoniste says he didn't phone anywhere to reserve a table for dinner."

"Did the maid mention anything about women? Evidence of female visitors here in his suite?"

"She said there were no cigarettes with lipstick. In fact, no stubs in any of the ashtrays. Monsieur Scott apparently didn't smoke."

"I found that out."

"And no sign that anyone had been in bed with him. The concierge says Scott rented a car when he arrived, at the airport."

"Get the make and license number."

"I've already done that. It's a red Peugeot and—"

"Hold on! I've just realized—something important's missing."

Graudin looked puzzled.

"Call headquarters for me." He motioned toward the white phone between them on the low table. "I don't want to waste time with that téléphoniste downstairs. Get Joffo!"

"Right." Graudin picked up the phone.

Damiot heard him give the number, but he was preoccupied, furious with himself for not questioning Joffo when he called to say the lab had received that parcel from Médico-Légal with the American's belongings. He didn't know then, of course, that Scott had been stabbed.

"Here you are, M'sieur l'Inspecteur!"

He snatched the phone from Graudin's hand and held it to his ear. "Damiot speaking! Tell me, Joffo—that parcel of clothing . . ."

"We're still working on it."

"Didn't think you'd be through this fast. But you can tell me this—did that knife cut through all the clothing?"

"Knife?"

"In the back. Did it penetrate his raincoat? The tweed jacket, the shirt and undershirt?"

"There's no knife cut in anything."

"You're positive? Doctor Bretty says he was stabbed in the back."

"We found no cuts in any of the clothing."

"Check again. It was a narrow blade. Easy to overlook."

"Hold on, M'sieur l'Inspecteur."

Damiot glanced at Graudin as he waited, his mind racing. Joffo had missed those cuts because nobody told him to look for them. That sometimes happened.

Bretty hadn't noticed the wound at first during the autopsy, because it had closed. The knife was small, he'd said, but the would was deep enough to kill. So the cuts in the clothing could easily have been overlooked.

"M'sieur l'Inspecteur?"

"Yes, Joffo!"

"We've checked again."

"And?"

"No cuts in anything."

"Include that in your report. I'll get back to you later." He returned the phone to its cradle and looked at Graudin. "No cuts in anything!"

"So?"

"Scott was probably stabbed when he was nude."

CHAPTER 6

THE BROAD SLOPE OF THE CHAMPS-ELYSÉES WAS SILVER gray in the rain.

Graudin drove carefully, peering through the spattered windshield at the early-afternoon traffic, as they slowed across the Rond Point.

Damiot, seated beside him, noticed that the sidewalks were almost empty, but lights blazed above each cinema. He read the huge sign over the entrance to the Marignan:

ALEX SCOTT—MARA VARNA
GUESSING GAME

The actor's image would be flashing across the screen inside the theater, while his body was being cut and probed on an autopsy table.

Poor bastard! He had played his last role in films.

Scott's death would be reported in the evening editions of the Paris papers. A film star's murder would be flashed around the world by satellite along with reports of distant wars.

"Here's the address." Graudin swerved the black police car onto the parking strip and slowed to a stop.

"Wait for me." Damiot got out, slammed the door, and dashed across the rain-slicked pavement into the building.

The lobby was small and dark, walls sheathed in plastic panels of imitation marble.

He checked a framed listing of tenants and saw that Tristan Murzeau Productions was on the third floor.

An empty elevator took him upstairs to a bare corridor with

four doors. One held a plaque with Murzeau in large gilt letters.

Damiot entered a windowless waiting room filled with soft music.

The only light came from a stark modern lamp on a chromium desk, where a plump blond looked up reluctantly from a magazine. She stared at him as he crossed toward her, between rows of low chairs placed against dark gray walls hung with framed photographs of actresses. He noticed Signoret and Girardot. The women at the desk was older than he had expected a film producer's secretary would be, wearing an expensive suit and blouse, her face a petulant cosmetic mask.

She continued to stare as he came closer.

"I wish to see Monsieur Murzeau."

"I'm afraid he's eating lunch. You have an appointment, nein?"

Damiot brought out the new leather case that contained his badge and flipped it open. "This is a police matter."

The blue eyes widened under their false lashes, and the magazine dropped onto the desk. "One moment, Monsieur." Reaching for the phone, she pressed a button.

"I thought you said—"

"He's eating lunch in his office."

Damiot heard the faint rumble of a voice as he slipped the badge into his pocket again.

"Someone to see you, Herr Murzeau."

Another rumble from the voice.

"But he's a policeman!"

A brief rumble.

She set the phone down and looked up at Damiot. "He's in a horrible mood today. The door on your left." She flicked jeweled fingers toward a narrow passage beyond her desk.

"Merci, Mademoiselle." He raised his hat and, entering the dark passage, saw that it contained two doors. He knocked on the left one.

"Herein!" A man's voice from inside, sharp and harsh.

He opened the door into an expensively furnished office where a gaunt-faced man sat in a black leather chair behind an antique desk. A tall lamp, with an opaque shade, cast light onto a mass of papers, including a stack of cables and piles of film scripts. The man's back was turned to a row of windows framing a distant view of the Tour Eiffel, an unsubstantial gray ghost, beyond a mass of unfamiliar buildings. He was eating soup, slowly, from a Sèvres bowl that rested on the only uncluttered surface of his desk.

"Bitte!" A skeletal hand, fingers gleaming with diamonds, motioned toward a smaller brown leather chair.

Damiot sat down, removing his damp hat and resting it on the rug before unbuttoning his raincoat. "Sorry, Monsieur, to interrupt your lunch."

"My soup will cool, and I won't eat all of it. Which will please my stupid doctor." His deep rumbling voice belonged to a fat man.

Damiot saw that Murzeau had been eating the steaming soup with a heavy silver spoon. It was chicken and smelled delicious, reminding him that he hadn't gotten any lunch.

"Can I offer you some?"

"Non, merci."

"I bring it from home. My cook prepares it every morning. Always the same! Very dull, I can tell you. I am on a strict regimen. Paying for having dined too well for too many years. My doctor forbids me the Lucallan pleasures of the table. Especially your French cuisine! He has ordered me never to go out for lunch because I will eat too much."

Damiot realized that, as he spoke, Murzeau had been appraising him.

Now he set his spoon down. "So! You are from the police." The cold gray eyes became crafty. "What could the Paris police want with me?"

"I am Chief Inspector Damiot and I—"

"Ach! I've read about you in the press. There was one interview in which you confessed that you were a gourmet."

"I enjoy food. Yes."

"I, unfortunately, was a gourmand. Something quite different! And I am paying for it. Aren't you usually involved with murder?"

"Murder had become my métier."

"Including today?"

"Including today."

"Wunderbar! I have produced several films about murder." He snatched a napkin from his knee and patted at his mouth. "Whose murder brings you to see me?"

"I spoke to you an hour ago, when you phoned Monsieur Scott's suite at the Hôtel du Pont."

"And what, dare I ask, were you doing there? What's happened to—" He stopped abruptly. "Scott? He's not . . ."

"Last night."

"Murdered?"

"His body was found in rue de Caumartin."

"Mein Gott!" He pushed the soup bowl away as though he would never finish what was left. "And who, may I ask, killed him?"

"That's what I must find out."

"How was he killed? Nein! I suppose you aren't permitted to tell me the weapon."

"The American consulate will be releasing news of his death, but even they have not as yet been told the weapon."

"Jawohl, mein lieber Herr Inspecteur. I understand. So? What can I tell you?"

"First, I'd like to know when you last saw Monsieur Scott?"

"Late Saturday morning. He came here to discuss changes he wanted made in our shooting script. With a list of ideas his dear wife had been kind enough to suggest. Serena Scott's a top writer in Hollywood, and I was hoping she might do a final revision on this screenplay. Unfortunately, she has a project of her own at the moment. Alex promised to phone me today, let me know when he'd be free to meet the writers, here in my office. I rang his hotel twice when I didn't hear from him, and was informed he'd gone out."

"Did he mention when you saw him that he was going to the theater Saturday night?"

"Matter of fact he did. Said he was going to the Folies-Bergère."

"Say anything more about his plans for the weekend?"

"Nothing. I assumed, natürlich, he would be with friends."

"Scott had friends in Paris?"

Murzeau shrugged. "Handsome young actors usually have too many friends."

"Women friends?"

"I have never heard that Scott was not normal." He lowered his voice, confidentially. "On his first visit to Paris without his wife—this was in August—Alex was, I felt, somewhat too attentive to my youngest daughter. We, my wife and I, warned her to avoid Monsieur Scott in the future."

"You were planning to make a film with him?"

"Contracts were signed when he returned in September, and we hoped to start shooting next spring. A group of our investors will be arriving from Saudi Arabia tomorrow."

"Arab money?"

"They invest in everything! They're coming here to meet their American star—Scott—and all the young actresses involved in our production. Giving a press party at the Ritz to announce that Alex will star in their film. I must inform them immediately of this tragedy before they read about it in the press. Their party, of course, will have to be canceled." A crafty look came into his eyes. "Mein Gott! Nein! That party must still be held. This should bring much publicity. Every news story will say Alex was to have starred in *Paris Pursuit!* We must announce that there will be a worldwide search for another top star to replace him. Danke schön, mein lieber Herr Inspecteur! You have brought us a treasure. Millions of francs and dollars in free publicity. Pardon me one moment. I must contact the firm handling our public relations." He snatched up the phone, jabbed a button, and snapped orders in German.

Damiot had little knowledge of the language, understanding only a few words, but this gave him an opportunity to study Murzeau. Balding skull, sparsely covered with oily hair that was much too black. He had recently lost weight. There was a wattle of flesh under his chin, and the collar of his white shirt stood out at the back. His dark gray suit looked expensive, but the jacket hung loose from his shoulders.

Glancing around the office for the first time, Damiot noticed heavy antique furniture and a black leather sofa. Framed posters on the walls for recent films—he had seen one of them—with Tristan Murzeau Productions across the top of each in scarlet letters. The Murzeau film he had seen was a good one, but he couldn't recall its name.

The producer banged the phone down and faced him. "I've told my secretary to arrange a conference here this afternoon, with our press representative. Scott's death changes everything."

"What sort of man was Alex Scott? As a person, in his private life."

"Who can say? He was an actor, and every actor is a dozen different persons. I have not as yet worked with Herr Scott. This would have been our first film together."

"Did you ever hear him mention anyone whose first or last name began with the letter L—man or woman?"

Murzeau frowned. "I don't believe so. No."

"Scott left a note on a pad in his hotel room reminding him to meet L after some show Saturday night."

"Did he?"

"You tell me it was the Folies-Bergère." He realized that the shrewd gray eyes had sharpened. What was the man thinking? "Did Scott, to your knowledge, have any enemies?"

Murzeau shrugged. "Doesn't everyone? Alex seemed to be respected by people with whom he had worked. I've discussed him with actors and directors who were associated with him on various films. They all said he was cooperative. Never delayed production. That's important these days! You can't afford actors who hold up shooting schedules. Wait a moment!"

Damiot saw the crafty look reappear in his eyes.

"I've remembered something that could be important. There was a party when Scott was here in September. He had a quarrel with another actor."

"American actor?"

"French—Dario Maurin. Actually, he's half Italian."

"I've seen him in films."

"This was a small party at my apartment. I always like to have one before starting a new film project so that key people meet each other and, at the same time, I can observe them in a relaxed situation rather than here in my office. The director sees the actors I'm considering for various parts. My costume designer can observe them, watch them as they move about in a room, at ease, discuss color preferences with them. I also try to arrange for my cameraman to be present with as many of our creative staff as possible. Madame Murzeau, who used to be a film star in Vienna, enjoys giving these little affairs. Much is accomplished. I watch everyone and make final decisions.

Whether to use certain people or not. Of course they never suspect what I'm doing."

"And Scott quarreled with this actor, Maurin, at your party?"

"I, foolishly I suppose, invited Maurin, whom I'd talked to earlier for the part Scott had been signed to play. There was a reason I wanted Maurin there. I'd told him if I didn't hire him for the leading role, there was another part, almost as good, that he could have. He and Scott resembled each other. Enough for them to play cousins in the film. The director and I wanted to see them together. We both agreed after watching them that Maurin could play Scott's French cousin, but, unfortunately, something was said—I never learned precisely what it was—and Scott suddenly knocked Maurin down. Several people who crowded around them heard Maurin say 'I'll kill you!' as he got to his feet."

"I'd better have a talk with Monsieur Maurin. Find out what happened." He reached for his hat and pushed himself up from the chair.

"My secretary will have his address in her file as you leave."

"Was that all Maurin said? 'I'll kill you.' Nothing more?"

"Isn't that enough, Herr Inspecteur?"

A card tacked to the door had Dario Maurin hand-printed in sprawling letters.

Damiot knocked and waited but heard no sound from inside.

There wasn't any elevator, and he had been forced to climb four flights of steps. Between the exercise and this damp weather his hip was troubling him.

He'd come here before returning to his office, because when Murzeau's secretary gave him the address—rue Tronchet—he realized it wasn't far from the spot where the American actor's body had been found. A short street, running north behind the Madeleine, parallel to rue de Caumartin.

He knocked again. Harder this time, the sound echoing through the empty corridor.

Now there was a sound of shuffling feet behind the door. An old woman? Probably a servant.

"Who is it?" A female voice, but young.

"I'd like to see Monsieur Maurin."

"One moment."

A bolt slid back, and the door was opened by a blonde in a man's striped silk pajama jacket. Legs bare, her feet in leather sandals several sizes too large, which explained the shuffling.

He reached for his badge.

"Inspector Damiot? Please come in."

He was so startled by her recognition that he could only acknowledge his identity with a nod and pull his hand away from his pocket.

She smiled as she held the door back for him to enter. "Monsieur Murzeau's office phoned. Said you were coming here."

"Oh?" He removed his hat as he went inside. So Murzeau had called to warn Maurin. To give him time to plan an alibi for last night?

"Dario will be with you in a moment." She led him through a narrow passage into a chilly studio apartment. "I'm going to make coffee. Will you have some?"

"Non, merci. This should only take a moment."

"We slept late this morning."

He watched her cross the studio and go into what seemed to be a closet, but as light flashed on, he saw that it was a tiny kitchen. A ceiling light shone down on her long blonde hair as she moved about preparing breakfast.

Damiot stood in the center of the cold studio and glanced around. The large room was unreal, like a drafty stage set, with a flight of steps rising past a high studio window, through which he glimpsed rooftops but no recognizable landmarks because rain was blotting out the city.

The light coming through the window was so faint it made everything seem faded. All the furniture appeared to be old, probably secondhand. A small television set, portable radio, and record player with stacks of discs. Lurid theatrical posters and color photographs of actors hung on white plaster walls. A collection of objects—masks, puppets, swords, and fencing foils—spilled from shelves crammed with books. Rich fragments of cloth and glittering scarves tossed over chairs and tables. Colors were dulled by the diffused light, but the room had a gaudy gypsy character.

He wondered if the girl was Maurin's wife or only a companion for the night.

In the past he had found actors quick witted and difficult to interview. Always avoiding direct questions and slipping away from the facts.

Unless you could flatter their egos! Unfortunately, he didn't remember the names of Maurin's films. Even those he had seen.

"What a pleasure! The famous Inspector Damiot."

He looked up to see Maurin hurrying down the steps, wearing an expensive robe of quilted black satin with a high collar that framed his head.

"Monsieur Maurin?"

"In person, though only half awake." He came toward Damiot, smiling, hand extended.

Damiot observed, as Maurin crossed the studio, that his feet were bare and his pajama legs matched the blonde's jacket. Curly black hair glistening with pomade. So the actor had taken time to make himself presentable. He shook Maurin's hand briefly. "I would like to ask you several questions."

"All the questions you wish! Shall we sit over here?" He moved toward a group of low chairs near a stone fireplace that held ashes from a large fire. "Would you care for coffee, Monsieur Inspecteur?"

"Nothing." He realized as he sank down, resting his damp hat on the bare floor, that the chair was much too low for comfort, making his raincoat bunch up awkwardly around his knees. "I'm surprised Monsieur Murzeau would phone to tell you I was coming."

"Not Tristan! It was his secretary. Said you'd just left their office. I asked to speak to Tristan, but she said he was having a conference. He's always in conference. Mostly, I suspect, with himself!"

"She told you about the American actor? Scott."

"Only that he had died suddenly. She said last night."

"She didn't tell you he was murdered?"

"Murdered? Mon Dieu!" Maurin glanced toward the kitchen, but the blonde was busy, her back turned.

The actor's reaction, surprise and shock, appeared to be

genuine. "That's why I've come to see you, Monsieur. Scott died in the street, not far from here."

"Near here?"

"On rue de Caumartin."

Maurin fumbled in a pocket of his robe, brought out a package of Gauloises, and offered it to Damiot.

"I've given them up."

"So have I. Hundreds of times!" He laughed as he shook out a cigarette and produced a lighter from another pocket.

Damiot watched him light the cigarette, aware that the fingers holding the lighter were trembling slightly. "Tell me, Monsieur. Where were you last night? Between ten and midnight."

Maurin put his lighter away and exhaled a cloud of smoke before answering. "I was here. All evening."

"You didn't go out, at any time?"

"Not for five minutes. And there's a dozen people who can prove what I'm saying." He turned toward the kitchen. "Chérie?"

"Yes?" The blonde appeared in the kitchen doorway.

"Did I go out last night? Between ten and midnight."

"You said the weather was too miserable." Looking at Damiot. "Some friends dropped in, around nine, and stayed until two o'clock this morning. We didn't get to bed until after three."

"Who were these friends?"

"Actors with an assortment of wives and mistresses," Maurin answered. "I can give you a list of names and you can check with them."

"If you will, Monsieur." He was aware that the blonde had withdrawn into the kitchen again. "When Monsieur Scott was here, in September, you both attended a party at Monsieur Murzeau's apartment."

"Yes. We did." His answer was hesitant. "Tristan always gives a party when he's preparing a new film, so that everyone involved can meet casually. That way you don't see each other for the first time on the initial day of shooting when you have other things to worry about. Who told you about that party?"

"Monsieur Murzeau himself."

"Why would Tristan bring that up?"

"He said you and Scott quarreled at the party."

"I wouldn't call that a quarrel."

"Scott knocked you down."

"He was so fast I didn't have time to dodge."

"Several people apparently heard you threaten him. Say you would kill him."

"I was angry enough to do so at that moment, but believe me, I did not kill Alex Scott last night."

"What made you so angry at the party?"

"Something he said. You see, Monsieur Inspecteur, I'd been promised the leading role in *Paris Pursuit*—the part Scott signed for—but a group of Arabs backing the film wanted an American star to guarantee a large box office in the United States. Unfortunately, none of my films ever played there, so the American public doesn't know my work. Tristan promised I would have the second lead—Scott's half-brother—and I agreed. Scott was pleasant when we met at the party, even congratulated me, but then, later, he said, 'Keep out of my way in our scenes together. Don't try any tricks. Like stealing one of my scenes.' And I said, 'French actors don't need tricks. They can steal a scene from an American actor without trying.' He knocked me down. I was so startled I didn't say anything at first, but then, as I got up, I told him I would kill him in every scene. I meant, of course, kill him as an actor. Not physically."

"What did he say to that?"

"Nothing. He turned and walked away."

"Did you see Scott last week? After he returned to Paris."

"I've made no contact with him since Tristan's party in September. I swear that's the truth."

"How does his death affect the making of this film?"

"I've no idea. I heard last week from Tristan's secretary that the Arab money men were arriving and there would be some sort of press party to announce that Scott was to be starred and I would be featured. Tristan's looking for a new girl—preferably English or Italian—to play the female lead."

"Is there a chance the leading role might still go to you, now that Scott's not . . . available?"

Maurin looked surprised. "I hadn't thought of that. . . . C'est impossible! The money guys will continue to demand an American star to guarantee their international receipts. There's not a chance I would get it! In fact, Monsieur Inspecteur, this raises a frightening possibility. If they do find another American star and he looks nothing like me, I'll never be able to play the half-brother."

"I thought it was a cousin."

"You're supposed to think that at the start of the film, but at the end you discover they're half-brothers. It's a thriller, and there's an important trick of the plot that will not be revealed in any of the publicity. Which is why I had to look like the star. Makeup, of course, can help, but there must be a real resemblance. So! If the new American actor looks nothing like me, I won't get the part."

"You've signed a contract?"

"Only Scott had been given a contract. That's how much they wanted him."

"I understand." He saw the actor's handsome face was troubled by the anticipation of being replaced. "Maintenant! If you'll let me have that list of people who might give you an alibi for last night . . ."

"Certainly." Maurin picked up a pad and pencil from the table and began to write as he talked. "But I must tell you, Monsieur Inspecteur, I've never killed anyone. Never fired a gun. Except on stage or in a film."

"The American was stabbed." He said the final word softly, watching Maurin's reaction.

He looked up, slowly, from his pad. "Stabbed?"

"A small knife with a narrow blade." Damiot glanced around the studio. "You have swords and fencing foils here, but nothing like a dagger or a stiletto."

"These swords were theatrical props, years ago, in a production of *Cyrano*, and I have studied fencing. But I've never stabbed anyone, Monsieur Inspecteur." He calmly resumed his writing. "Never."

As Damiot pushed himself up awkwardly from the uncomfortable chair, he noticed the ashtrays overflowing with dead butts. Perhaps Maurin was telling the truth about not going out last night.

Or was he?

Maurin was, first of all, an actor. All theater was illusion and acting a form of lying. Actors were trained to lie in order to create illusion. They learned how to do it skillfully and believably.

Damiot stooped to pick up his hat.

Maurin ripped the page from the pad and got to his feet. "You don't think I killed Alex Scott?' He held out the list of names. "Do you?"

"I've no idea as yet who killed him." He took the list from the actor's still trembling fingers. "That's what I must find out."

CHAPTER 7

DAMIOT DRANK HIS FIRST PASTIS OF THE EVENING GRATEfully, at a table on the dimly lighted terrace of the Café de la Paix. This was a favorite winter spot, when there were no tourists, facing Boulevard des Capucines.

It had been a long day—still not finished—and he was weary.

Rain streamed down the wall of glass that in cold weather enclosed the café terrace from the public sidewalk.

He hadn't left the Préfecture until after six o'clock, when the radio in his office was predicting more bad weather tomorrow.

He'd taken a taxi back to the Champs-Élysées and seen perhaps an hour of the Scott film at the Marignan. Afterward he found another taxi to bring him here.

His hat was sticky against his forehead, his raincoat stank of wet rubber, and both trouser legs, as usual when it rained, felt uncomfortably heavy and damp. And his feet were cold.

Tonight he wanted to walk through rue de Caumartin, visualizing the way it had looked when Scott came stumbling through the rain last night.

He had told his two assistants, Graudin and young Merval, to meet him there at nine. They would cover the street, on both sides, looking for anyone who had seen the American.

But first he would have another pastis before going into the restaurant for dinner.

He glanced inside and saw that it was half empty. Waiters moving about, through a rosy glow of light, reflected in the tall mirrors.

Only four other people were seated at the small round tables on the shallow terrace—three men and a woman—nursing their drinks as though they didn't wish to venture out into the storm again.

Two men at one table, middle-aged and drinking whisky, discussing a business deal or, more likely, comparing their mistresses before going home to have dinner with their wives.

A young man was seated alone, with a beer he hadn't touched in several minutes, furtively glancing at the woman sipping a Pernod.

Plump and attractive, in her early thirties, wearing a smart tan raincoat, a varicolored scarf covering her hair, brown leather handbag resting on the table, and a tan silk umbrella propped against a chair. She might be a secretary from some nearby office, waiting for a dinner companion to show up, or a prostitute putting off, as long as possible, walking in the rain. She was aware that the young man was eyeing her.

As Damiot savored his pastis, beginning to feel the warmth from the nearest heater, he glanced toward the corner where the boulevard crossed Avenue de l'Opéra. No sign of life except for an occasional passing bus or taxi.

The American consulate had given out a press release on Scott's death, and early editions of the evening papers carried the first brief stories. Tomorrow they would have more complete reports, padding their few facts with biographies of the dead actor and publicity on his films.

After Damiot had returned to the Préfecture, from Maurin's apartment, there had been calls from several newspapers, but he had instructed Graudin to tell them he wouldn't be available until tomorrow. Unfortunately, they had been informed by the consulate that he was in charge of the Scott investigation. Tomorrow morning the corridors outside his office would be crowded with reporters. The murder of a cinema star was big news.

He began to sort out the few facts he had turned up today.

First Maurin. That quarrel at the Murzeau party.

Why did Murzeau tell him that Scott knocked Maurin down? And why would Murzeau's secretary phone Maurin to warn him that the police were coming to question him?

Was Maurin telling the truth about what had happened? For instance, what he had said to Scott at the party.

In the car, after leaving Maurin, Graudin had reported talking with the building's concierge while Damiot was upstairs. He had learned there was a second entrance to Maurin's apartment, a door in the bedroom that led to a corridor of the upper floor. Graudin had asked if Maurin had left the premises Sunday night, but the concierge couldn't say because he'd been watching television.

So Maurin could've gone upstairs and slipped out through that bedroom door while his friends were talking and drinking, left the building to meet Scott somewhere near rue de Caumartin.

He'd turned the list of names Maurin had given him over to Graudin for questioning, but he would talk to Murzeau's daughter himself.

Reports from the forensic lab and the coroner's office had been waiting on his desk.

He read the autopsy report first. They had found water in the actor's lungs, and the condition of his liver indicated Scott was a heavy drinker. Damiot had phoned Médico-Légal and questioned Dr. Bretty. "You're not saying Scott drowned? That water in his lungs . . ."

"No, M'sieur Inspecteur. He swallowed that when he fell face down in the gutter. The knife wound killed him before he could drown."

"And his liver?"

"Maladie de foie! Just like a Frenchman. Would've gotten him in five years or less if he'd continued drinking."

"Then cause of death was solely that stab wound?"

"Absolutely."

He had then read Joffo's neatly typed report from the forensic lab. They had turned up little of interest. Scott's pockets contained a gold chain with seven American keys, a man's white handkerchief, and a ticket stub for the Folies-Bergère dated Saturday night.

Which confirmed what Murzeau had told him.

Graudin had overlooked that ticket stub when he went through the dead man's pockets.

The Folies was on rue Richer, which became rue de Provence as it continued west. And rue de Provence crossed the northern end of rue de Caumartin. Had Scott gone to rue de

Caumartin Saturday night as well as Sunday? Did he meet L both nights?

Damiot had called Graudin in and given him a list of items that were missing. Scott's wallet and passport. Probably an expensive wristwatch. And the wallet would have contained credit cards and his identification papers. Americans never traveled without them. He instructed Graudin to get word to known informers and fences about all the missing items. Tell them the wallet probably contained a large amount of cash. The money would never be recovered, but the police wanted everything else. No questions asked.

Graudin had already sent out the license of Scott's rented car—which he'd obtained from the concierge at Hôtel du Pont—to every arrondissement. He'd also checked the two restaurants, Tour d'Argent and Lasserre, where the actor had dined Friday and Saturday evenings. Learned that he'd been alone both times.

Damiot had told him to find out what time Scott left the Folies-Bergère. Someone must've recognized him.

Much still to be done.

Something odd about those packages of new hundred-dollar bills . . .

Graudin had carried the attaché case with the hidden American money up to the lab when they returned to the Préfecture. There would be no report from that until tomorrow.

While Graudin was in the lab he had learned from the forensic boys that they had turned up nothing in Scott's hotel suite. Just the actor's prints and those of a maid who had cleaned there this morning.

The only positive fact in all this was that Scott had died as a result of that stab wound in his back.

But where was Scott last night, at the moment he was stabbed? Had he met Maurin in a café, then gone on alone to meet L in a nearby hotel room? That seemed more likely.

He couldn't have been stabbed in the street.

No cuts in his clothing. He must have been undressed when the killer lunged with his knife. The actor's back had to be turned.

Nude. In a hotel room.

A woman? It had to be a woman! A whore.

Scott could've known her since one of his previous visits to Paris. Those times when his wife wasn't with him.

He met her Sunday night and she took him to a hotel that rented rooms by the hour on their lower floors, no questions asked.

Afterward the woman had demanded too much money. They quarreled and Scott turned his back as he picked up his clothes to dress.

She brought out the knife from her purse and stabbed him.

The actor had managed to dress and leave the hotel. Reached rue de Caumartin before he collapsed.

That's how it must have happened.

Must keep this out of the papers, at least for the moment, while he looked for a prostitute who carried a knife in her purse.

A knife with a long narrow blade.

His attention was drawn to a taxi pulling in to the curb. A young man and a girl got out, happy looking in spite of the weather, laughing as they ran across the wet sidewalk to the protected terrace.

As his eyes followed them into the restaurant, he finished the last of his pastis.

The two middle-aged businessmen were still talking at their table, but the young man had moved over to sit with the woman.

Damiot smiled and faced the rain-swept boulevard again.

He had called his hotel before leaving the office and told the concierge not to walk Fric-Frac tonight. Just give her dinner from one of the cans of food piled on a shelf in the bath and she would sleep until he got there. He would walk her before going to bed. Maybe this rain would stop later tonight.

It had been strange seeing Scott's film at the Marignan. Not a very good film. Too much violence and too many ridiculous love scenes. The voices had been dubbed. All the actors, including Scott, spoke fluent French. That had disappointed him, because he had wanted to hear Scott talk. An actor's voice revealed much about him as a person. He had been aware as he watched Scott, in scene after scene, that this young man—slightly too handsome but vital and masculine—was at this moment in one of those refrigerated drawers, like something filed away, at the Institut Médico-Légal. He was aware of Scott's resemblance to Dario Maurin and could see why Murzeau wanted to cast them as cousins or half-brothers. The film had, finally, bored him, and he had come out from the almost empty theater into the cold reality of the driving rain.

He looked toward the entrance of the restaurant again, but there was no sign of his waiter.

A young woman in a faded duffle coat was standing in the doorway. She appeared to be in her late twenties. Not so well dressed as the woman drinking Pernod but more attractive. Face partially hidden by a hood that covered her hair and made her look like a tourist, American or English. She was staring at him.

He looked away, avoiding her eyes. She must have read about him in some newspaper and recognized him from a photograph. This was happening much too frequently these days.

There would be wine with dinner when he went inside but right now he needed another pastis.

This past year—especially since that Vermeer fric-frac on the Riviera that had caused international headlines—too many people were recognizing him. Some of the more sensational Paris papers went out of their way to print his photograph whenever one of their cameramen caught him off guard. It was getting to be annoying and eventually would cause him trouble. A policeman's face should never be familiar to the public.

The only good thing resulting from the publicity was that in recent months he seemed to have less trouble getting a good table in a restaurant. Which he rather liked.

"Inspector Damiot?" The question was whispered, barely audible.

He looked around, startled, to face the girl in the duffle coat. "Yes."

"I knew it was you, but I asked the waiter to be certain."

"Mademoiselle?" Raising his hat, which stuck momentarily to his forehead, he rose from the table.

"I've seen your picture many times, and I was reading, as I ate dinner, about the murder of that film actor." Holding up a newspaper in her mittened hand. "That you're in charge of the investigation. And now. . . . It's unreal! You sitting here."

"A favorite spot of mine, this terrace, at the end of the day. I can have a quiet drink. During the summer I like to watch the crowds passing, but when the tourist season ends I enjoy it even more."

"And I'm intruding! I am so sorry."

"Not at all, Mademoiselle. Won't you join me for a drink?"

"Thank you, no. I'm on my way to meet some friends."

He realized as she spoke that she was even prettier than she had seemed from a distance. Blue eyes, sensuous mouth. Impossible to see what she was wearing because the wretched duffle coat covered her body and he couldn't tell whether she was slim or plump and her legs were hidden by slacks tucked into boots. An expensive brown leather bag hung from her left shoulder. "One drink, Mademoiselle? Surely you could spare time for that. Perhaps a glass of champagne? Have pity on a lonely detective."

"The famous Inspector Damiot is lonely? I can't believe that!" She hesitated, smiling like a child who hopes to be coaxed.

"One drink?"

"Eh bien! My friends can wait." She dropped her newspaper on the table as she sank onto a chair, resting her shoulder bag beside the newspaper. "I'd love to have a drink with you."

Damiot sat facing her, amused and interested, placing his hat on a chair.

"But no champagne! I'll have what I was drinking with dinner, if I may. A glass of Chablis." She smiled. "I saw you observing these other people just now."

"Was I? That becomes a habit if you're a policeman. Even when I'm not working. Although, I suppose, I'm never really off duty."

"I've often wondered. Does a detective keep regular hours? Nine to five?"

"Certainly not! I frequently work all night. And this may be one of those nights. However, I didn't stop for any lunch, so I'm going to allow myself a good dinner before I meet two of my assistants on rue de Caumartin and try to find out how that American actor met his death last night."

"How exciting!" She pulled off her mittens and set them on top of the newspaper.

"Something more, M'sieur l'Inspecteur?"

Damiot looked up to see his waiter. "A glass of Chablis for Mademoiselle and another pastis for me."

The waiter smiled slyly and returned inside.

"I haven't told you my name!"

"No, Mademoiselle. You haven't."

"It's Andrea."

"Andrea?"

"Andrea Brandon."

"And you're American."

"So my accent still gives me away!"

"Your accent is charming and your French excellent. How long have you been in Paris?"

"Almost three years. But I'm still trying to improve my French."

"You're studying?"

"Not any more. I took French lessons when I first arrived, then I taught English to make a little money and had some courses in French literature at the Sorbonne." She unfastened the top button of her duffel coat as she talked and shook the hood away from her head. "That was during my first year in Paris."

He watched as the hood dropped back and a silken curtain of hair fell to her shoulders. It was long and straight and white-blond. Without the hood to hide her cheeks, he saw that she was extremely pretty. Delicate, barely visible blond eyebrows, pert nose, a mouth that was sensitive as well as sensuous. But the blue eyes were wary, as though there might be something in the past that made her timid with strangers. "And what are you doing now? Your third year in Paris."

"I've created a marvelous kind of job for myself. I apartment-sit!"

"Apartment-sit?"

"It's been done a lot back home, of course, but I discovered that nobody was doing it here—as a legitimate business, I mean—until I began to run little ads in the Paris *Tribune*."

He was aware of the waiter serving their drinks as she talked, but didn't take his eyes from her lovely face.

"You may have seen them. Always the same—'Let me sit in your charming house or apartment while you're away'—then it says 'American girl of taste and impeccable background will apartment-sit while you scarp on a Himalaya or laze on a Seychelle. Infinitesimally small fee. Minimum period four months.' Then there's a phone number where people can reach me."

"This pays you?"

"Extremely well! I live in a style I couldn't afford on my own. My fee gets higher as more people recommend me to their friends. At the moment, I'm sitting a lovely pied-à-terre, not far from here, with a maid who comes in to clean. The people who own the apartment have a villa in Mexico where they spend every winter. Their Paris apartment has three bedrooms. So I change beds every week!"

He laughed as he raised his glass of pastis. "Santé, Mademoiselle!"

She picked up her wineglass. "Santé, Monsieur!"

They drank, eyeing each other expectantly.

Andrea spoke first. "You probably think I'm one of those forward Americans. Terribly pushy and rude."

"Certainly not!"

"Coming to your table and striking up a conversation."

"I'm delighted you did."

"Lots of people do, I suppose. And ask for your autograph."

"I am not a cinéma star, Mademoiselle. Only a policeman."

"I've never heard of any detective in New York as famous as you. And I read all the crime news back home in the newspapers and magazines."

"Do you?"

"Been reading detective novels since I was a toddler!"

"We call them romans policiers."

"I know you do. My father passed them on to me. After he'd read them. He said novels of detection were a true reflection of modern life."

"I also read them. Like most other detectives."

"Do they really?"

"Your family lives in New York?"

"My mother is dead. Killed years ago in an accident." Her

face became solemn. "And my father has remarried. Twice. That's why I came to France, I suppose, to escape from the past. Get away from unpleasant memories."

"Have you succeeded?"

"Not really. No."

"No one ever does. Memories follow us. We drag them along, unfortunately, wherever we go."

"I've certainly found that out. You have a family, Monsieur?"

"Not any more."

"But I read somewhere that you were married."

"We've separated."

"Oh."

"Both my parents are dead and, to my knowledge, I have no other relatives."

"You were born in Provence?"

Damiot laughed. "Yes, I come from Provence."

"I've heard that the Provençal cuisine is terrific!"

"I think so."

"One of the newspapers called you 'the gourmet detective.' Someday I hope to drive through every province of France. Eat all the different cuisines."

"Take secondary roads and avoid the main highways. Then you'll see the real France."

"I'll drive only a short distance each morning to the next stop. Have lunch in some enchanting country inn, then continue on for a few hours until I find a wonderful restaurant for dinner. Stay the night, then set out again next morning. That way I'll learn firsthand about real French cooking!"

"You have a car?"

"A beat-up old Volkswagen. A friend gave it to me last year when he had to fly back to New York because of illness in his family. I dream of driving through each province, preferably in the spring, when there won't be many tourists on the road. Everyone tells me it would be dangerous, traveling alone. Do you agree, Monsieur Inspecteur?"

"It's always dangerous for a young woman alone. So many unexpected things can happen. Especially with an old car."

"I can change tires if I get a flat. My father made me learn to take care of my car when I was a teenager. Pull the motor apart and put it together again."

As she talked, looking much too fragile to know anything about motors, Damiot remembered something he'd wanted to do for years. He had suggested the idea to his wife many times, but Sophie wanted no part of such an experiment. Perhaps this American girl might be interested.

". . . heard about girls stranded in the Alpes-Maritimes when their cars break down. Far from any village. I've been told that women alone are turned away from many hotels and inns."

"They'd rather keep their rooms empty on the chance that a couple will turn up and, of course, pay more for a night's lodging. As you've been talking, I've thought of something!"

"Yes, Monsieur Inspecteur?"

"First of all, it would take weeks of driving for you to visit all the provinces of France. But I can suggest another sort of tour for you. One you could make at your leisure. Visit each French province without leaving Paris!"

"Not leaving Paris?"

"There are restaurants here with chefs from every department of France. You could eat in a different one each week and it would take you nearly two years to sample the regional cuisines of each province."

"What an enchanting idea! Has anyone done this before?"

"I suppose they have, although I've never heard of anyone."

"Sounds terrific! I'll be able to apartment-sit during the day and dine in a distant province in the evening!"

"Would you care to undertake this project with me as your guide?"

"You, Monsieur Inspecteur?"

"Dine with me—perhaps twice a week—as my guest. That way we could cover all of France in less than a year."

"Well, I—I don't . . ."

"The idea bores you."

"Dining with Inspector Damiot? It's an enchanting idea."

"Then you'll do it?"

"Of course!"

"There will unfortunately be some evenings when I can't be

free. Like tonight. But I'll phone you late in the afternoon to let you know, and we can make it the following evening."

"I'm seldom home late afternoons. Why couldn't we pick a place where we could always meet? Perhaps some café or . . ."

"What about right here? You said you're apartment-sitting nearby."

"This would be perfect! The Café de la Paix has been one of my favorite places ever since I arrived in Paris. I have the most horrible claustrophobia and small places make me smother. But this is so spacious! The high ceilings inside and this long terrace. I sit here for hours, even in the summer when it's crowded, because the boulevard is lined with lovely trees and I don't feel the buildings across the street crowding in. I like it best, like tonight, in the rain or when the streetlamps make blue shadows on the snow. I never feel smothered here."

"Then this is where we'll meet for an apéritif, before we go somewhere for dinner."

"And if you can't make it I'll be waiting the next evening."

"What about tomorrow? I shouldn't have to work two nights in a row."

"Tomorrow? Yes. I'll be free." She gulped the last of her wine. "Oh, this is such a lovely idea." She hung the brown leather bag over her left shoulder again.

"Seven-thirty? If I don't show up by eight you'll know I can't get away. Better still, I'll phone here and have them give you a message."

"Where will we dine tomorrow night?"

"I've no idea. Have to think about that. Make some calls. I know several chefs, and they keep track of most of the other chefs in Paris. Where they come from and which cuisine is their specialty."

"All day tomorrow I shall be looking forward to dinner." She gathered up her newspaper and ski mittens. "Now I really must be going or my friends will be furious. Thanks for the wine."

"My pleasure, Mademoiselle." Damiot got to his feet as she rose from the table. "I look forward to tomorrow night."

She thrust out her hand, awkwardly, like a child.

Damiot took the small hand and held it. Her flesh felt firm.

"This has been the most exciting thing that's happened to me since I came to France! Meeting you . . ." She slipped her hand free and tucked the newspaper under her arm. "I hope you catch whoever stabbed that American actor. Bonne chance!"

"À demain, Mademoiselle!"

"À demain." She turned abruptly and went toward the exit to the street.

Damiot watched as she pulled on her mittens, then raised the hood to cover her hair. That done, she looked back and waved before opening the glass door and hurrying away through the rain.

The storm hadn't slackened.

He glanced around and saw that the young man and the woman in the tan raincoat had gone, but the two middle-aged men were still talking. Their wives would give them the devil!

Sinking onto his chair again, he watched Andrea running toward the corner.

Where was her Volkswagen parked?

Of course, she hadn't said she was driving tonight. After all, she was "apartment-sitting" nearby.

It would be amusing to take her out for dinner twice a week. His evenings wouldn't be so empty. Later, if she proved boring, he could say he was busy.

He had a feeling she would never become boring.

Checking his wristwatch, he saw that it was just past eight. Plenty of time to go inside and have dinner, then walk up the avenue to meet Graudin and Merval.

Andrea was turning the corner, up Place de l'Opéra, hurrying as she lowered her head and shoulders against the rain.

Damiot smiled.

He had never had an affair with an American girl before.

CHAPTER 8

GRAUDIN WAS WAITING IN AN UNMARKED POLICE CAR, headlights dark, on Boulevard des Capucines at the corner of rue de Caumartin. Young Merval sat beside him.

As Damiot approached, they got out of the car. "Any activity?"

"Nothing, M'sieur l'Inspecteur." Graudin, conscious of his seniority, always answered before Merval. "No one walking and little traffic. Looks about the same as last night."

Damiot stood on the corner and squinted through the driving rain. The Comédie Caumartin, halfway up the street, was a pale blur of lights. "That theater wasn't lighted last night."

"There's a performance at nine o'clock," Merval explained. "I spoke to the manager while I waited for Graudin to get here. The show ends at eleven-thirty and the theater's dark ten minutes later. I showed him Scott's photograph. He'd read about the actor's death in the newspaper, but of course it didn't say he died here. He recognized the photograph and was certain Scott didn't attend last night's performance. Would've noticed him. Wasn't much business because of the weather."

"What's planned for tonight?" Graudin asked, eager to get started.

"Drive up to the end of this block and park your car. Then work your way back on foot, one of you on each side of the street. Go in wherever you see a light and ask if anyone noticed Scott last night. I'll start from this end and do the same."

"We haven't had one of these door-to-door jobs in months."

"And such good weather for it!" Damiot laughed as they

returned to the car. "Meet you. Middle of the block." He was in a good mood tonight, thanks to that American girl.

After she left, he had gone inside the Café de la Paix and ordered dinner. More money than he usually paid for a week-night meal, but he hadn't felt up to hunting for a cheaper restaurant in the rain, knowing he would be walking the streets later.

Graudin switched on his headlights and eased the car around the corner into rue de Caumartin.

Damiot followed.

Andrea! Nice name. Andrea.

Must decide which cuisine they would have for their first dinner together. Cooked by a chef from which province? Burgundy, Val de Loire, Alsace.

Standing on the corner, his back to the flickering streetlamp on the other side, he watched the silent police car moving up rue de Caumartin. Waited until it stopped and the headlights were turned off.

Now the street was completely dark. This was the way it looked last night. How the American had seen it.

Impossible to know from which direction Scott had come into the street, but he had a strong hunch it must have been from the other end.

Cars parked along both sides again.

The actor must have been returning to his car when he died. So knowing where the car was in relation to the spot where his body was found would give them the direction from which Scott had been walking.

Damiot started up rue de Caumartin, peering from side to side, noticing that the glow of light from the theater was mirrored in each puddle. That wouldn't have happened last night. The puddles would have reflected nothing.

He hadn't noticed any windows lighted when he arrived on the scene. And none was lighted now.

Of course, this was Monday. People retired early on the first night of the week. Always more tired after their day's work following a weekend.

The shops on both sides of the street had metal shutters lowered over their display windows. No lights visible, upstairs or down.

He heard footsteps behind him.

A woman hurrying, high heels tapping against the pavement.

Damiot turned and looked back.

She was carrying an umbrella that hid her face—a young woman, from the way she walked—and wearing a short raincoat that showed her skinny legs. The umbrella lifted as she approached him, revealing a blank oval of face that quickly developed features. Eyes accentuated with mascara, sharp nose, too much lipstick.

"Mademoiselle?"

"Mon Dieu!" She looked out from under her umbrella, smiling automatically. "You startled me, M'sieur."

He brought out the leather case from a pocket of his raincoat where he had placed it for easy access and flipped it open to show the badge. "Police Judiciaire."

"I'm a waitress. On my way home from work."

"If you say so." He returned the badge to his pocket. "But I'd like to ask you a question, Mademoiselle." He pulled the photograph from an inside pocket. "Have you ever seen this man? Here in rue de Caumartin or nearby?"

She leaned forward to stare at the picture in the spill of light from the theater.

"Last night? Or any other time."

She looked up, studying his face. "You're Damiot! I read in the paper tonight you're investigating this actor's death. They printed his picture. Was it near here he was murdered?"

"Not too far." He glanced at the spot across the street where Scott's body had been found. "Have you ever seen him in this neighborhood?"

"Never, M'sieur l'Inspecteur. But then I don't come this way often. Business was rotten tonight. I didn't have the price of a bus. So I'm walking home to Pigalle."

Damiot thrust the photograph back into his pocket. "Don't mention to anyone for at least another twenty-four hours that you saw me here in rue de Caumartin. We're not saying as yet where the American was found."

"I understand."

"If you go back to the boulevard you'll find a taxi to take you home." Fumbling in another pocket for money. "You'll ruin your shoes in this weather if you walk to Pigalle." He handed her two twenty-franc notes. "And if you happen to hear any talk about this actor Scott—if anybody says they saw him—give me a call at the Préfecture."

"I'll do that, M'sieur l'Inspecteur. My name's Carine."

"Carine?"

"I've heard some of the girls talk about you. When you used to be on the vice squad."

"That's a long time ago."

"They say you were always fair. Never took them in without a reason or an order from your bosses. One girl, Minon, says you're a good guy."

"How is Minon? Haven't seen her in years."

"She's had another baby. Three kids to support now. Lousy men!" She smiled again. "I'll tell Minon I saw you, and you're still a good guy." Turning back the way she had come. "Au 'voir, M'sieur l'Inspecteur!"

"Bonne chance, Carine." He smiled, knowing she would catch a bus home and use the rest of his money for supper, as he watched her hurry, heels tapping, back toward the boulevard.

Starting up rue de Caumartin again, he noticed another light. Across from the theater, on the side of the street he was walking. A small blue neon trembling in the cold rain.

No sign of Graudin or young Merval, and it was too dark to see where they had parked the police car.

"Chou-Chou! Where are you, mon petit?"

He looked across the street and saw that a door had opened. The figure of a fat woman was silhouetted against a lighted entrance passage.

"Come, Chou-Chou! You hear me? Immediately!"

Damiot slipped between two parked cars toward the open door and saw as he came closer that the woman was white-haired, wearing a denim work apron over a housedress, espadrilles on her bare feet.

She heard his footsteps and turned. "M'sieur?"

"Police, Madame." Displaying his badge again.

"What is it now?"

"You're the concierge?"

"My husband and I. For twenty years never any trouble."

He produced Scott's photograph and held it toward her. "Have you ever seen this man?"

She dropped spectacles over her eyes from on top of her head and squinted at the picture. "Looks like a criminal, all right! A face like that's not to be trusted. Too handsome."

"Ever noticed him here on rue de Caumartin?"

"I don't have time to watch people in the street." She shoved the glasses back on top of her head. "Never saw that one before."

Damiot thrust the photograph into his pocket, out of the rain. "Merci, Madame." He heard a cat miaow softly and looked down to see the same gray cat he had noticed last night, in another doorway.

"Chou-Chou! Little devil!" The old woman shook her fist at the rain-soaked cat. "Where've you been?"

The cat slunk past her through the open door, into the entrance passage.

"Good night, Madame!"

"M'sieur." She followed Chou-Chou inside, banging the door.

Crossing to the other side of the street again, Damiot saw that the neon letters—Chez Pavy—made a pool of quivering blue light on the wet sidewalk at the entrance to a café. It must get business from the theater during intermissions. He hadn't noticed the blue neon last night. Maybe the bar wasn't open Sundays. Eh bien! He could use another pastis.

"M'sieur l'Inspecteur!"

He looked around to see Graudin coming toward the blue glare of neon followed by Merval.

These were his two favorite assistants. Merval, the new man, always at Graudin's heels like a puppy. Carrot-haired Graudin, tall, long-faced, and solemn. With a wife and three small kids. Merval short and chubby, the sort who would never lose his baby fat. Always laughing. Probably because he wasn't married yet.

"Learn anything?" he asked as they came closer.

"Nothing," Graudin answered. "No lights in most windows. We rang a few bells, but none of the people who looked at that photograph had ever seen Scott."

"Or even recognized his picture." Merval added.

"You did better than I. I only saw two people—a whore and a concierge looking for a cat. Neither had any information." Damiot glanced toward the entrance to Chez Pavy. "You two wait in the car while I go in here. Then we'll continue up the street. Another hour of this and we'll be soaked."

"I'll back the car down," Graudin answered. "So we'll be waiting when you come out."

Damiot pushed the door open and went into the café.

The place was larger than he had anticipated from outside. Softly lighted, however, so it was impossible to judge its true size. A long English-type bar ran along one wall, on his right, with a row of polished wooden tables and comfortable brown leather chairs opposite. There was a much larger room in the rear with more tables—these had red-checked cloths—and a fireplace with lighted logs. Perhaps a dozen people in the back room eating dinner and two rodent-faced young men wearing hats and raincoats hunched on stools at the far end of the bar, drinking beer.

As he crossed to stand at the bar, near the entrance, a balding heavyset man wearing a tweed jacket appeared through a curtained door behind the bar and came toward him. "Could I have a pastis?"

"Certainly, M'sieur." He reached for a bottle without looking and placed a glass in front of Damiot.

He saw that the barman was in his fifties, with a flat nose that had been punished many times, probably a former boxer, prematurely bald. His fighting weight had sagged to fat tending bar. Damiot also noticed that he was pouring a generous drink.

His beefy hand pushed the glass across the bar. "A great honor to have Chief Inspector Damiot in my café."

"You know me?" He tasted the pastis.

"Matter of fact, I was going to call the Préfecture first thing in the morning and ask for you."

Damiot gulped his pastis. "You were calling me tomorrow?"

"My name's Pavy and I'm a partner in this setup." Shoving the pastis bottle out of his way and leaning both arms on the edge of the bar. "The evening paper said you're handling the case of that American actor who got himself killed last night."

Damiot straightened, waiting for whatever was coming.

"That's why I was calling. To tell you Scott was here last night."

"Alone?"

"With a girl."

"How old?"

Pavy shrugged his massive shoulders. "I never know a dame's age any more."

"What did she look like?"

"Couldn't tell. They walked past me, in and out, and sat at that last table over there." He nodded toward a table in a dark corner, near the entrance to the dining room. "Didn't get a good look at her because I recognized Scott right away and was watching him. I'd seen some of his films and like his type. A young Gabin or Gable. He'd been a boxer—like me—when he was younger."

"You talked to him?"

"He never gave me a chance. Never looked at me. And didn't say anything as they left. Too busy talking to the girl. Some of these actor types don't like you to recognize them when they're with a dame. Know what I mean?"

"Was the girl a prostitute?"

"Who can say? Some of these new girls look like respectable married women."

"Some of them are." He took another swallow of pastis. "What color hair?"

"Couldn't see. She was wearing some kind of plastic rain cover over her head and shoulders, which she never took off."

"Color of her eyes?"

"Never saw them. She wore sunglasses. You'd better talk to their waiter. He's in the dining room. Let me get him." Pavy turned and slipped through the curtained doorway again.

A group of people were leaving the restaurant, crossing the bar toward the entrance. A man and two women, middle-aged, laughing and talking. Probably going across the street to the theater.

Damiot avoided their eyes in case one of them recognized him and looked at the two young men at the end of the bar. He realized as they darted glances in his direction that they knew who he was. Probably car thieves or burglars, discussing a job for later tonight. Not his problem. When they saw him observing them they tossed off their beers and followed the others outside.

As Damiot finished his pastis, he heard a car taking off with the sudden roar of a powerful motor.

He wondered why that girl with Scott wore sunglasses on a rainy winter night. Must've had something to hide.

The curtains were shoved apart and Pavy returned. "Jan's coming. Good kid! His father used to be a boxer, like me. We were talking earlier, me and Jan, about that actor being in here last night before he was killed. We both recognized him. Jan had seen his films back in Holland."

"You weren't open last night around midnight."

"We closed early. Soon as they turned off their lights across the street at the Comédie. This weather's ruining everybody's business." He had picked up the pastis bottle and refilled Damiot's glass. "This one's on the house."

"Merci." Damiot saw a blond youth push through the curtains behind the bar. Tall and muscular, but with the ingenuous face and clear blue eyes of a child, white apron tied over his black suit.

"Here's Jan," Pavy said.

The youth thrust a huge hand awkwardly across the bar. "Monsieur l'Inspecteur."

Damiot shook his hand, sensing the boy's strength. "You're from Holland?"

"My father owns a restaurant in Amsterdam. He sent me to Paris to learn French cuisine. At night I work for Monsieur Pavy, my father's friend, as a waiter. I have the necessary papers."

"I'm sure you do."

"During the day, I study at the École de Cordon Bleu to become a chef, and next summer I go to Zurich to learn restaurant management. I must know everything about a restaurant because one day I will inherit Papa's."

"My father was a chef."

"Was he?" His young face brightened.

"Had his own restaurant in Provence. But I am a policeman. All I can cook is an omelette."

"But that is an art! To make a good omelette."

"Pavy tells me you served this American actor—Scott—last night. And he was with a girl."

"That's right, mÿnheer Inspecteur. But only drinks. They didn't order any food."

"What did they talk about? Were you able to hear?"

"They would stop talking when I went near their table."

"Didn't you overhear anything they said? Either of them?"

"I'm sorry." He shook his head. "The girl's voice was very low. Barely a whisper."

"Did they seem to be arguing?"

"I couldn't say."

"Who did most of the talking?"

"That's easy! It was Scott. The girl said very little."

"Did they speak French or English?"

"Sounded like French."

"You speak English, do you?"

"I speak four languages, mÿnheer Inspecteur. That is the absolute minimum necessary for me to be able to run a first-class restaurant."

"What did this girl look like? Was she attractive?"

"I couldn't see. She never took off her sunglasses. But I could tell she was young."

"Was she a whore?" He saw the boy's face crimson.

"I wouldn't know, Monsieur. I thought—wearing sunglasses—she might be a film actress."

"Tall or short?"

"Didn't see her standing. But I could tell she was small. Not fat but not thin. She had black hair."

"Black? You're certain?"

"Her hair was hidden, but I noticed when I took their order that a long black strand had slipped down from under the plastic covering she was wearing because of the rain. She had pushed it out of sight when I returned with their drinks."

"So her hair was long and black. What did they drink?"

"Monsieur had whisky with water and the young woman had a cognac."

"What time were they here?"

"About ten-fifteen," Pavy answered. "I remember because they came in after the other people returned to the Comédie for the second act. Usually we get quite a few during the intermissions, but last night there were only half a dozen. I remember the girl came in after they left."

"The girl arrived first? Ahead of Scott?"

"That's right."

"How soon afterward did he show up?"

"In about five minutes. And they stayed less than ten minutes."

Damiot turned to Jan again. "Is that how you remember it?"

"Yes, mÿnheer Inspecteur. That's how it was."

Damiot dropped money on the bar for his first drink. "If you think of anything more, either of you—no matter how unimportant it might seem to you—get in touch with me at the Préfecture."

"We'll do that, M'sieur l'Inspecteur!" Pavy answered.

"And if the girl comes in again—alone or with someone else—call me at once. If she leaves before I get here, send Jan after her to see where she goes."

"Was Monsieur Scott killed near here?" Jan asked, his eyes puzzled. "The newspaper didn't say where his body was found or how he was killed. And I was wondering . . ."

Damiot smiled, amused by the youth's curiosity, which would be useful when he had his own restaurant. "I can tell you the facts, as far as we know them, because they'll be in the newspapers tomorrow. Scott's body was found in the gutter. Across the street. A policeman walking through rue de Caumartin noticed him sprawled in the rain. He thought at first it was a drunk, but when he turned Scott over he saw that he was dead."

"Murdered?" Jan asked, his blue eyes wide. "In this street?"

"That's right. He was stabbed." Damiot turned and headed for the door. "Thanks for the drink."

CHAPTER 9

DAMIOT GLANCED BACK AS HE TURNED OFF AVENUE DE l'Opéra into rue Saint-Augustin and saw that the white Volkswagen still followed.

There was no traffic, and the rain was heavy again.

This day had been long and tiring. Starting with an early-morning session with his chief. After Damiot had filled him in on the Scott case, the old man had told him to catch the whore with the knife as quickly as possible—the murder of a foreign visitor always brought unpleasant publicity—and keep him informed about each development.

Nothing important as yet was developing.

Damiot and Graudin had checked out all the names on Maurin's list. Each person told the same story. Maurin didn't leave his apartment Sunday night, and nobody remembered his going upstairs to the bedroom.

A motorcycle officer had noticed the license number of Scott's missing car and reported to headquarters that it was parked on Boulevard de la Madeleine near the lower end of rue de Caumartin.

Damiot had gone with Graudin to inspect the car before it was towed away. A red Peugeot. It had been parked there since Sunday night, and the police must have passed it many times, not knowing it belonged to the actor.

The lab had found nothing of interest—not even Scott's prints—so he had been wearing his gloves while driving. They had reported late in the day that Scott's attaché case had revealed nothing except the actor's prints on the leather case and the hidden money. Nothing more.

Attaché case and money would be handed over to Scott's widow, who, according to the American consulate, would be arriving tomorrow.

Young Merval had gone to the Folies-Bergère and, after showing Scott's photograph, learned from the manager that the American had left the theater after the first act. The manager had noticed him leave but didn't realize his identity. He rarely went to the cinema because of his working hours and hadn't read about Scott's death in the papers.

Everything today had led to a dead end.

Damiot knew, of course, that Scott had left the Folies early to meet L somewhere at ten o'clock.

Now he had to find L.

There had been no time to get any lunch, but during the afternoon he had called a gourmet friend who agreed that the best example of cuisine de la Loire to be found in Paris would be at the Relais Touraine . . .

He realized that his trouser legs were damp from the walking he'd done in the rain today.

Slowing his car, as he reached the Square Louvois, he checked his mirror and saw the white Volkswagen close behind.

He turned down rue Lully, through the rain, along the edge of the small square, then left on rue Rameau—happy to see that no cars were parked here—easing toward the curb in front of the lace-curtained window displaying Relais Touraine on a rain-splattered expanse of plate glass.

The Volkswagen pulled in behind him.

He had taken a black police car for the evening, as he often did during an important investigation, because he planned to explore the side streets of the 9th arrondissement after dinner. Check all streets off rue de Caumartin in the hope of finding where Alex Scott had taken that girl Sunday night. She had to be a prostitute, and because of the rain Scott would have looked for the nearest small hotel.

Last night he had postponed a further check of the area after leaving Chez Pavy. The rain had been heavy when he rejoined Graudin and Merval, so he had told them to drop him off at Place Dauphine . . .

Standing beside his car, he watched Andrea hurrying toward him, avoiding the puddles in the cracked sidewalk.

Tonight she was wearing a brown and white striped scarf over her hair, a gray raincoat instead of last night's duffle coat, expensive high-heeled brown boots, and leather gloves instead of ski mittens. The same brown leather bag hung from her left shoulder.

"Isn't that the Bibliothèque Nationale?" she asked.

He glanced up at the dark mass of the ancient edifice, looming above the square, as he walked beside her toward the restaurant. "You've been there?"

"Many times. But I never knew this little square was hidden back here."

"Most Americans never discover it. Which is fine! Tourists can ruin a good restaurant." He held the door open for her.

Andrea stepped inside, pushing through red plush curtains that protected the interior from drafts. "It's empty!"

Damiot followed into the discreetly lighted restaurant.

"But something smells terrific!" She looked around, sniffing the warm air.

"My father used to say he could tell a fine restaurant when he entered because good food leaves traces, like perfume, for days." He saw a portly man in a dark suit hurrying from the kitchen. "Here's le patron."

"Ah, Damiot! Been reading about you in the papers again. The murder of that American. Welcome, mon ami! You have the place to yourselves this miserable evening. Like une salle privée at Maxim's but with your own personal chef!" He came toward them, through a glow of light from shaded candles on the tables, balancing his weight delicately on what appeared to be unusually small feet for such a large man.

"May I present le patron—Monsieur Martin, Mademoiselle Brandon."

"Monsieur Martin?"

"Welcome, Mademoiselle." Martin's eyes twinkled as he waved for them to follow him. "Tonight you may have any table!" He turned to Andrea. "Although Damiot, comme toujours, will probably wish to have his usual table facing the kitchen doors."

"By all means!" She laughed. "His usual table."

"The young lady is American," Damiot explained. "I've brought her here to enjoy the Val de Loire cuisine." As he talked he was shrugging out of his raincoat.

Martin bowed to Andrea. "My chef and I are honored. He's from Chinon, and I was born in Tours. Both of us came from the Département of Indre-et-Loire. I regret that Madame Martin decided to go upstairs after nobody had turned up for dinner by eight o'clock. When business is bad my dear wife always develops a migraine." He paused before a table in an alcove with a faded rose velvet banquette. "Perhaps Mademoiselle will set here?" Gesturing toward one of the side seats. "So that the chief inspector has his customary vantage point from which to observe developments in our kitchen."

"In your restaurant I'm happy to sit anywhere!" Damiot exclaimed, hanging his hat and raincoat on metal wall hooks.

"No! You must take your usual place." Andrea slid in to sit on the side banquette. "This is perfect." She rested her shoulder bag beside her. "I know very little about cooking. So I'm only interested in the result—what's served on my plate."

Martin beamed. "The perfect attitude, Mademoiselle!"

Damiot edged around the table from the other side and sat in the center of the banquette facing a pair of chromium-sheathed doors with round windows through which the kitchen was visible in a blaze of light. He glimpsed the chef in his toque blanche, with two sous-chefs, talking and laughing. In another moment they would scurry about like dancers in a precisely choreographed ballet.

"Perhaps Mademoiselle would care for an apéritif?"

Damiot turned to Andrea. "Shall we repeat what we had earlier?"

"Perfect." She pulled off her gloves and glanced around the room at the rows of empty tables with lighted candles waiting for diners who hadn't appeared.

"A dry vermouth for Mademoiselle," Damoit ordered. "And a pastis for me."

"I'll have your waiter bring menus." Martin bowed and returned to the kitchen.

Andrea untied the striped scarf, shaking her hair free. "You've obviously been here before."

"Many times. Yes." He watched the long yellow hair fall to

her shoulders. "During the years I've lived in Paris I have made a personal survey of one-star restaurants. They're always trying for another star, but to achieve two stars their chefs must be ambitious as well as talented. And really care about food."

She slipped out of her raincoat as he talked and tossed it over the back of the banquette.

He saw that she was wearing a dark yellow wool dress that made her hair appear even more pale and golden. The only jewelry was a thin gold chain around her throat. She looked much younger, even more attractive than she had seemed last evening. "This is my favorite of all the Paris restaurants serving a cuisine from the Loire Valley. There are others, more famous, but in my opinion this one's the best!"

"Have you been there? To the valley of the Loire?"

"Unfortunately, no." He saw that, by candlelight, her eyes were a clear and dazzling blue. "Theirs is one of the classic cuisines of France, but then every French citizen swears his own department has the finest. The province where he was born." He looked up as a waiter brought their drinks. "Good evening, Michel!"

"M'sieur l'Inspecteur. Mademoiselle." He placed an apéritif in front of each, then produced menus from under his tray before heading back toward the bar.

"For the second time this evening." Damiot raised his glass. "Vôtre santé, Mademoiselle!"

"Santé, Monsieur."

They studied each other with interest as they drank.

"Monsieur Inspecteur . . ." Andrea hesitated.

"Mademoiselle?"

"I'm bursting with questions! The evening paper said Alex Scott was stabbed."

"I gave that information to the American consulate this morning and they released it to the press." He sipped the pastis as he explained. "Tomorrow morning I've agreed to hold a briefing for the reporters who cover crime news in Paris. All the foreign press will attend because Monsieur Scott was an international star. They'll gather at the Préfecture like wolves scenting blood. Unless I toss them a few scraps of information they'll turn their claws on me."

She laughed. "You make them sound like monsters."

"Most of them are."

"And have you discovered who killed Alex Scott? Or mustn't I ask?"

"You may most certainly ask, and I would be delighted to answer your questions if I were able. Before the departure of my wife, I often discussed my work with her. It's useful to have an outsider's opinion about what you're doing on an investigation. Although I don't recall that my wife was ever any real help." He shrugged. "It sometimes cleared my mind when I explained to her what I was trying to do. Helped me see things more clearly. But, to answer your questions, I'm beginning to turn up things—seemingly unrelated bits and pieces, as well as people—in this Scott case. However, I've no idea—as yet—who killed him."

"It only happened two nights ago. This is Tuesday."

"That in itself is a bad sign. Usually, if an investigation's going to end quickly, there'll be immediate clues. Not bits and pieces, but important items of information and witnesses. Sometimes they turn up immediately at the scene of the crime. But when nothing of real value develops in twenty-four hours I've learned we're in for a lengthy and difficult investigation. Possible weeks or even months!"

"Months?"

"Some cases drag on for years. Fortunately, I've never yet had one of those. I'd say most important cases take a few weeks. If the puzzle isn't solved within a month, you may never find the answers."

"Are there many like that?"

"More than you'd think." He realized, from her questions, that she was genuinely interested. "I've just come off a murder case that I suspect will never be solved."

"I had no idea! That cases go unsolved."

"Frequently."

They looked up to see the proprietor, bowing and smiling.

"I've had a brief conference with my chef and informed him that Mademoiselle wishes to experience the cuisine of our native province. He will be delighted to cook such a dinner for Chief Inspector Damiot and his charming guest."

"Wonderful!" Andrea exclaimed.

"My chef and I wish to make several suggestions."

"Why don't we leave everything to you, mon ami?" Damiot asked. "Start to finish."

"I am honored, Monsieur Inspecteur." Turning to Andrea. "Is there something Mademoiselle dislikes? Seafood, perhaps? Garlic or—"

"No, Monsieur. I like everything. And, fortunately, I've never had to diet."

"Splendid!" Facing Damiot again. "And the wines?"

"You choose them for us."

Martin beamed. "There are several bottles I've been saving for such an occasion. Parisians overlook the glorious wines from my native province. They prefer their usual Beaujolais. I can promise you some treasures!" He bowed, snatched up the menus from the table, and hurried toward the kitchen.

Damiot turned back to Andrea. "You don't smoke, Mademoiselle?"

"Not anymore. And you?"

"I've given it up. Food tastes much better now."

"I told a friend this afternoon that I'd been invited to sample cuisines from the different provinces of France without leaving Paris. She thought it was a sensational idea! Couldn't imagine why some commercial company hadn't arranged such gastronomic tours of the city. Of course, I didn't say I was being guided by Chief Inspector Damiot! She would've been truly impressed."

"Perhaps we can do this every Tuesday and Thursday evening. If I'm free and Mademoiselle doesn't become bored."

"Marvelous! Only I mustn't take you from your work."

"Even a detective has to eat dinner." He finished the pastis and set his glass down.

"Will you be going back to work tonight?"

"I plan to check the side streets, off rue de Caumartin, looking for any small hotel where Scott could've gone immediately before his death Sunday night. He was seen around ten o'clock in a café—Chez Pavy—on rue de Caumartin. The owner and a waiter recognized him."

"So you'll be retracing his footprints before the murder?"

"He left no footprints in the rain. You might say that I'll be following his psychological footsteps."

"Was he alone? At this Chez Pavy?"

"There was a girl with him. They're unable to describe her, except that she was young, her eyes hidden behind sunglasses, her hair covered. They could tell me only two things. She and Scott spoke French, and her hair was long and black."

"But you just said her hair was covered."

"A strand escaped from the plastic covering she wore over her head and the waiter noticed it was black. Scott and the girl left Chez Pavy together. I would guess he took her to some nearby hotel."

"You mean she was a prostitute?"

"That seems likely."

"And you think Scott was killed at this hotel that you hope to locate tonight? His body dumped on the street?"

"I think he may have been stabbed in the hotel. Perhaps he quarreled with the girl over money and her mec appeared."

"Mec? What's that?"

"Her protector. Mec is a polite word for pimp. He may have stabbed Scott, or the girl could've done it herself. I suspect Scott left the hotel and managed to get halfway down rue de Caumartin, hoping to reach his car, before he collapsed.' As he talked he observed through the round windows in the kitchen doors that the ballet of chef and sous-chefs had begun. "Tell me, Mademoiselle, did you ever hear anything back in the United States about this film actor Alex Scott?"

"I'm afraid I know little or nothing about movie stars."

"You've been to California? Hollywood?"

"Never to Hollywood. When I was an infant, my mother took me to visit her parents in Santa Barbara, but we didn't go to Los Angeles. That's the only time I was in California."

"Have you heard any gossip about Scott? His personal life? Read about him in the American newspapers or magazines?"

"Are detectives interested in gossip?"

"Always! Most gossip contains at least a soupçon of truth that might be developed into an important fact."

"I'm afraid I never read news about film people. Especially the gossip columns. They're so frivial."

"Is this an American word? Frivial?"

"It's one I invented years ago. Combination of frivolous and trivial. Meaning even less important."

"Frivial?"

"I rarely go to movies anymore—they're all so frivial—and when I do I prefer to see old films. The great ones I've missed or was born too late to see."

"So you recall nothing you've heard about Scott?"

"Unfortunately, I've never even seen Alex Scott on the screen. The sorts of films he made don't interest me. All that macho nonsense is for adolescents."

"Frivial again?"

"The worst! I do, however, seem to remember . . ."

"Yes?"

"He's married, and his wife, I believe, writes screenplays, but I've no idea which ones or whether he appeared in any of them."

"She's flying over to Paris tonight. Arriving in the morning. The American consulate phoned her in California to inform her of her husband's death. Sorry I can't tell you more."

They looked across the restaurant as a procession erupted from the kitchen, where the two sous-chefs were holding the double doors open.

Monsieur Martin led the others through the silent dining room. Followed by their waiter, rolling a serving cart, ahead of an old waiter bearing a bottle of wine in an ice bucket.

"Bravo!" Damiot applauded.

Andrea watched, wide-eyed, as the procession approached.

Martin bowed. "Permit me, Mademoiselle. Monsieur Inspecteur." He motioned for their waiter to remove the silver cover from a platter in the center of the serving cart.

"How beautiful!" Andrea exclaimed, staring at the pâté revealed, like a rare jewel, in a nest of chopped amber aspic surrounded by fresh parsley.

"Pâté of eel!" Martin announced as the waiter cut into it, setting the first slice aside. "My chef made this yesterday, and it has been resting for twenty-four hours. This is served only to special guests."

"I am honored," Andrea whispered, watching the knife slice through the pâté.

The other waiter had uncorked his wine bottle and was holding it up carefully for inspection.

Damiot read the label. "Montlouis—1978?"

"An exceptionally good year," Martin answered. "The grapes floated in sunshine that autumn."

The waiter poured pale golden wine into Damiot's glass and waited, bottle poised.

Damiot sipped a little, holding the wine on his tongue briefly, allowing it to trickle down his throat. "Excellent!"

The waiter poured wine into both glasses, deftly avoiding the younger waiter who was placing a slice of pâté in front of each.

"Bon appétit, mes amis!" Martin bowed and waved the waiters ahead of him, back to the kitchen with the serving cart.

Andrea stared at her pâté in its nest of amber aspic. "I've never eaten eel."

"Then you're about to have a true gastronomic experience."

"You've had eel pâté before?"

"Of course!" He reached for the basket of bread and offered it to her. "I prefer mine, like a true peasant, on buttered bread."

She broke a thick piece and watched him do the same, butter his bread, then dig into the slice of pâté and spread it on top of the butter.

"This is the only way to eat it."

Andrea followed his example. Took her first bite, cautiously, chewing slowly before swallowing. "It's delicious!"

"Bien!" He lifted his glass toward her. "This is a wine from the Touraine."

She raised her glass in response, and they both drank.

He sighed with pleasure. "It came, I suspect, from le patron's private cellar. In your honor. He's never served it to me in the past."

"It's really lovely."

He watched her sip the wine, pleased that she was appreciating this first course. "Have you always been interested in food?"

"Ever since I was a child. My mother knew nothing about cooking, but she adored good food. Papa, however, was a gourmet—like you—and we had a series of wonderful cooks."

"Your father must've been rich."

"He is rich—very rich." She frowned slightly, glancing at Damiot, then continued eating.

He realized that she was even more intriguing than he had thought last night at their first meeting. Something curiously innocent about her, a gamine quality, which intrigued him. He saw that her hands were small and compact, with short, unpolished nails. Like the hands of a child. Something touchingly vulnerable about them and about her. She was gulping her food and wine. "You're eating too fast."

"Isn't it awful? I always do! Like most Americans."

"Eat more slowly. Analyze each ingredient in the food. You will enjoy it more."

"I'll try."

"Your father lives in New York?"

"Oh, no! He always lived in Germantown."

"Wheres that?"

"A section of Philadelphia. Which is a city in Pennsylvania."

"I've heard of Philadelphia. But why is your village called German Town?"

"They wouldn't appreciate you calling it a village. It was settled hundreds of years ago by Germans, but I never met any of their descendants when I lived there."

"And this German Town is your home?"

"Oh, no! My passport says New York, but that isn't really true either. I lived in New York for five years before I came to Europe."

"You keep in touch with him—your father?"

"No. We are not . . . friendly."

"No brothers or sisters?"

"I was an only child. My father had a son by each of his second and third wives, but I never saw them. The first son died. I'm glad he has a son because he never wanted a daughter."

"His second wife also died?"

"They were divorced."

Conversation was interrupted by the return of le patron leading the same procession. This time there was a large covered china tureen on the serving cart.

One waiter removed their plates while the other ladled steaming soup into china bowls.

Martin looked at Damiot with anticipation.

"The pâté was superb!"

"Delicious!" Andrea exclaimed.

"Bien!" Martin's smile expanded. "This soup is a bouillon of chicken. Its simplicity is exceptional."

Damiot sniffed the steam rising from his soup bowl as the waiter placed it before him. "There is the pure essence of a happy hen!"

"Happy hen? I must tell that to my wife." He waved the waiters away and marched after them toward the kitchen.

Andea was the first to taste. "I've never had anything like this! Incredible!"

Damiot held the broth in his mouth, relishing its richness before swallowing it slowly. "My father used to make such a bouillon when he could spare the time. Takes two days."

"I've read that your father was a chef."

"He owned a small auberge in Provence. We had this same bouillon for our family dinner on special occasions, but it was never listed on the menu."

"Then this isn't found only in the valley of the Loire?"

"A variation can be found in most provinces."

They ate their soup without further conversation.

Damiot wondered briefly whether she was on the streets tonight. That prostitute with her knife. Was she at this moment picking up another man in the rain? Was the knife small enough to hide in her purse? The lab said it was like a stiletto.

"And you'll be looking for a hotel tonight, near rue de Caumartin, where that actor may have gone with a prostitute?"

"Yes." It was as though she had sensed his thoughts.

"You think he was in a hotel when he was stabbed?"

"He had to be!"

"How can you be so positive? Is it intuition, or do you have facts that lead you to think this?"

"I prefer facts to intuition. Although both can be valuable. In this instance there is one fact. I will tell you, confidentially, what the newspapers will not be printing for the moment. There was a stab wound in Scott's back. But there were no cuts in any of his clothing. There's your fact."

"No cuts? I don't understand."

"When Scott was stabbed he must have been nude."

"Oh?"

"He managed to dress himself and leave the hotel, but he died before he reached his car."

"He had a car?"

"One he had rented. We found it this afternoon, parked on Boulevard de la Madeleine near rue de Caumartin. Which indicates Scott was returning to his car from the northern end of the street. So the hotel must be in that direction." He looked up to see that the small procession, led by le patron, had returned from the kitchen. "That bouillon was superb. My compliments to the chef."

"And mine." Andrea added.

Martin bowed as the two waiters swiftly and expertly went about their work. "This is a pike," he explained, "which, a few hours ago, was swimming in the river Loire. A prince of pikes!"

Damiot saw the magnificent fish on its silver platter as the young waiter divided and served it while the other waiter refilled their wineglasses.

Andrea watched in eager anticipation until she was served. "It's beautiful! Like a painting."

Daimot looked down at his portion of the fish with its patina of beurre blanc surrounded by fans of dark green parsley. "Magnifique!"

"I will tell the chef," Martin responded.

"Much too beautiful to eat!" Andrea exclaimed.

"No, Mademoiselle. No dish is too beautiful to eat. The chef would be unhappy if I told him that." He waved the waiters ahead of him with their serving cart.

Andrea separated a morsel of fish with her fork and raised it to her mouth.

Damiot took his first taste as he watched her. "Well?"

"Simply delicious! In fact, this is the best dinner I've had since I came to Paris. And I've eaten in some rather famous restaurants. Fouquet's, La Régence, Drouant's . . ."

"Those are too fancy for me! I can't afford a three-fork restaurant on a policeman's salary."

"This dinner must be costing you a fortune."

"This is a one-fork restaurant, which I can afford." He saw that she was eating too fast again. Perhaps she, too, hadn't taken time for lunch. "I hope you'll be free Thursday night for another dinner. Our second province of France."

"Did you really mean that? Dinners every Tuesday and Thursday?"

"You're not backing out!"

She looked directly at him. "Well, I . . ."

"You will have dinner with me Thursday evening? After I've had two more days of hard work on this Scott case?"

"Yes. I will. I'd love to hear about everything that happens. How you catch the murderer—this prostitute with a knife, if that's who it is—hear about it first hand from the famous Inspector Damiot."

"Then we'll meet again, same time, Café de la Paix?"

"If you wish."

"I do."

She smiled and lowered her eyes as she continued eating.

Damiot wondered where to take her for their second dinner? Which of the hundreds of Paris restaurants? Those he could afford. Must remember to cash a check before Thursday night.

Would he be any closer to the solution of the Scott murder by then?

"I've just had the strangest thought!"

"Yes?" He saw that she was staring across the silent restaurant.

"I imagined that every seat was taken at all these empty tables. Handsome men and beautiful women. Laughing and talking and, of course, eating this wonderful food and drinking."

"This place would be so noisy we wouldn't be able to have a quiet conversation. I prefer it like this."

"Oh, so do I. This is perfect. A crowd would give me instant claustrophobia."

The next course was agneau à l'estragon, the tender lamb fragrant with fresh tarragon, served with vegetables and a hearty Saumur, also 1978, which Damiot had never tasted before.

They finished the red wine with small pyramid-shaped goat cheeses followed by a tarte au citron and a white wine from Chinon that was not too sweet.

Damiot remained silent as they finally drank their black coffee.

"You're thinking about that American actor," Andrea murmured.

"Matter of fact, I was."

"Planning what you'll do tonight in rue de Caumartin?"

"Wondering what I'll find. Which missing pieces of the puzzle may turn up."

"Pieces?"

He laughed. "I'll be happy to find even one."

CHAPTER 10

THE RAIN WAS MUCH HEAVIER AS DAMIOT TURNED HIS CAR up rue de Caumartin.

Once again, this must be how the street looked Sunday night when Scott was murdered. Dark, except for that haze of light from the theater on the left and the faint blue neon of Chez Pavy on his right.

Parked cars, as before, on both sides. Nothing moving. No traffic and nobody walking.

He wondered if that young policeman would be on duty tonight. What was his name? It had sounded like some new kind of soap. Rispol!

The lobby of the theater, as he drove past, was brightly lighted but empty—the audience, if any, would be inside watching the play—its box office closed for the night. No sign of life at Chez Pavy. They would have no business on a rainy Tuesday night. Theater or café.

Pavy and that Dutch youth would be at the bar, drinking beer, discussing the Scott murder and getting drunk. Jan would outlast the older man.

Two small hotels toward the end of the block, but Graudin and Merval would've checked both of those last night. He must look for hotels on the side streets where his assistants hadn't gone.

The actor wouldn't have taken that prostitute to a hotel in rue de Caumartin with his car parked around the corner on Boulevard de la Madeleine. His instinct would have been to take her in the other direction.

He turned right into the first side street, without noticing its name on the corner sign. Saw that there was a hotel halfway down the block. A narrow five-story building, the sort that would rent some of its rooms by the hour.

Not as many cars parked along here.

He eased toward the curb and slowed to a stop.

Leaving the car in the rain, he wondered if Andrea was getting wet. He hoped she didn't have to walk after she parked her car. She was going back to that apartment whose owners were in Mexico.

Their dinner together had been extremely pleasant, and he looked forward to their next. Thursday evening.

Crossing the puddled sidewalk, peering up and down the poorly lighted street, he saw that it was one of those tiny side streets that twisted in every direction around the opera house. He wasn't familiar with this area. In fact, he'd never worked on any investigation that had brought him here in the past.

He passed a small sign with faded letters—Hôtel Amadeus—as he hurried up the worn marble steps, out of the rain, to the entrance door.

The lobby was a narrow passage with a staircase at the far end to the first floor. A sagging sofa, no pictures on the cracked walls, one potted plant dying on a gilded pedestal.

Damiot followed the strip of faded linoleum to a small reception desk, where a green-shaded bulb over the switchboard revealed a mail rack that held no letters.

He tapped the bell squatting froglike on the marble-topped counter, and pulled Scott's photograph from an inside pocket of his raincoat.

No sound of life from upstairs, and the air was stale, smelling of disinfectant.

He struck the bell again. More sharply.

A door opened behind the switchboard, releasing a blur of music and voices from a television set, followed by a thin woman with dust gray hair wearing a man's heavy gray sweater over her faded housedress. Cold gray eyes observed him with suspicion. "Yes, M'sieur?"

He held the photograph across the stained marble counter. "Ever see this man?"

She stared at the picture. "Who wants to know?"

"Criminal Police." He flipped the leather case open to show his badge. "Chief Inspector Damiot."

"Damiot!" She stared at him. "Then it's murder?"

"You recognize his face?"

"I may have seen it somewhere."

"He was here, wasn't he, two nights ago? Sunday night?"

"So you know."

"He had a girl with him."

"I didn't see any girl."

"Would've been easy for her to slip upstairs." He glanced toward the staircase. "You rent rooms on your first floor to men with whores?"

"I never ask questions."

"Did you know this man was American? A film star?"

"I noticed he was better-looking than most. And polite." She stared at the photograph. "Why would that girl want to kill him?"

"I didn't say she killed him."

"You mean he killed her?"

"His body was found in rue de Caumartin. A stab wound in his back."

"Then he wasn't killed here!" She was so relieved that the words poured out. "I heard him leaving, stumbling downstairs, but I didn't see him. Sounded like he'd been drinking."

"And the girl?"

"Didn't see her come in and didn't see her when she left."

"Didn't you hear her? There's no carpet on those steps."

The old woman hesitated, scowling. "I heard someone run downstairs, right after the man left. But I didn't come out to see who it was."

"When the man took the room did he speak English?"

"He spoke French, but I knew he wasn't a Frenchman."

"Did he pay with American dollars?"

"With francs. He had a wallet full of money!"

"Did he?"

"You say he was a film star?"

"Scott. Alex Scott."

"Never heard of him."

"I suppose that room's been cleaned since Sunday?"

"Well, no. . . . Linen's changed on the bed, but I don't clean a room every time somebody uses it."

"Bien! I was hoping you hadn't." He shoved the photograph back into his pocket. "Let's have a look at it. Bring the key."

She turned to the mailboxes and lifted a large key with its crimped metal tag from a hook. "I hope this doesn't give the hotel a bad name, M'sieur l'Inspecteur."

"No worse that it probably has already."

The old woman shuffled from behind the counter, key dangling from her arthritic fingers. "At least this American wasn't killed on the premises."

"I said he didn't die in your hotel." He followed her toward the stairs. "But I suspect he was stabbed here."

"Stabbed?" Glancing back as she started up the steps. "Was it that girl?"

"She probably knifed him while they were upstairs. We have reason to think Scott was nude when it happened."

"We have no control over what goes on in the rooms."

"Quite right, Madame." He followed her up the splintered wooden staircase to the first floor and through a shabby hall, where he counted six closed doors, three on each side, with another worn strip of linoleum down the center.

The old woman unlocked a middle door and swung it open. "This is the room." Snapping a wall switch, lighting an ugly lamp on a bedside table.

Damiot followed her inside, leaving the door open.

Both of them paused for a moment, staring at the bed.

He saw that it was an old-fashioned double bed with a plain wooden headboard and a flowered cover faded from many washings. An open door revealed a small cubicle with a lavabo and a bidet. The tub and toilet would be somewhere down the hall.

"Has anyone used that lavabo since Sunday night?"

"I haven't. And there's been no one else here. This weather kills our business."

"Don't run any water in it. There may be traces of blood."

"Blood!"

"The girl would've needed to clean her knife. I'll have the police lab go over everything in this room."

"More work, as usual, for me!"

He wondered how many bodies had coupled on this bed. His eyes circled the room, missing nothing. A small armoire with a cracked mirror in its door, directly opposite the foot of the bed.

Facing the entrance door was one heavily curtained window. Framed prints on the walls of voluptuous female bodies in a froth of lace. They must have been popular fifty years ago, because he had seen these same prints in many cheap hotel rooms, their lurid reds always faded to dull pinks. Two wooden chairs with a bare table between them. And that was all.

He walked into the cubicle and leaned down to squint at the linoleum around the base of the lavabo. "Did you notice any bloodstains here?"

"I wouldn't be looking for bloodstains!"

"Nothing on the sheets when you changed the linen?"

"I never examine the sheets. Just carry them down to the laundry."

"Have they been laundered?"

"Yesterday."

"Too bad." He glanced at the ancient phone on the bed table. "May I make an outside call?"

"I'll have to go downstairs and put it through for you." She headed toward the door. "Don't give me the number now because I'll only forget it." Looking back. "They won't mention this hotel in the newspapers, will they?"

"They usually do."

"Eh bien! Maybe it will bring us business. I might charge double for the bed that film star used."

Damiot grunted.

"What did you say his name was?"

"Scott. Alex Scott."

"I'll never remember."

"It's in the newspapers. And I'm afraid it will continue to be in the papers until we find out who killed him."

"I'll buy a paper tomorrow. And I'll call you from downstairs, M'sieur l'Inspecteur, to get that number you want."

"Merci, Madame! I must call the Préfecture. Get some men from the lab to go over this room." As she closed the door, he walked toward the armoire and stared into the cracked mirror. He could see the bed reflected but, moving his head from side to side, found it was impossible to see the chairs or table, only the bed. For obvious reasons.

If only there were some scientific device to bring back images that had been reflected in a mirror!

That whore could've stabbed Scott while he was on top of her. The knife must have been hidden under the bolster or in her purse on the floor beside the bed. She managed to reach it while he was mounting her. Clasped both hands around the handle and stuck the knife into Scott's back with all her strength. She would have needed to know exactly where to place the point of the blade. A spot where it would avoid striking bone as it penetrated. Their two bodies pushing together would have forced the knife into his flesh. He visualized Scott as the sharp blade cut through flesh and muscle. Pulling back, automatically, which only sent the knife in deeper. Unaware, at first, of what was happening.

There must have been a brief sting of pain.

She pulled the knife out quickly, or the cut would have been wider.

Damiot moved closer and saw his own image obscure the vision of the bed. His crumpled hat and old raincoat. The crack in the mirror cutting across his scowling face.

The phone rang and startled him.

CHAPTER 11

HE TOUCHED THE BUTTON BESIDE THE CLOSED DOUBLE doors and heard a discreet buzzer respond inside.

Glancing up and down the long corridor, he was grateful for the silence that enveloped the Hôtel du Pont in a protective cloak. It was like a living presence after the uproar at the Préfecture this morning, when he had faced a noisy pack of reporters and answered some of their questions. There had been representatives from most of the international news services and, for the first time in his experience, from half a dozen magazines.

"Chief Inspector Damiot?"

He looked around to see that one of the doors had opened and a slim redhead in an expensive tailored blouse and tan slacks was extending her hand in welcome. "Madame Scott?"

"I can't begin to tell you, Monsieur Damiot, how pleased I was to learn that you'd be handling the investigation of my husband's death. Do come in!" She released his hand and went ahead through the foyer.

Damiot closed the door and followed, removing his damp hat, aware of the heat as he entered the salon again.

"It was weird, sitting in my California office yesterday—I'm working at one of the majors—to receive a call from our consulate in Paris and learn that Alex had been murdered. I wasn't actually shocked, because it was as though I was hearing about a total stranger."

He saw that all the lamps were lighted and fresh flowers had been arranged in every vase. The salon looked more cheerful. Even the rain, obscuring the windows, wasn't so depressing.

"Toss your raincoat over a chair. How long has the weather been like this?"

"Several days now." He placed his hat on a glass-topped table and removed his raincoat. "We always get rain in November."

"This can also be one of our rainy seasons in California. I for one love it! We have, as you must know, a surfeit of sunshine."

He faced her as she relaxed on the striped sofa and retrieved a lighted cigarette from an oblong pottery tray.

"Please." She motioned toward a chair. "Would you care for a drink or some coffee? Cigarettes?"

"Nothing." He sank into the fauteuil, noticing the three shiny magazines still spread out on the coffee table. There was also a pile of opened cables, several American books with garish jackets, and an enormous brown leather shoulder bag that lay open, its contents spilling out. "You speak excellent French, Madame."

"My parents insisted I study languages because they were such compulsive travelers. They would drop me off at school in Switzerland before flying on to India or some other fabulous place. Later, when I was older, they took me along with them. My father was a film director who worked all over the world. He's dead, but you may know his name. George Ronkle?"

"Ah, yes." He smiled, hoping to hide the fact he'd never heard of George Ronkle.

"Papa made thrillers. Many of them were shown in France."

"Of course." If he'd seen them he didn't remember.

"Although he was never quite so famous as Hitchcock. Hitch was the absolute master of the genre. I became interested in the fine art of detection at an age when most of my contemporaries were still reading *Snow White*, because, you see, I read all the books my dear father was considering for filming. Of course, thrillers and detective stories are really fairy tales for adults."

He studied her more closely as she talked. Intelligent but not beautiful. This was the face in that photograph in the other room. She appeared to be slightly older than her husband but was probably several years younger. Auburn hair brushed in soft waves, falling to the collar of her blouse, partially hiding high cheekbones. A long nose and the sharp line of her jaw were defeated by a generous mouth. Her eyes, in this artificial light, seemed hazel or light brown and in person they were more searching than brooding. He suspected from her manner that Madame Scott was accustomed to getting what she wanted from life.

". . . and, of course, I've read about you many times, Monsieur Inspecteur, in the newspapers and magazines. American as well as French! In fact, last year I began to keep a file on you."

"For what possible reason?"

"Background material, in case I ever write a script about a dashing Parisian detective. You see, Monsieur, I write screenplays—thrillers—involved with crime and detection, and I'm always seeking fresh ideas. I did a preliminary story treatment for one Hitchcock film—he used more than one writer on many of his scripts—and, of course, wrote many original screenplays, including several for my father. Which is why I keep files on people who intrigue me. So I know much more about you than you could possibly know about me!"

"Do you, Madame?"

"For instance, you're a gourmet."

"Well . . ."

"One American magazine called you 'the gourmet sleuth'! That intrigued me because I profess to be something of a gourmet cook."

"I don't cook, unfortunately, but I do enjoy good food."

"You must tell me your favorite Paris restaurants while I'm here. Not the ones patronized by the Hollywood crowd."

He nodded, but promised nothing.

"I also know that both your parents are dead. You're separated from your wife, and, according to one story, you live in a hotel near the Préfecture with an adorable black Scottie-poo named Fric-Frac."

"Quite true!" He realized that this interview was getting out of hand. He hadn't as yet asked any questions.

"Let me immediately tell you several things about myself. I am, as you can see, a very direct person, Monsieur Inspecteur.

I will answer whatever questions you have for me as honestly and as completely as possible."

"I'm sure you will, Madame."

"My name is Serena, but I was never called Rena, even as a child. Imagine—Rena Ronkle! Sounds like bird talk. I've always insisted everyone call me Serena. Even my late husband." She exhaled a white cloud of smoke. "I should tell you at once that Alex was an utter and complete bastard, in every way, and I'm glad the bastard's dead."

"You surprise me."

"I'm telling you the absolute truth. I hated Alex. There've been times—many times—when I could have murdered him myself. But, unfortunately, I'm not the type."

"There's no single type that commits murder. At least not in my experience." As he leaned forward to question her, he was distracted by his reflection in a large wall mirror and pulled back quickly in order not to see himself. "Why didn't you leave your husband?"

"Because of our two young sons."

"Had you considered divorce?"

"Not for a moment. The boys needed their father for another four or five years. Or, at the very least, the illusion of one. And that's all Alex has been for some time. An illusion! As father and as husband. But neither of us, I assure you, ever contemplated divorce. For one thing, we are both devout Catholics."

"I see."

"My husband's real name is Timothy Kelleher. He comes from Chicago, and his father is a farmer somewhere in Illinois. I've never met his family. He was Tim Kelleher when we first met, playing a small part in one of my father's films. That's when I fell in love and married him. Papa changed Tim's professional name to Alex Scott and gave him a featured role in his next production. I'd written the script and, quite naturally, rewrote the part for Alex. Building and adjusting it to fit his talent. Which wasn't enormous. Alex had never seriously studied acting. He always got by on his looks. I suppose that's why I fell for him. His handsome face! And that's why he was starred in his next picture, after the fan mail poured in from thousands of lonely teenagers. The publicity boys started the big buildup and he was on his way. His first starring role was in a film my father did not direct and I hadn't written." She crushed out her cigarette and rose from the sofa. "Sure you won't change your mind about a drink?"

"No." He started to rise. "Merci."

"Don't get up! I suddenly crave a large whisky. It's all this talking about Tim." She opened one of the double doors and slipped into the bedroom, leaving the door ajar.

Damiot glanced toward the windows again and saw rain streaming down the panes, blotting out the rooftops across rue du Bac.

When he finished here, he would take Madame Scott to identify her husband's body. Always an unpleasant part of his job.

He wondered what Andrea was doing today. Had she come out in this weather? Shopping somewhere.

Tomorrow night they would dine together again. He still had to select a restaurant that served food from a province remote from the Loire Valley.

"Won't change your mind, Monsieur Inspecteur?"

"No, Madame." He turned as she returned from the bedroom, a tall glass in her hand. "I never drink when I'm on duty."

"I'm sure that's very wise." She settled onto the sofa again. "I don't usually before late afternoon, but I still feel chilled from that damn plane last night." She drank the whisky thirstily, then rested her glass on the coffee table near a thin gold cigarette case and a jeweled lighter. "What was I saying before . . ."

"Your husband's career. How he became a film star."

"Actually, I was about to say that it was during his first starring picture that I began to suspect Alex was sleeping around. And he was. From script girl to leading lady. I became aware of gossip early on. I don't usually listen to such trivia, but this time it was obviously true. I discovered people were calling him 'the Great Scott' for his sexual prowess. One day, lunching alone in the studio commissary, I overheard two little actresses talking. Heard one say, 'Great Scott's done it agin!' The other actress giggled. 'Another new doll?' And her friend said, 'I hear it's two new dolls this week!' They had no idea, of course, that I was his wife." She picked up her glass and took a long gulp of whisky. "I think Alex had a doll here in Paris. Maybe a whole house of dolls."

"I suspect your husband may have been killed by a woman."

"That certainly doesn't surprise me." She set her glass down and took another cigarette from the golden case, then lit it as she talked. "The young man from the consulate who met my plane told me that Alex had been stabbed in some street near the Madeleine. Is that true?"

"Yes. His body was discovered sprawled in the rain by a policeman."

"What a miserable way to die." Her voice, for the first time, was touched by genuine emotion. "For anyone to die."

"Do you know any of the women your husband may have been seeing in Paris?"

"How could I? I wasn't with him."

"You were with him last summer, on his first visit. You and both your sons, I believe."

"That was actually a holiday for the two boys. I'd visited Paris countless times, but Alex and our sons had never been here before. We made reservations at this hotel, where I'd stayed in the past, and it was so pleasant that Alex stopped here each time he returned. He flew over in August and again in September—alone both times—to discuss making a film with Tristan Murzeau. He signed his contract in September, and they were to start filming next spring."

"You knew Murzeau?"

"No. He's never produced any films in Hollywood. We hadn't even heard about this Murzeau project when we were here in the summer. That's how things happen these days in the picture business. Alex got a call from his agent soon after we returned from Paris. Murzeau was interested in him for the lead in his new film. They talked back and forth for weeks, then Alex flew over here in August to meet Murzeau and again, in September, after his agent had worked out a deal."

"Did your husband ever mention a French actor—Dario Maurin?"

"Oh, yes! Maurin was to play the second male lead in the picture. I'd seen him in French films and rather liked him, but

Alex met him at some party during his September visit and detested him."

"Did he say why?"

"No. And I didn't ask. I knew they'd be working together for weeks, and I didn't want them to be antagonistic before they even started shooting. It gets rough enough later on."

"Do you know the names of any women your husband might have been seeing in Paris?"

"I'm afraid not. No."

"Was there a special type of woman your husband liked? Perhaps one who resembled you?"

"He liked them all! But especially the young ones. The soft and pretty ones. He told me many times that I was too domineering. Although, God knows, I constantly avoided influencing him in any way. I learned long ago that was completely useless. Alex would do precisely as he pleased."

"What about whores?"

"He wasn't a bigot." She smiled. "About any minority."

"There's a possibility that he was killed by a prostitute."

"I doubt he would've picked up a woman in the street." She shrugged. "Of course, one never knows. What any of us will do, given the right moment and the opportunity."

"Quite true, Madame. We've traced your husband's movements to the hour prior to his death. He kept a rendezvous with a young woman in a café—Chez Pavy—on rue de Caumartin. Two people have identified him. They say the girl had long black hair and spoke French. She arrived first. Your husband joined her almost immediately, and they had a drink together. After that they walked around the corner to the Hôtel Amadeus, where your husband engaged a room. The concierge didn't see the young woman but was certain that someone was with your husband, whom she identified from a photograph. He left the Hôtel Amadeus and managed to reach rue de Caumartin before he collapsed."

"And the girl?"

"The concierge heard her run down the stairs after your husband left, but again, she didn't see her. The forensic lab found traces of blood in the lavabo that matched your husband's blood type. The girl must've cleaned her knife there."

"It's all so—so louche!"

"Can you tell me how much money your husband might have been carrying on his person?"

"I've no idea."

"No money was found in his pockets. No wallet or cash."

"But Alex always carried a wallet with cash and several credit cards. As well as small bills and change in his pockets. I gave him that wallet. Dark brown leather, from Dunhill's. He usually had at least several hundred dollars in it."

"Do you have any idea how much money he may have brought with him to Paris?"

"Matter of fact, I wondered about that myself after I learned he'd been murdered. I phoned our bank before leaving California, and they informed me Alex had withdrawn ten thousand dollars in new hundred-dollar bills the day before he flew to Paris."

"Ten thousand?" His hunch had been right! And a thousand dollars was missing from that attaché case.

"Another five hundred in tens and twenties. I was surprised to learn about the ten thousand because Alex never carried that much cash. When we were here last summer we brought most of our money in travelers checks. The five hundred, I assumed, would be to cover expenses en route and after his arrival, but I had no idea what that ten thousand could be for."

"No suspicion?"

"I did wonder briefly if he might be paying someone off. Perhaps a debt—he liked to gamble—or even blackmail. Someone here in Paris."

"Any idea who that could be?"

"None."

"A woman?"

"Most likely."

"Had your husband received any mail from France after his last visit? Personal mail?"

"I never saw his mail. We have a secretary who takes care of that. Greta answers everything but our personal mail, which she gives to each of us unopened. I've never liked anyone to read my letters."

"So your husband could've been corresponding with someone in Paris without your knowledge?"

"I suppose. . . . I'll ask our secretary if you wish, when I phone California."

"That might be helpful." He hesitated. "I found a leather attaché case among your husband's luggage."

"Oh, yes! He bought that recently to carry scripts and contracts. So he could read them on the plane."

"The attaché case has a secret compartment."

"Does it? I had no idea! How curious."

"Which contained nine thousand dollars in new hundred-dollar bills."

"Nine thou— Then he'd already spent a thousand!"

"Our forensic lab has examined the attaché case and the money."

"Any fingerprints?"

"Only your husband's. They—attaché case and money—will be returned to you."

"I found his contracts and shooting scripts on a shelf over the bed."

"Yes. I saw them when we went over the room."

The telephone rang on the coffee table.

"Pardon, Monsieur Inspecteur." She snatched it up. "Madame Scott speaking. . . . Yes, Monsieur Valentin?" Her eyes remained on Damiot as she listened. "Certainly not! Refer them to the American consulate. I refuse to see anyone, and, as I told you, I'll accept no phone calls." She set the phone down. "Reporters in the lobby."

"Your consulate must've told them you're staying here."

"I was thinking, before the phone rang. . . . There's a girl Alex met when he was here in August and again in September. He talked about her, both times after he came home. How attractive she was, and so intelligent. Tristan Murzeau's youngest daughter. I don't recall her first name, but I could tell that Alex was somewhat more than interested."

"You think he might've been having an affair with her?"

"I took that for granted." Smiling enigmatically and leaning forward to tap ashes from her cigarette into the pottery tray.

"Did your husband speak French?"

"He'd picked up a few basic words. The language of sex is universal. Actually, during his two previous visits—when I wasn't with him—he told me the hotel had arranged for someone to come and teach him every day. I suppose for an hour or so. I know his French seemed to improve."

"I saw that new film at the Marignan on Monday, hoping to hear his voice and observe him when he was alive."

"You mean *Guessing Game?* That one's a bomb! Alex hated it."

"Unfortunately, all the voices were dubbed by French actors."

"They usually are."

"Did your husband wear a wristwatch, Madame?"

"A very expensive one. It was a gift from someone—I suspected a woman—although he never said and I didn't ask."

"The watch is missing."

"It's worth several thousand dollars, I should think."

"Your husband telephoned you, didn't he, last Saturday?"

"Yes, he did. The call came through in the afternoon, around three. How could you know he phoned me?"

"There was a notation on a pad next to the phone in the other room, saying call Serena in California. Another note to meet L after the Folies Saturday night, and a third to check the time with Tristan for a Monday conference."

"Tristan, of course, is Tristan Murzeau."

"But who is L?"

"I've no idea. A woman, I suppose."

"This was a first marriage for you—and your husband?"

"My first. Alex had been married in Chicago before he set out for the golden ghetto of Hollywood. His marriage had been annulled and he never discussed it, except to say they'd been much too young. I didn't want to know what had happened. 'The snows of yesteryear!' I was having a blizzard of my own."

"And you, Madame, since your husband sought other women, you have had—affairs?"

"Only one. And Alex knew about that. In the last three years it's been taken for granted we go our own ways."

"And this other man?"

"We'll be married now. I love Julio more than I ever loved Alex. And my sons worship him! He's a genuinely good man and, fortunately, Catholic."

"An actor?"

"God forbid! Julio's a brilliant pianist but not quite good enough for a concert career. He's in the music department at the university. Enjoys working with young people. He's Mexican, gentle and totally affectionate, and I adore him. I'm a sucker for Latins! We spent all of last weekend together and it was heaven. Ironically, there'll be no financial problems because my sons and I get everything Alex has left in his estate. Which, of course, could've given me a motive for murder—except for the fact I have a highly successful career of my own and inherited a sizable fortune when my father died. Anyway, I was in California and have a dozen witnesses to prove it. And there's the fact that Alex called me from Paris."

"We don't know that he spoke to you."

"That's very true."

"How much was your husband to be paid for this film he was going to make in France?"

"A million in American dollars, which I understood would come from a group of Arab backers with vast holdings in the United States. But, naturally, he hadn't received a dollar of that as yet. Only signed the contract. He got almost a million for his last picture—that one you saw—much more than he was worth."

"I've talked to Murzeau. He and his wife had been aware of your husband's interest in their daughter."

"With Alex it was always rather noticeable!"

"There was a party at the Murzeau apartment in September. Your husband had an argument with Dario Maurin, according to Murzeau, and knocked him down."

"Alex always was too fast with his fists. Mucho macho! Did he and Maurin fight over the Murzeau girl?"

"Maurin claims your husband struck him because he said a French actor could steal any scene from an American actor."

"Maurin's absolutely right. The good ones can. Although any American actor would naturally give him an argument. Dario Maurin is a better actor than my husband ever was."

"We've checked Maurin's alibi for Sunday night. Several people were with him at his apartment. They say he didn't go out all evening. Maintenant, Madame. I've asked enough questions for the moment. If you'll permit me to escort you to our Institut Médico-Légal, you can identify your husband's body."

"If I must." She crushed her cigarette on the tray. "Actually, I've always wanted to visit a morgue. In case someday I might need to write a scene about one." She rose gracefully.

Damiot pushed himself up from the fauteuil, his hip paining again.

"Never thought it would be to identify the body of my husband."

"I have a car downstairs. A police car, if you don't mind."

"Lovely! I've never ridden in a Paris police car. With a handsome chief inspector. Siren sounding!"

"This car's black and unmarked. And we won't need the siren."

"Perhaps another time." She went toward the bedroom. "Let me find my coat."

Damiot slipped into his raincoat and picked up his damp hat, turning for a final look at the handsome salon with its expensive flowers whose fragrance, in the overheated room, reminded him of a funeral.

He glanced at the three shiny new magazines spread across the coffee table. The only visible evidence that Alex Scott had ever been in this room.

CHAPTER 12

"WHAT LUCK THIS MORNING?" DAMIOT ASKED, LOOKING from Graudin to Merval, seated on the other side of his desk.

"Practically nothing." Graudin, as usual, replied first.

Damiot turned back to him. "You went to Pigalle?"

"Spent two hours going from café to café. Talking to mecs, informers, and any prostitutes I could find. Most of them sleep until afternoon. No trace of Scott's wallet, and nobody knew of any whore who carries a knife."

He turned to Merval again. "What about Montparnasse?"

"Same thing there. I told everyone I spoke to that if they remembered any girl who carried a knife or heard about the American's wallet, they should report it."

"I learned several things from Scott's wife. The wallet was expensive—brown leather—probably containing a large sum of money, francs and dollars. Also, he was wearing a wristwatch. She says her husband drew ten thousand dollars from his bank before leaving California. We found nine thousand in that attaché case. So a thousand is missing. There's a possibility—and the wife agrees—that Scott brought the ten thousand to Paris as a payment for someone. Possibly a woman. Probably blackmail."

"You think the woman who killed him took that thousand dollars?" Graudin asked.

"That's likely. Or it could've been in the wallet and removed from his body as he lay in rue de Caumartin."

"What's Madame Scott like?"

"She hated her husband. Says he was a bastard."

"You think she killed him?" Merval asked.

"I doubt it. Says she was in California with her lover all weekend. But check the airlines. Find out when she left Los Angeles and if she did actually arrive here this morning."

"How did she react when she identified Scott's body?" Graudin asked.

"With no emotion. Looked at him, nodded, and said, 'That's the bastard.' She signed all the necessary documents. I told them at the Institut to release the body whenever they finish their tests. She's taking it back to California right away."

"Sounds like a cold bitch," Graudin muttered.

"She has a Mexican lover, and Scott obviously had many affairs. Madame Scott thinks he knew several women here, including Murzeau's youngest daughter. I'm going to question the Murzeau girl this afternoon."

"What do you have for us?"

"I've an idea. Came to me last night when I couldn't sleep." He swiveled his chair toward the window and saw the rain beating against the panes. The light outside wasn't much brighter than in his office where the desk lamp seemed even fainter than usual. He was aware of steam hissing from the radiator, but the air was chilly. "Another lousy day. . . . You can both stay here this afternoon. Merval, you take all phone calls and keep notes on what each person says."

"Yes, M'sieur l'Inspecteur."

"Even the cranks. Especially the cranks!" He turned his chair around to face them again. "Here's my idea. Graudin, I want you to go upstairs and see that new man who's in charge of the computers."

"I thought you didn't believe in that."

"I dislike the idea of computers in the Préfecture. No machine will ever deduce the truth from a series of taped lists. But it came to me in the night that the damn computers must have a complete list of every whore that's been picked up in the past several years. They've been feeding information into them from our files for months. They must've covered prostitutes among the first groups."

"I would think so." Graudin looked solemn.

"Have whoever's in charge do a check—or whatever he calls it—for any prostitute who carries a knife and for any man found dead in the street in the past three years with a knife wound in his back and no cuts in his clothing." He saw that both sergeants had straightened, their interest aroused. "I'd like to see whatever turns up when I come back."

"Yes, sir." Graudin got to his feet.

"And, Merval . . ."

He jumped up. "M'sieur l'Inspecteur?"

"Order me a car for the afternoon. I'll drive myself."

Damiot parked in front of the elegant apartment house on Boulevard Maillot, hurried across the sidewalk and up the broad steps to the entrance, where he paused. Shaking raindrops from his raincoat, peering toward the Bois, where white mist was rising from a small lake and the trees were dripping water.

Pushing one of the heavy glass doors open, he entered the enormous lobby, where a marble staircase circled an elaborate elevator and murals depicting a sunny Bois with carriages filled with elaborately dressed women holding varicolored parasols were framed by thick marble columns. He went directly to the desk.

A porter in a gray uniform, who had been reading a newspaper, observed his approach. "M'sieur?"

"Monsieur Murzeau's apartment?"

"You have an appointment?"

"Police Judiciaire." He showed his badge. "Inspector Damiot."

"Damiot?" He put his paper down as he rose behind the desk. "Been reading about that American actor who was making a film for Murzeau, but I didn't think you'd turn up here. M'sieur Murzeau's never home at this hour."

"I want to see his daughter.

"There's three of them."

"The youngest."

"That's Mademoiselle Linette. She's the little beauty. And the wildest! Always up to something."

"Is she in at the moment?"

"You're in luck. They all went out this morning, but Mademoiselle Linette came home about an hour ago. Shall I announce you?"

"Perhaps you'd better."

He turned to the switchboard, lifted the phone, and dialed.

Damiot waited, wondering what his reception would be.

"Mademoiselle Linette? Someone to see you from the police. Chief Inspector Damiot. . . . Yes, Mademoiselle." He set the phone down. "She answered herself. Said you're to come up." He motioned toward the staircase. "It's the next floor and faster if you walk. There's one apartment on each floor, so you'll have no trouble finding it."

"Merci." Damiot crossed the black and white tiled lobby and went up the crimson carpet covering the marble steps, clutching the elaborate bronze railing to ease the pressure on his hip.

The same crimson carpet, in the upstairs corridor, led to a pair of paneled doors directly opposite the elevator shaft. A discreetly engraved plaque to the right of the doors indicated that this was indeed the apartment of Tristan Murzeau.

He pressed the button in its circle of bronze and glanced toward the usual pair of distant windows at the end of the corridor. Saw tree branches, through a mist of rain, whipping in the gale.

"Chief Inspector Damiot?"

He turned to see that the door had been opened by the blonde girl who had opened the door of Dario Maurin's studio. "You are—"

"Linette Murzeau."

He removed his hat. "Why didn't you—"

"Tell you who I was the other day? Because you'd come to see Dario. I thought it would only confuse matters if you knew who I was." She stepped back for him to enter. "Please come in."

As Damiot went inside he heard a woman singing, somewhere in the depths of the apartment. The voice was that of a trained lyric soprano. Reminded him of his former mistress, although Olympe was a coloratura.

"That's my mother singing." Linette closed the door and led him through the foyer into a long, brightly lighted corridor.

He was aware of heavy antique furniture—unlike any he'd ever seen, probably Austrian—shaded lights, bowls of fresh roses, and elaborately framed paintings under individual lights.

"Maman was a star in Vienna. Opérette and films. Before Papa brought her to Paris with my two sisters. I was born here, so I'm a French citizen. Maman still works with a coach every morning, and after lunch she practices for hours. I don't know why. I'm afraid she'll never make another film or sing in opérette again. Here we are, Monsieur Inspecteur." She swung a door open.

Damiot followed her into a small salon.

She closed the door behind them and led the way to a pair of facing sofas. "Better take off that raincoat."

"Merci, Mademoiselle." As he slipped out of it he glanced at the tall windows facing those dripping trees in the Bois. Again the furniture must be Austrian. There was a clutter of bibelots and small porcelain figures on every table, walls lined with framed theatrical posters and photographs of actors in elaborate costumes. He hesitated, uncertain where to deposit his hat and coat.

"Put it on that chair." She motioned toward a small gilt chair as she sank onto one of the sofas. "Can't hurt it."

Damiot folded his raincoat onto the chair, setting his hat on top of it.

"Now we can talk, Monsieur."

He sat on the other sofa. Saw that her long blond hair was arranged in a knot at the back of her neck and she was wearing a simple light brown dress with golden slippers, like a ballet dancer's, on her feet. "So Dario Maurin is your friend."

"We are lovers." She giggled. "You must've realized that!"

"It was my impression. How long have you—"

"Two years. We wanted to get married, but Papa wouldn't give his consent. Maman approves, but Papa doesn't want me to marry an actor. Although he married an actress! People—especially parents—are so inconsistent. And Dario's afraid to go against Papa's wishes because he knows Papa has tremendous influence in the film business. Could keep him from getting jobs."

"Why did your father tell me that Maurin quarreled with Scott? That the American had knocked him down?"

"Papa was hoping to cause trouble. Make it look bad for Dario. But I was there and saw all that happened."

"Your father says Maurin threatened to kill Scott."

"He only said he'd kill him in their scenes together."

"You actually heard him say that?"

"Well, no. . . . I was across the room with some friends, and I couldn't hear what was said. But I do believe Dario. What he told you. He would never threaten to kill anyone!"

"Why did your father suggest I go to Maurin's studio, then phone to warn him I was coming?"

"Papa didn't phone. That was his secretary. And she called to warn me—not Dario—that you would probably be there at any moment. She told me Alex had been murdered, but I didn't tell Dario. Papa doesn't know that Fräulein Hoffmann is always trying to help me—Dario and me—warning us when Papa's up to something. She's an old friend of Maman's. They worked together in Vienna, on the stage. Of course, Maman is older."

Damiot was aware of the soprano, slightly muffled now, by the closed door, singing a familiar melody. Lehar or Stolz. "Your name is Linette. That means flaxseed in French."

"I know. Papa says when I was born my hair was so blond he named me Linette. It's much darker than it used to be."

As he looked at her hair he thought of Andrea. The American girl's hair was much lighter, almost white blonde and not so long as Linette's. And, curiously, Andrea seemed younger, although she was probably slightly older. As he studied Linette, he remembered that notation Scott had left on his pad. "You were with Alex Scott last Saturday night."

"How could you know that?"

"He wrote several reminders for himself on a pad in his hotel suite. One of them was to 'meet L after show Saturday.'"

"He met me at Fouquet's. You know everything, Monsieur Inspecteur! Even what I was wearing?"

"Unfortunately, no. I do know that Scott dined alone Saturday night at Lasserre and went to the Folies-Bergere but left during the first act."

"So he told me. We did have dinner together Sunday night at Drouant's."

"That I didn't know."

"After dinner he found me a taxi."

"What time?"

"Must have been before ten. He had a rented car, but he said he couldn't drive me home because he had to keep an appointment."

"With whom?"

"He didn't tell me, but I suspected it might be a woman."

"It may have been the woman who killed him."

"The papers are suggesting she was a prostitute."

"That's one possibility." He wasn't going to be more definite than that. "Can you tell me, Mademoiselle, what you and Scott talked about? Saturday night at Fouquet's and Sunday when you dined at Drouant's?"

"Quite simply, at Fouquet's he tried to persuade me to have an affair with him. He made the same blunt approach in September, after he came to that party my parents gave for people involved with Papa's new film. I had met Monsieur Scott in Papa's office during his previous visit in August, but we hadn't talked. At the party, with both my parents watching, he tried to persuade me to have dinner with him. I refused, but Dario was watching and became furious. That's really why he was rude to Alex later, but he did not threaten to kill him. He wouldn't do a thing like that! Dario is wild and crazy, but he doesn't like quarrels. At least not physical ones. He shouts, but that's all."

"What did your parents say when they saw you with Scott?"

"Papa warned me to avoid him. But they always tell me to avoid every attractive young male. If this were Vienna, fifty years ago, they would put me in a convent. But this is Paris, and I do what I please. My parents and I live in different worlds."

"So you continued to see the American actor?"

"Only in restaurants or cafés. I refused to visit him at his hotel." She hesitated. "You really think, Monsieur Inspecteur, that Alex had a rendezvous with his murderer Sunday night, after he left me?"

"I suspect that is very probable."

"The last I saw of him, as my taxi pulled away from Fouquet's, he was getting into his car. I watched him through the rain, thought how handsome he was."

"And I'm thinking, Mademoiselle, what a fool he was. To leave you and drive off to meet some other woman."

She shrugged. "Chacun à son goût." Glancing toward the

door. "If Maman should come in here, don't repeat any of this."

He realized that the singing had stopped. "I must be on my way." Getting to his feet. "If you remember anything more about Scott, please phone me at the Préfecture." He picked up his hat and raincoat as she rose from the sofa. "Don't say anything to your father about my questioning you. At least for the moment."

"I certainly won't. Now or later." Going ahead, toward the door. "And I hope you find whoever this woman is who killed Alex Scott."

"So do I."

"I'll come to the door with you." She turned, her hand on the knob, and faced him again. "There is something that perhaps I should tell you."

"Yes, Mademoiselle?" He shrugged his arms into the raincoat.

"When Alex was here in September . . ." She frowned as she remembered. "It was after that party my parents gave. I was walking with some friends on the Champs-Élysées. We'd been to the cinema and were on our way to have some supper at the Crazy Horse. As we passed one of those open café terraces—it was still warm in September—I saw Alex, seated at a table, with a girl."

"Can you describe her?"

"I didn't really see her face. She wore sunglasses, although it was night—after eleven o'clock—and she had a scarf over her hair. I didn't want Alex to see me, so I looked away. I'm sure he didn't notice me passing. He was talking to the girl."

"You didn't happen to see the color of her hair?"

"Yes, I did. It was long and black. Hanging down from under the scarf."

So it was the girl who waited for Scott in Chez Pavy! "Did she look like a prostitute?"

Linette shrugged. "What does a prostitute look like, Monsieur Inspecteur?"

"Very true, Mademoiselle."

She smiled, opening the door. "We are all prostitutes. . . ."

* * *

What does a prostitute look like?

The question circled in his mind as he climbed the worn carpet on the gracefully curving wooden staircase. These old buildings in Montmartre were more familiar to him that those fancy apartments facing the Bois.

He hoped at this hour that Picolette would be awake.

She had never looked like a prostitute. He'd known her since his first year with the police.

Reaching the second floor, he went straight to the familiar door.

What if Picolette had moved?

A small card was thumbtacked to the door. All four thumbtacks painted a glossy red. Leaning down to read the hand-printed name, he realized that the red was nail polish. This made him smile, as did the name on the card. Madame Arque! It had always amused him that a whore was named Arque. He knocked on the door discreetly and glanced up and down the twisting hall, lighted by a single bulb in the ceiling.

"Who is it?" The remembered voice, warm and inviting.

"A friend."

"At this hour? Mon Dieu! I'm barely awake."

"An old friend."

"Eh bien! In that case . . ."

He heard a bolt pulled back, a key turned. The door opened, and he saw a plump figure with frizzy hair against a halo of light. "Picolette?" He moved forward so she would see his face.

"Damiot! It's been years." She held her face up to be kissed. "You rascal!"

As he touched her cheek with his lips, he caught a ghost of the same perfume she had always worn. He used to know what it was called. "I'm a married man now."

"I heard she'd left you."

"She did. But we're not divorced." He closed the door and followed her down a narrow hall.

"I also heard you've been seeing some of the new girls."

"Jealous?"

"I knew you'd turn up here sooner or later. And you have!"

He followed her into a room crowded with furniture and overflowing with pillows. There were three pillowed sofas and more pillows on the floor. Countless small statues, porcelain and plaster, of nude women and men in every space large enough to hold them. Some were obscene, but most were only vulgar. "This place hasn't changed."

"I guess some things have been added, but nothing's ever thrown out!" She laughed as she lowered her plump body onto a sofa.

Damiot removed his hat as he sat on one of the other sofas, facing Picolette, observing her more closely. "You look about the same."

"I've put on a little weight."

"Not too much." He saw that she was wearing no makeup, but her frizzy hair was blonder than it used to be. The revealing robe was designed to tease with glimpses of pink flesh. "Did I wake you?"

"I'd finished breakfast and was reading the morning paper. About Chief Inspector Damiot and the handsome American actor who got himself murdered. Would you care for some coffee?"

"Nothing. Merci. I'm here because of that actor."

"What's he have to do with me?"

A phone rang in the distance, but Picolette made no move to answer it.

"Any day now, the papers will be saying that Scott may have been killed by a prostitute."

"That'll be bad for business. The girls are having trouble enough with all this rain every night." Her eyes became more serious. "Why have you come to me?"

The phone continued to ring as they talked.

"I'm hoping you may be able to help us."

"Help the police?"

"Help me."

"How?"

"Everything seems to indicate Scott was stabbed in a hotel room while he was nude. We think it was a girl who had a knife hidden in her handbag."

"I heard that one of your men was in the neighborhood this morning, asking questions about a whore with a knife."

"That was Graudin. He learned nothing, so I've come to you."

"Why me?"

"I thought you might know of any girls who carried knives."

"When I heard the police were looking for such a person, I made several phone calls. Asked some questions of my own. I thought if I learned anything I would pass the information on to you. It's bad business for all the girls when you guys prowl the streets."

"What did you learn?"

"Not much. It seems there were two girls who always carried small knives. Maria La Folle and Ginette from Algiers. Crazy, both of them! Their knives were always causing them trouble. Maria La Folle got into a fight with another girl in Pigalle and pulled her knife, but the other one had a gun and killed her. That's two years ago."

"And Ginette?"

"She knifed a guy last month in Marseilles. She's still waiting to be tried."

"You're no help at all." He rose from the sofa, hat in hand.

"I tried, mon ami."

"And I'm grateful." He looked back at her before leaving. "Good to see you. Even on a business matter."

"What about some evening when you're not working?"

"After this Scott case is wrapped up."

"Then I hope you wrap it up in a hurry. That girl should be caught. I loathe people who kill each other."

"À bientôt." He turned toward the door.

Her voice followed him through the hall. "You have my phone number. It hasn't been changed. À bientôt, chéri!"

CHAPTER 13

FRIC-FRAC WAS STEPPING CAREFULLY, SHAKING THE DAMP snow from her paws, as she walked ahead of Damiot along Quai des Orfèvres.

The wet pavements were dull silver, but under each streetlamp a ring of fresh snow dazzled like white fire.

He was troubled. One of the evening papers had printed a story by their top crime reporter. The headline had jumped out from the page when Graudin set the paper on his desk: Was American Film Star Murdered by Prostitute?

The article underneath had printed the reporter's conclusions, arrived at from the facts released by the Préfecture. They were the same conclusions Damiot had reached from those same facts.

He sighed. Tomorrow the corridor outside his office would be filled with reporters again. Demanding answers to questions he would still be unable to answer. And he would be summoned upstairs to face more questions from the chief. He would be able to give the old man no answers.

Fric-Frac paused as usual, to perform her final effort of the evening, at her favorite spot on the Quai du Marché-Neuf.

Damiot looked up at the dark façade of the Préfecture and wondered what the great Vidocq would do in such a situation. A thousand whores in Paris, but how could you find one with long black hair who wore sunglasses and carried a knife in her purse?

Picolette had managed to turn up only two, one of them behind bars, the other murdered.

He had spent the remainder of the afternoon in his office,

avoiding the rain, hoping to hear something positive from the keeper of those computers upstairs, but Graudin had reported there would be nothing until morning.

He had always thought a computer gave an instant answer to any question fed into its mechanical gullet, but apparently such was not the case.

Fric-Frac pulled on her leash as they continued on toward rue de la Cité.

Damiot could barely see the lights of the Périgourdine, on the Left Bank, through a soft curtain of snow. They were open tonight. Of course, this wasn't late. He had eaten dinner alone at Paul's on Place Dauphine and afterward walked the few steps to his hotel as the first snowflakes began to fall. Hurried upstairs to get Fric-Frac and brought her out for her last walk of the day.

At first she hadn't minded the damp snow, but now it was staying on the pavement and sticking between her pads.

There had been another story in the evening paper. Tristan Murzeau had announced that Tristan Murzeau Productions deeply regretted the tragedy of the talented young American actor's death but that this would not halt production of the film *Paris Pursuit,* which should start shooting in the spring. He was now looking for another top American star to replace Alex Scott in the leading male role, and he would personally be leaving for Hollywood to interview actors and make a final selection. There was a photograph of Murzeau with a group of robed Arabs and two young actresses whose names were not given. There was no mention of Dario Maurin.

Fric-Frac pulled on her leash.

He saw that they had reached rue de la Cité and she wanted to cross to the other side. "Go ahead, Madame." Following her to the opposite corner where they turned, past the Préfecture, toward their hotel.

It was getting colder, and the snow seemed to be heavier.

He glanced back toward Place du Parvis, but it was impossible to see the cathedral beyond the drifting veils of white.

If the air got any colder the pavements would dry and this snow would stop melting. That could mean the streets would be frozen tomorrow, with drifts of snow that would quickly turn black from the filth in the air.

Tonight he would have a hot shower and get to bed early.

In spite of the dampness, his hip hadn't bothered him all evening.

After a good night's rest he would be able to face another busy day tomorrow.

Fric-Frac continued to fling the wet snow from her paws.

Damiot smiled. She was like a woman who had stepped in a puddle.

Must remember to weigh himself when he showered. He suspected that he'd put on a little weight. Last night's dinner with Andrea and another tomorrow night. Two dinners every week! Must cut down on what he ate every other night.

The wind struck his face as they turned the corner toward Place Dauphine. It was getting colder. He could feel flakes of snow, larger and heavier, striking his hat and hitting the shoulders of his raincoat.

Must remember to stop at his bank tomorrow and cash a check. He would be spending more money than usual—two dinners a week with Andrea—but he had saved money living alone, and he could afford them.

He was looking forward to more such dinners. Delicious food and a charming young woman.

Andrea!

Had she gone out, tonight, in this weather? He hoped that her "beat-up" Volkswagen could handle snow.

Crossing toward his hotel, Fric-Frac tugging on the leash, he looked across Place Dauphine and saw that the small triangle of park was covered with a layer of snow in which, as yet, there were no footprints. The streetlamps were dimmed by the falling flakes, but around their bases were circles of light that made the snow a brilliant blue white.

As they approached the entrance to Hôtel Dauphin, Fric-Frac pulling ahead, Damiot saw the shadow of a man on the glass of the doorway.

The door opened before he cold get his key.

"Been watching for you, M'sieur l'Inspecteur."

He saw that it was old Pierauld, the night porter, which

meant there had been a message since he'd brought Fric-Frac out for her walk.

"The Préfecture called. Said it's urgent. You should call soon as you came back."

"Merde!"

"Yes, M'sieur l'Inspecteur."

"Want to get them for me?"

"Certainement." The old man in his faded denim uniform scurried ahead of them and went behind the desk to the switchboad.

Damiot released Fric-Frac's leash, and she ran past the lounge to sit facing the elevator.

He saw that the old man had finished dialing and was waiting for someone to answer. Sometimes, at night, the Préfecture switchboard got busy.

"Hôtel Dauphin calling back. I have Chief Inspector Damiot for you. Hold on!" He picked up a phone and handed it across the desk.

Damiot took the phone and held it to his ear. "Damiot speaking."

"Had a call for you, M'sieur l'Inspecteur, from a M'sieur Pavy."

"Yes, Chamard. I know Pavy."

"He said tell you there's a woman in Chez Pavy asking questions about that American actor, M'sieur Scott."

"Frenchwoman?"

"She speaks French but he thinks she might be British."

"Call Pavy back. Tell him I'll be there in ten minutes. And tell him to hold the woman until I get there. If she leaves, he should send one of his waiters to follow and see where she goes."

"Yes, M'sieur l'Inspecteur. I'll tell him."

"And send a car to pick me up."

"Right away."

"Make it fast!" Damiot handed the phone to Pierauld. "I have to go out again."

"Want me to take Madame la Duchesse upstairs?"

Damiot looked at Fric-Frac sitting in front of the elevator. Her tail wagged when she saw he was watching her.

"I think I'll take her with me. She likes to ride in a police car." He snapped his fingers. "Come, Fric-Frac! We're going out."

She knew what that meant and came bounding toward him, dragging her leash.

"Good girl!" He bent to snatch up the leash. "We'll have a ride through the snow. Talk to an Englishwoman and, who knows, you might even have some wine."

Pierauld chuckled. "How you spoil that dog!"

"Madame Fric-Frac isn't a dog. She's a human being. And my best friend!"

Fric-Frac walked ahead, toward the entrance, tail waving.

The snow covered rue de Caumartin like a white shroud, but as the black police car slowed to a stop, Damiot realized that the street seemed darker than before.

The neon above the entrance to Chez Pavy was lighted, but the theater was dark.

"Here we are. That blue neon on your right."

Risard slowed to a stop.

"Wait for me. Don't know how long I'll be."

"I'll double-park until one of these cars moves out. Be watching for you."

Damiot got out. "Come, Madame."

Fric-Frac jumped down and slid in the snow.

He closed the car door and followed her between two parked cars to the sidewalk. As they went toward Chez Pavy he was aware of a cold wind slashing through the street from the north, sending billows of snow dancing and spreading.

The door to Chez Pavy opened as they approached.

He saw Pavy holding it back for them. "What happened? The theater's dark."

"No performance tonight. Afraid this weather has closed their show for good. Which means bad business for me. Come in! I was watching for you. The Préfecture called and said you were on your way. You've got a dog!"

"Any objection?"

"Certainly not. I have one here, in the kitchen, and two more at home. Dogs are welcome at Chez Pavy."

"Bien!" He stepped inside, Fric-Frac trotting ahead and sniffing the air for evidence of cooking.

"That woman's still here. She's had three cognacs and asked a lot of questions about what happened when Scott was here Sunday night."

Damiot saw a sabled figure seated at a banquette table across from the bar.

"Got suspicious how she knew Scott was here because there's been nothing in the papers."

"I told her he was here. This is Scott's wife."

"Oh?"

"Thanks for phoning me. Gives me a chance to have another talk with her. Bring her another cognac, and I'll have a glass of white wine."

"Right away, M'sieur l'Inspecteur."

Damiot moved on, into the light, Fric-Frac tugging on her leash and her nose pointing toward the kitchen. He was aware of Pavy going behind the bar where tonight no customers were seated, but a few people were having dinner in the back room. He removed his hat as he walked toward Serena Scott.

"Monsieur Damiot! What a delightful surprise."

"Madame."

"And you have your dog?"

"Her name is Fric-Frac."

"Fric-Frac! How clever of you. That makes her truly a policeman's dog. I adore dogs! We've half a dozen in California. All prizewinners!" She leaned down to pat Fric-Frac's head. "What a love! Do sit down, Inspector."

He dropped his hat on a chair and peeled out of the raincoat. "At least these are more pleasant surroundings than our last."

"You mean the morgue? But I enjoyed that. Not seeing Alex again. Certainly not like that. After all, I did once care for the man. So that was rather painful. But I did learn a lot there. Made all sorts of mental notes in case I ever have to write a scene set in such a locale. Why can't Fric-Frac sit here beside me?" She patted the red leather seat of the banquette. "Fric-Frac! Sit here."

Fric-Frac looked up at Damiot for approval.

"It's all right, Madame."

She moved under the table and jumped onto the banquette, immediately inspecting the top of the table for any food.

Serena stroked her head. "Do you take her out on your investigations?"

"From time to time." He sat facing her.

"How exciting! For her. To be Chief Inspector Damiot's dog. Prowling the midnight streets of Paris in search of some murderer."

"Good evening, mÿnheer Inspecteur."

Damiot looked up to see the young waiter. "Good evening, Jan!"

"More bad weather tonight." He served their drinks quickly and withdrew.

"They know you here, obviously." Serena reached for her fresh cognac.

"I only discovered Chez Pavy two nights ago."

She darted glances toward Pavy at the bar as she talked. "Did they call and tell you I was here?"

"Monsieur Pavy, the owner, called the Préfecture to say there was a woman—he thought you were British—who was asking questions about Monsieur Scott."

"They thought I was British? Which may be because I lived in London for several years and picked up an accent, or, more likely, because the teacher in Switzerland who taught me French was an English lady. All these years, I must've been speaking French with a British accent and didn't realize it!" She raised her glass. "À vôtre santé, Monsieur Inspecteur!"

"Santé, Madame!" Damiot lifted his glass and took a swallow of wine.

"I went to the Hôtel Amadeus before I came here."

"Did you?"

"Told that dragon of a concierge I was Monsieur Scott's wife and I knew you. Explained that I wanted to see the room where my husband took that girl. Of course, I gave her some money."

"That should've opened every door."

"I was only interested in one. What a miserable, grubby little room! I asked if she'd ever seen my husband before, and she swore she hadn't. I got out of there as fast as I could and came straight here. Questioned the waiter first and he brought the owner. Monsieur Pavy! They, too, had never seen Alex before. So I learned nothing from any of them. Only what you'd already told me."

Damiot smiled. He saw that she was wearing a large diamond ring and her gloves and shoulder bag were on the table.

"I, of course, had hoped I might solve the mystery of my husband's death. Imagine the publicity I would get in Hollywood! Writer of thrillers finds husband's murderer."

"Bonne chance, Madame."

"This will be my only intrusion on your territory, Inspector. I knew there was little chance I would be able to find anything. A clue to the murderer or anything else. But I did want to see the street where Alex died. This café where he and the girl had a drink and that disgusting hotel room where he took her. Eh bien! I saw them. Now I will return to California. As soon as I can arrange to send back his body."

"That should be handled by your consulate, Madame. There will be official papers to sign."

"I might just do that. Let them take care of everything."

"When do you plan to leave Paris?"

"This is Wednesday. Perhaps Friday."

"You could probably have that attaché case with the nine thousand dollars tomorrow."

"I'd forgotten about that!"

"You'll also have to sign for them."

"Of course."

"I'll check with the lab in the morning, and if they've finished their tests I'll have someone bring them—attaché case and money—to your hotel."

"You've no idea what became of that missing thousand dollars?"

"I suspect your husband gave it to someone."

"To that girl who stabbed him?"

"Very likely. Or he might have paid it to someone who had nothing whatever to do with his death."

"And his wallet?"

"I'm afraid that was taken while he was unconscious. After he collapsed in the street. I've sent word out to known informers and fences to look out for it. For his passport, credit cards, and the wristwatch he was wearing."

"You think they'll turn up?"

"One never knows."

"What does Fric-Frac want?"

He saw that she was sitting up, both paws on the table. "She's hoping for some of my wine."

"Wine?"

"Only white wine." He pushed his glass across the table. "A little white wine is good for her digestion. There you are, Madame."

Fric-Frac leaned forward and lapped the wine from his glass.

Serena laughed. "I've never seen such a thing! Would she care for some of my cognac?"

"That would be too strong for her." He reached for his glass. "Enough, Madame La Duchesse!"

Fric-Frac licked her whiskers but continued to sit with her paws on the table.

Damiot finished the wine. "Another cognac, Madame Scott?"

"Not tonight. Actually, I've been drinking more than usual since I arrived in Paris. Phoned some friends—film people who happen to be here—and had them come over to the hotel for drinks earlier this evening. Of course, they all wanted to know the inside dirt about Alex. Afraid I couldn't tell them anything. They insisted I have dinner with them at Ledoyen. You've been there?"

"No, Madame."

"You must try it one day. Incredible food! And naturally we all drank a bit too much. But afterward I was cold sober. My friends drove me back to the hotel, through the snow, and after I got rid of them I came here. Had to see rue de Caumartin before I went home."

"I understand, Madame."

"Tell me, Monsieur Damiot. Have you ever heard of a French detective—he lived in the last century—named Vidocq?"

"Oh, yes!" He thought of the lithograph hanging in his office and the books in his hotel room. "I am a great admirer of François Eugène Vidocq."

"I've an enormous file on him. And every book that's been written about him. In French and English."

"Do you?"

"One day I hope to write a screenplay about Vidocq. I think

an incredible film could be made from his life. Of course, there's a tremendous amount of material that would have to be discarded. Next time I return to Paris I plan to make a tour of the places he lived. See the actual streets he walked. The houses and apartments—if they still exist—his office at the Préfecture."

"I've no idea which office was his! Never thought to ask."

"Perhaps when I come back, you might be kind enough to give me a personal tour of the Préfecture."

"I would be delighted, Madame. In fact, before you arrive, I will try to find out which parts of the building are unchanged since Vidocq was alive."

"That's a deal! Perhaps next summer."

"Plaisir, Madame."

"Eh bien!" She fastened her sable coat beneath her throat as she talked, collecting her shoulder bag and gloves. "I am suddenly feeling my drinks and terribly tired. Couldn't sleep Tuesday night, after I learned about my husband's murder, and didn't close my eyes last night on the plane. So tonight I shall probably die. Figuratively, that is! Tomorrow I'm seeing Tristan Murzeau, who wants me to write an original screenplay for him." She pushed herself up from the banquette.

Damiot left money as he rose from the table. Put on his hat and raincoat as Serena, with some difficulty, edged around the table. Fric-Frac followed, trailing her leash. "I have a car, Madame. Permit me to drop you at your hotel."

"That won't be necessary. I rented a car this afternoon."

"In that case, permit me to escort you to your car. Come, Fric-Frac!" He reached for her leash, then turned to nod toward Pavy and Jan behind the bar.

The Dutch youth immediately darted ahead of them to open the entrance door.

Fric-Frac hesitated before going outside.

"All right, Madame. We go home."

She stepped down to the pavement and trotted ahead through the snow.

Damiot saw that Serena was swaying and reached to support her arm, his fingers sinking into the luxurious sable. "Where's your car?"

"This way." She motioned down rue de Caumartin.

Jan bowed them through the door. "Plaisir, Madame. Monsieur."

"Perhaps I will see you again, Monsieur Inspecteur." Serena followed Fric-Frac outside. "Before I leave Paris."

"I hope so, Madame." He supported her firmly as they walked in the snow with the wind pushing them down the street.

"If I agree to write a film for Tristan Murzeau I should have to be in Paris for several months. Perhaps we might see something of each other. You could help me with the material for my screenplay."

"That would be my pleasure."

"Oh! I didn't tell you. . . . I called our secretary in Beverly Hills. About the mail Alex received from Paris."

"Yes, Madame?"

"She keeps no record of personal mail—my husband's or mine—but she did remember seeing letters from Paris. Mostly from Tristan Murzeau Productions."

"That's to be expected."

"As well as several from women. Also to be expected."

"Did she remember any names?"

"Only one. Linette Murzeau."

"Murzeau's daughter."

"So I assumed. She remembered it because of the name. She'd never heard of anyone called Linette before. She doesn't remember the address."

"And that's all?"

"Not quite. She says there were two or three letters from another woman, but she can't recall the name. Only that they had American Express as a return address. I'm afraid this isn't much help, is it?"

"One never knows. Every puzzle has many pieces. The trick is to find the important ones."

"This is my car." They had reached a dark green Volkswagen. "Let me find the key." She opened her shoulder bag and fished inside.

Damiot held her firmly as she stepped down from the curb, pulling on the leash to keep Fric-Frac out of her way, and guided Serena around the car to the driver's side.

"Here we are!" She held up the key and closed her handbag.

"Let me unlock that for you."

"I'm perfectly capable." Fumbling the key into the lock and, finally, opening the door.

Fric-Frac jumped up onto the seat.

"No, Fric-Frac!" Damiot ordered. "Down! Immédiatement!"

Serena laughed. "The little love! Wants to come with me."

She jumped down, reluctantly, into the snow.

Serena arranged her fur coat and sank down behind the steering wheel, turning to look up at Damiot. "Don't suppose you'd care to come back to my hotel at this hour?"

"It's getting late. And I have much to do tomorrow."

"Perhaps another time, Inspector. You're a fascinating man. I would like to know you better. Much better. . . ." She slammed the car door.

Damiot stepped away from the car, pulling Fric-Frac back, and waited until the Volkswagen eased out from between the other cars and sped up the street.

He glanced down and saw that Fric-Frac was paying her respects to rue de Caumartin. "Good girl! Now I won't have to walk you again."

Waiting for her to finish, he squinted up and down the street for his car. Impossible to see any distance. He wondered if Risard was asleep or had gone around the corner to find a café where he could have a drink.

The street looked much narrower in the snow. Buildings seemed to be taller, their roofs invisible.

Fric-Frac pulled on her leash, eager to be on her way.

"Bien, Madame. We find our car."

She growled suddenly and pulled him toward the opposite curb.

"What is it, Madame?"

Now she was tugging on the leash, pointing toward a dark archway and barking.

"No, Madame! No!"

She was pulling him across the sidewalk.

"If it's that damn cat again . . ."

"M'sieur Damiot!" A woman's voice.

"Who is it?"

A pale oval of face floated out of the darkness. "I've been waiting here. Hoping to see you. Remember me? Carine."

"How long have you been standing here in this weather?"

"I was coming up the street when you got out of your car and went into that café. So I waited for you to come out again, but you were with the lady and I didn't want to bother you."

"Why did you want to see me?"

"I read in the newspaper that you're looking for a girl with a knife."

"That's right. I am." He saw now how thin she looked, wearing that same short raincoat, umbrella clutched in one gloved hand, plastic hood over her head. "You know of such a girl, Mademoiselle?"

"I might."

"Tell me!"

"I met her one night last summer. We were having a drink—at separate tables—on a café terrace. I noticed her because she had little knives stuck in her shiny black hair. It was so unusual that I spoke to her. Told her how pretty they were."

"Was her hair long?"

"Yes, although she was wearing it on top of her head."

"And straight?"

"That's right. You know her?"

"No, but this may be the girl I'm after. Did you talk to her?"

"She moved over to sit with me. Told me she was lonely in Paris. No real friends. Guess I shouldn't have been so friendly, but I was feeling lonely myself. I realized right away she was only an amateur. The kind that takes business away from professionals. I shouldn't have talked to her, but she looked so sad. Sitting there by herself. . . . We had a drink together."

"Where was this?"

"A café on Boulevard Raspail."

"Did she tell you her name?"

"Only that people called her Lolo."

"You've seen her again?"

"That was the only time. I don't go to Montparnasse any more. It's too far from where I live."

"She was young?"

"Under thirty."

"And French?"

"Oh, no! She told me she was born in Saigon."

"Oriental?"

"Vietnamese."

"Mon Dieu! I hadn't thought."

"Is that important?"

"Very important, Mademoiselle Carine."

He knew now why the girl in Chez Pavy had worn sunglasses. Covering her eyes to hide the fact that she was Oriental.

CHAPTER 14

THE SNOW HAD DISAPPEARED, WASHED AWAY.

Damiot sat at his desk, facing the window, watching gusts of wind propel curtains of rain across the Pont Saint-Michel.

Everything was gray again this morning. River, bridge, and sky, as well as his mood.

He had been sitting here for more than two hours waiting for something to develop. And waiting always made him irritable.

First thing today he had sent Merval off to the Montparnasse police station with instructions to check on a Vietnamese whore who called herself Lolo.

Last night he had given Carine a lift, in spite of her protests. Fric-Frac had liked the young woman and jumped into her lap, sat there until they dropped the thin little prostitute on a snow covered corner near Place Pigalle.

He was grateful to Carine for waiting in that archway with her information about the Vietnamese girl.

That was more than Picolette had been able to tell him. In the old days, Picolette knew most of the girls in Montparnasse, but this time she'd let him down.

Now if only Merval could locate this girl quickly. That's if she was still calling herself Lolo.

He'd gone upstairs for an early-morning meeting with the chief but told him only that he was looking for a prostitute who was known to carry a knife. He hadn't mentioned Lolo.

The phone rang on his desk.

He didn't turn to pick it up and, after another ring, it was silenced.

Graudin was intercepting all calls in the outer office.

There had been messages from several reporters, but he hadn't called any of them back.

The newspapers this morning carried stories elaborating on yesterday's suggestion that Scott had been stabbed by a prostitute. They went as far as they dared without more facts.

He would avoid reporters today until he had something positive to give them.

If nothing developed in the next half hour he would hit the streets himself. Go from bar to café in Montparnasse and ask for Lolo. The only danger was that she would quickly hear Chief Inspector Damiot was looking for her. Then, if she had killed Scott, it would be easy for her to lose herself in the large Vietnamese colony. Her friends and relatives would hide her until she could be smuggled out of France.

No. He must wait here, seething with impatience, until Merval or one of the other inspectors tracked her down.

The telephone rang again, only once this time.

Damiot smiled. Graudin was also getting impatient.

His office was cold, in spite of the radiator wheezing and steaming. Must be freezing outside.

He must decide where to take Andrea tonight. What cuisine they would eat this time. Which restaurant.

No need to make a reservation for dinner in this weather.

He'd cashed a check this morning. Enough for dinner tonight and again next Tuesday, as well as his usual weekend expenses.

He heard sleet striking the windowpanes. So it was getting colder! Did that mean it might clear today? Or tonight.

The phone rang. Three times.

Graudin must still be talking to that last caller.

He was tempted to pick up the receiver and listen to the conversation but restrained his impulse.

Did Lolo have the thousand dollars in American money that was missing from Scott's attaché case? If she tried to spend any of those hundred-dollar bills, somebody would certainly report it.

She'd be too smart to try a thing like that. Easy to get rid of the money. By now—it had been missing since Sunday night—

those bills could be in Tunis or Hong Kong. Impossible to trace back to Lolo—if that really was her name.

He looked forward to meeting Andrea tonight. Their second dinner together. The first had been extremely pleasant, his most relaxing evening in months. And tonight, after dinner, he would very casually suggest they continue the evening in some nearby hotel.

There were side-street hotels in most arrondissements where he knew the manager or concierge.

Make the suggestion to Andrea, as though he had just thought of it, do nothing that might offend her or turn her off.

He had a feeling that her sexual appetites were as insatiable as her obvious zest for living and her enjoyment of food. There was something revealing about her mouth. One of those women who looked sensuous even when they were spooning soup.

She'd been living in Paris several years, so she certainly couldn't be a virgin.

There was a brisk knock on the door, and Damiot turned as Graudin appeared, holding the door ajar as he spoke.

"Madame Scott would like to speak with you, M'sieur l'Inspecteur."

"Thought she'd be asleep this morning." He reached for the phone.

"No. She's in the outer office."

"Show her in." He rose and switched on his desk lamp to make the dusky office more cheerful as Graudin pushed the door wide open.

"Inspector Damiot will see you, Madame."

Serena swept past him, toward Damiot.

He saw that she was wearing the same sable coat with gray slacks tucked into expensive boots. "Bonjour, Madame!"

"Bonjour, Monsieur Inspecteur!"

He was aware of Graudin, behind her, retreating and closing the door. "You reached your hotel safely last night?"

"And slept like an innocent babe. I know you're terribly busy, but I wanted to thank you for moving everything with such dispatch. The consulate called this morning and said all the documents had been processed. My husband's body could be released and that attaché case with the nine thousand dollars would be returned to me. I've been upstairs signing dozens of forms with one of those handsome young men from the consulate who came along to be sure everything was in order."

"You've made more progress than I, Madame." He motioned toward the old leather chair facing his desk. "Won't you sit down?"

"I mustn't keep you. Also, this young man's taking me back to the consulate, where they'll arrange for the shipping of the body to California. I refuse to travel on the same plane, so they're finding someone else. It seems there are always young Americans stranded in Paris who are happy to have a free plane ticket."

The phone continued to ring as they talked, and Damiot wondered each time if it was Merval reporting that he had found Lolo.

"There has been one new development, Madame."

"Oh?"

"I have reason to suspect that the young woman seen with your husband at Chez Pavy, immediately prior to his death, may have been a Vietnamese."

"Alex always did like Orientals!"

"We're looking for this young woman. At least it narrows the search slightly."

"Bonne chance, Monsieur Inspecteur! What I really wanted to tell you is that I've decided not to fly back to the States until next week. I've agreed to do that screenplay for Tristan Murzeau."

"Congratulations!"

"But not an original. It's to be based on some French novel. Frankly, I'd never heard of it, but he's giving it to me at lunch. So I'll read it tonight." She hesitated briefly. "Don't suppose you're free for dinner?"

"Unfortunately, Madame, I already have a dinner engagement."

"Pity." She smiled. "I was hoping to pick your brains. Learn about murder in Paris. Hear first hand the details of your life as a chief inspector with the Police Judiciaire."

"Perhaps another time, Madame."

"I presume you're dining with a young lady tonight."

"Your deduction is brilliant."

"Then I couldn't hope to persuade you to change your mind." She laughed. "I mustn't keep my escort from the consulate waiting. I've a feeling they keep these young men wrapped in plastic. When there's a job to be done they unwrap them, wind them up, and send them off in a shiny car." She turned toward the door. "À bientôt, Monsieur Inspecteur."

"À bientôt, Madame. I will contact you when I have something more to report." He watched her open the door and glimpsed a blond youth waiting in the outer office before the door closed.

It swung open again almost immediately as Graudin returned, kicking it shut with his heel and coming straight to the desk.

"What's happening?" Damiot asked, sinking into his chair.

"There was a call just now. Somebody tossed a wallet through the entrance at the Pigalle police station. One of the officers noticed it when he came on duty but didn't see who threw it."

"Naturally."

"Picked it up and looked inside."

"Scott's wallet?"

"With identification papers and credit cards."

"Passport?"

"No passport, money, or wristwatch."

"The passport, of course, will be sold to someone. Eh bien! We now know for a fact, Scott was robbed as he lay dying in the gutter. Watch and money will never be found, but I want that passport. No questions asked. American passport issued to Timothy Kelleher. Occupation—actor."

"I'll get the word out. I've told them to send the wallet and all that's in it to the forensic lab."

"There won't be any prints. Whoever tossed it into Pigalle headquarters would have wiped it clean."

"What about the American money? That thousand dollars."

"Whoever killed Scott has that. Either he gave it to her or she took it from his wallet after she stabbed him."

"Dr. Bretty called."

"What now?"

"He heard from Madame Allanic. Her husband was taken to the hospital last night with pneumonia."

"Which hospital?"

"Bicêtre."

"That's serious, at his age. Remind me tomorrow to send flowers."

"One piece of bad news."

Damiot smiled. Graudin always saved the worst news for the last. "Yes?"

"That inspector in charge of the computers called."

"And?"

"He had some trouble today with his machines. Says it may have something to do with this damp weather. When they started working again, he tried to find out if there were any whores known to carry a knife. No idea how he does it, but one of the other inspectors said he punches some kind of card full of holes and drops it in a slot. I'm told his machines break down all the time."

"Anything turn up on whores with knives?"

"That's why he called. The computers are working again, but he said the card came out blank."

"What about similar stabbings? Knife wounds in the back but no cuts in the victim's clothing?"

"He's working on that now. Said he would have an answer for you this afternoon. If the machine don't break down again."

"Merde! All this waiting, nothing happening . . ."

The telephone rang and Graudin picked it up. "Chief Inspector Damiot's office."

Damiot turned his chair toward the window and saw sleet sliding down the panes. He scowled. The morning had been wasted.

"I'm sorry, Madame. I can't put you through to Inspector Damiot unless you tell me why you wish to speak to him. I'm his assistant, Sergeant Graudin."

He had hoped those computers would come up with something. Although he still resented the idea of some mechanical device helping to catch a murderer.

"Many people say they know the Chief Inspector, but unless you give me your name. . . . Picolette? I'm sorry, Madame. . . ."

Damiot swiveled his chair. "I'll take it."

"One moment, Madame. Here's Inspector Damiot." He handed the phone across the desk.

Damiot held it to his ear. "Bonjour, Picolette!"

"You're so important these days, you don't answer your phone."

"Never too busy to talk to an old friend."

"I'm calling about that matter we discussed yesterday."

He straightened in his chair, eyes on Graudin. "Yes?"

"I made some phone calls last night and again this morning. Two of my friends tell me there's a new girl who sometimes wears knives in her hair. They say she's an odd one. Keeps to herself. Never talks to anyone, except handsome young men. She has long black hair and—"

"Wears sunglasses?"

"Nobody mentioned that. This is Paris in November! Not the Riviera."

Damiot sighed, deflated.

"The girls see her in the cafés, but they're not friendly. She's Vietnamese."

Damiot straightened again. "Is she known as Lolo?"

"So you've heard about her!"

"Last night. One of my men is out now looking for her."

"I have an address. Where she lived last month."

"Give it to me!" He reached for a pen and pad.

"She lives in Montparnasse."

"I know that. Which street?"

"Rue Vavin."

"The number?"

He wrote it on his pad. "You came through for me, Picolette! And I'm on my way to rue Vavin!" Handing the phone back to Graudin. "Order a car. You'd better drive. Maybe we'll find Merval wandering in the street."

The police car, Graudin at the wheel and Damiot slouched beside him, sped down Boulevard Saint-Michel, through rue August Comte, and up rue d'Assas without glimpsing Merval or his parked police car.

Damiot ordered him to slow down in rue Vavin and park in front of the address Picolette had given him on the phone.

They got out into a barrage of cold sleet and ducked under an archway leading into a small courtyard. Stood there, brushing pebbles of ice from their hats and shoulders, as they looked up and down the desolate street.

Damiot saw one old woman huddled under an umbrella, walking carefully on the icy pavement, carrying a string bag full of groceries. Some small shops in this block, but the character of the street changed after it crossed Boulevard Raspail, with supper clubs and cabarets on either side. At night the far end of the street would blossom with garish neons, but in this gray morning light rue Vavin was depressing.

"Want me to come with you?" Graudin asked.

"You'd better stay here and watch for Merval. I'll question the girl alone. Two of us might seem to be threatening her."

As Damiot went through the arched passage toward the courtyard, he was met by an aroma of cooking that drew him straight to the lace-curtained window of a door with a sign indicating that this was the lair of the concierge.

He knocked and, while he waited, analyzed the aroma. Puzzling out the ingredients that were simmering in white wine.

The door opened, and a fresh wave of the delicious smell engulfed him.

A tiny pleasant-faced woman with spiky white hair looked up at him, smiling, wiping her hands on a spotless apron. "M'sieur?"

"You're stewing rabbit."

"For my husband's dinner."

"With mushrooms and basil. Onions but—no garlic?"

"My husband can't eat garlic."

"Your stew smells delicious. Eh bien! You have a young woman living here known as Lolo?"

"Second floor. Number ten." She frowned, recognizing the voice of authority. "Lolo's not in trouble?"

"Not at the moment." He turned toward the courtyard again.

"I certainly hope not. Such a nice girl." The quavery voice floated after him. "The steps are on your left, M'sieur."

He saw an open door and, ducking through the sleet, entered a small vestibule with a cracked marble floor and a handsomely proportioned old wooden staircase.

His hip began to complain before he reached the top of the second flight of steps and found a door with the number he sought.

Not a sound from inside and no voices or music coming from behind the other closed doors.

Then, as he raised his hand to knock, there was a shrill and inhuman shriek from behind the door.

He knocked lightly.

The shriek was repeated.

He knocked again, more sharply, and heard something moving in the apartment.

"Who is it?" A young female voice. Apprehensive, barely audible.

"Is that Lolo?"

"What do you want?"

"May I come in, Mademoiselle? An important matter. I must speak with you."

"One moment, Monsieur."

Another shriek from behind the door as a bolt was pulled back.

The door was opened by a girl in some sort of Oriental robe.

He saw that she was young and extremely pretty. "Mademoiselle Lolo?"

"Who are you?"

"Chief Inspector Damiot." He held out his badge.

"Police!"

"May I come in?"

"Of course, Monsieur l'Inspecteur." She backed away from him, one hand clutching her robe.

Damiot followed, closing the door, into a room filled with an overpowering combination of exotic scents, probably incense as well as perfume. He saw, in the faint light from two paper lanterns hanging from the ceiling, that Lolo's robe was made of some dark blue material with a pattern of strange white birds. It dragged on the floor, but as she walked ahead of him he glimpsed her bare feet in white sandals with blue thongs.

She sank gracefully onto an unmade divan-bed, motioning toward an awkwardly low chair.

He sat down, resting his hat on a bamboo table. The chair was more comfortable than he had anticipated.

A harsh shriek filled the room, much louder than it sounded from the hall.

Damiot looked around and saw a large white-plumed bird perched in an ornate white pagoda cage hanging near a row of tall windows with a bleak view of rain-soaked rooftops.

"Did Chee-Chee startle you?" Lolo giggled nervously. "He is my friend. My only friend."

The bird watched them with shiny, too human eyes.

Damiot, turning back to Lolo, realized that she was looking at him with no apparent fear or apprehension. He was about to ask his first question when he noticed that her glossy black hair was wound into a thick knot on top of her head and held in place by two small jeweled daggers. The sight of them caught him with his mouth open.

"Why have you come to see me, Monsieur?"

"There are several questions I must ask you."

She shrugged. "I have nothing to hide from the police. What can I tell you?"

"You are called Lolo?"

"Lolo is my legal name. Since before I came to France, more than five years ago. My full name is Lolo Yeung—spelled Y-e-u-n-g. That's the name that was on my passport and my visa. I became a citizen of France last year, and that is my legal name on all my papers."

"You are Vietnamese?"

"By birth. My father is Vietnamese, but my mother is French, and I was born in Saigon. It was my mother who named me Lolo. It is the name of a character in some opérette she saw, here in Paris, when she was very young."

The bird shrieked again.

"That was before her parents brought her to Vietnam. My French grandfather was in the diplomatic corps."

"This explains why you speak French like a Parisian. Where are your parents now?"

"They have a Vietnamese restaurant on rue Gomboust. Very successful. My brother and sister both work there. I became tired of serving the tourists and left my family to live on my own. My parents did not approve, and I do not see them anymore. But I survive."

"Do you like Paris?"

"It is a sad city. Before I came here I always thought it was a happy place, but it is cold and gray. I do not like the winters—this rain—but even in the summer it is cold and gray. And sad."

"You are a prostitute?"

She shrugged again. "If you say so, Monsieur."

"You enjoy such a life?"

"I enjoy meeting young men. Talking to them. Hoping to find one that is gentle and kind."

Damiot studied her exquisite face as she talked. Her skin was like translucent silk, the slightly slanted eyes enigmatic black pools under their dark eyebrows. She seemed to be wearing no makeup. He wondered if she had been asleep when he knocked on her door.

". . . but they are neither—gentle or kind—these young men. They are, all of them, crude and coarse."

"Then why do you continue?"

"I suppose because I am bored with life. It is not pleasant, living alone."

"Why not go back to your family?"

She smiled sadly. "Haven't you discovered, Monsieur, that it is never wise to go back? To one's family or to any other person."

"Yes. I have learned that. Tell me, Mademoiselle—did you ever know a man named Scott?"

"Scott."

"Alex Scott?"

"I think not."

"An American film actor."

"Where would we have met?"

"Perhaps here in Paris."

"No."

The bird shrilled again.

Damiot winced. "Monsieur Scott was in Paris last June. Again in August and September and, finally, last week."

"I do not go to see American films, and I have never met Monsieur Scott."

Damiot had a strong feeling that she was telling the truth. And obviously she did not read the newspapers or she would have reacted to Scott's name. He glanced around the small apartment and saw no radio or television set. Only a small record player.

The bird screeched again.

"Why do you ask me about Monsieur Scott?" she asked.

"We are trying to find anyone who may have seen him since he arrived in Paris last Friday." He produced Scott's photograph from an inside pocket of his raincoat and held it toward her. "This is his picture."

"He is very handsome." She stared at the picture, frowning. "I have never seen this face. I am sorry." She looked up at Damiot and smiled. "I would like to help you, Monsieur."

"Help me?" He slipped the photograph back into his pocket. "Eh bien! If you hear of anyone who did see Scott or talk to him, would you phone me at the Préfecture? Chief Inspector Damiot."

"Of course, Monsieur l'Inspecteur."

"Those knives in your hair—are they antiques?"

"Oh, no. We sold all our antiques before leaving Saigon. Everything! These are cheap imitations I picked up in a bazaar before we left. I used to have a dozen, but these two are all I have now."

"Could I see them?" He held out his hand.

She looked puzzled, then shrugged. "But of course!" She reached up with both hands and pulled out the two small daggers.

Damiot watched as the long black hair coiled down over her robe. He breathed deeply of the fragrance that came from her hair. Disturbed and unaware for a moment that she was holding out her hands with the two daggers, their jeweled handles toward him. He took them from her and saw that the jewels were imitations, their glitter tawdry. The points of the blades were sharp, but the knives didn't appear long enough to cause a deep cut.

"I have never stabbed anyone with them, Monsieur Damiot, if that's what you're thinking."

Her use of his name startled him, until he remembered that he had given it to her when he brought out his badge.

"I could never kill a human being. Not even those soldiers who raped me during the war."

"Which soldiers?"

"First the Communists and then the Americans. That is why I no longer enjoy having sex. Even though I continue looking for a handsome man who is gentle and kind." Her eyes searched his face.

The bird screeched and shattered the mood.

Damiot held up the two daggers. "Could I have these for a few days, Mademoiselle?"

"If you wish."

He brought out a handkerchief, opened it, and placed the daggers on the white cloth, folding it over them and returning the handkerchief to his pocket as he rose from the chair.

Lolo remained seated. "I have not killed anyone, Monsieur l'Inspecteur. In Saigon or in Paris."

Damiot retrieved his hat. "Thank you for answering my questions."

"Will I see you again, Monsieur?"

"When I return your daggers." He put his hat on and headed for the door.

"Perhaps some evening, when Monsieur is not working."

Damiot turned, his hand on the doorknob, and looked back. Her face was a lovely mask of innocence, but the luminous Oriental eyes held the knowledge of centuries. Knowledge of good and evil.

"You are an extremely handsome man and, perhaps, a kind man."

"Au 'voir, Lolo."

"À bientôt, Monsieur Damiot."

As he opened the door, the bird screeched one final time.

CHAPTER 15

THE SLEET HAD STOPPED, BUT THE RAIN CONTINUED. For the moment, as the small police car avoided the deep puddles at some of the street corners, Damiot didn't feel like talking. Andrea, snuggled beside him, had sensed his mood and remained silent.

They had talked about unimportant things over apéritifs at the Café de la Paix—she had been waiting when he got there—but both their moods had changed as the black car headed up Avenue de Clichy and they retreated into their own private thoughts.

Damiot was exhausted but exhilarated because things were finally moving. His hunches seemed to be paying off. Those despised computers had, to his surprise, come up with something promising.

When he returned to his office, two dossiers were waiting on his desk with an unfamiliar name on each. Luc Darbois and Victor Montal. Both men had been found in a Paris street, five months apart, with a single stab wound in their backs and no cuts in their clothing. The two murders were never solved and had been filed as incomplete.

Like that case he had left unfinished last week. He wondered if Jacques Bertrand's dossier would ever be pulled out of the files again. Not likely! These two guys, Darbois and Montal, were lucky.

Maybe . . .

The two cases had attracted little attention. Both were believed to be casual street murders. Like that of Jacques Bertrand. Nobody had realized the importance of one fact—

their clothes hadn't been cut—so the two cases had never been connected . . .

He glanced at Andrea beside him, gloved hands folded in her lap. "We're almost there."

She looked up and smiled.

Damiot peered up Avenue de Clichy as the wiper swept drops of rain from the windshield. Hardly any traffic. Taxis had vanished again. Restaurants were lighted, but nobody was going in or coming out.

He had phoned earlier to make their dinner reservations and had engaged a room in a nearby hotel where he was known.

The evening looked promising.

Andrea had agreed it might be wise for her to ride in his car, and they had left hers—the battered white Volkswagen with its two patched tires—parked near Café de la Paix. He would drive her back there, at the end of the evening, and not have to take her wherever she was "apartment-sitting."

He was looking forward to dinner and, in anticipation, hadn't eaten any lunch.

When he called the restaurant he had talked to le patron—ordered their dinner, food and wine—and was salivating at the thought of the lapereau à la chasseur which, at this moment, would be giving off a more complicated aroma than the one coming from that concierge's apartment in Montparnasse this morning.

Lolo's concierge. Lolo Y-e-u-n-g . . .

Her two small daggers, when he last saw them, rested on a white enamel tray in the forensic lab.

Was this Vietnamese girl the killer?

There was something . . . triste about her. He'd been aware of it constantly as they talked. She was one of the most pathetic individuals he'd ever questioned. A victim of that miserable Vietnamese war. Raped so many times, apparently, that she no longer found pleasure in having sex. Searching for a man who was "gentle and kind."

Her life in Vietnam destroyed by the war. Uprooted and brought to Paris. Returning to the prostitution she'd been forced into at an early age in Saigon. Brutalized by soldiers. Imprisoned now in a world of whores, which she hadn't sought and didn't enjoy. That is, of course, if she was telling him the truth.

And he had a strong feeling she was.

At no time during their conversation did he sense that she'd been avoiding his questions or was lying.

In spite of that, she could be the prostitute who had stabbed Scott and, probably, Darbois and Montal as well.

If the lab said neither of those knives had killed Scott, he would have to visit Lolo again. Take Graudin and Merval with him. They could search her apartment, looking for other knives, while he questioned her. Next time his questions wouldn't be so cautious. He'd been much too easy with her.

There'd been other women who had fooled him at first meeting. Still had to watch that. A beautiful woman could convince you of anything.

Lolo was sad. Alone and vulnerable.

She seemed as much of a prisoner as that ridiculous white bird in its fancy cage.

Amazing how people who were imprisoned by circumstance—he had known others—frequently owned caged birds. It was as though it made them feel free, watching a bird behind bars . . .

He glimpsed the lighted restaurant. "Here we are!"

Andrea leaned forward to read the sign above the entrance. "Café Toulouse? As in Lautrec?"

"Actually, this restaurant's named for the capital of the Department of Haute-Garonne. The painter Lautrec was born in Albi, which is in the next department."

"And the food tonight?"

"You are going to sample the cuisine and drink the wines of Languedoc. The couple who own Café Toulouse are from Narbonne. I hope you don't mind that I took the liberty to phone this afternoon and order our dinner. Including a main dish that must be cooked for several hours."

"How exciting!"

No parked cars, so Damiot eased close to the curb in front of the restaurant and quickly escorted Andrea through gusts of rain toward the entrance and into the small restaurant.

Stepping out of the damp air, into the warmth of the low-ceilinged room, Damiot breathed deeply, inhaling the rich aroma of the lapereau à la chasseur.

"M'sieur Damiot!"

He saw that young Madame Gisquet, coming from behind her high desk near the entrance, had gained weight. "Madame!" He shook her hand. "This is Mademoiselle Brandon."

La patronne smiled and shook Andrea's hand. "Mademoiselle."

"Madame Gisquet is the wife of le patron. Her husband is one of the finest young chefs in Paris."

"If that were true, M'sieur, we shouldn't be empty tonight. Only three other persons for dinner."

"It's this weather."

"Let me have your coat, Mademoiselle. M'sieur."

He removed his damp hat and slipped out of his raincoat as Andrea pulled the flowered scarf from her head, peeled off her gloves and stuck them into her bag, which she slipped from her shoulder. Damiot handed his things to la patronne, who hung them in a small cloakroom, then helped Andrea with her raincoat. He saw that she was wearing another simple dress, this time some kind of dark beige material with white collar and cuffs that made her look even younger. Her white-blonde hair swirled down below her shoulders.

"This way, Mademoiselle, Monsieur." Madame led them through the restaurant. "My husband has everything ready for you. He appreciates it when people call ahead to give their dinner order. That allows him time to prepare everything more carefully."

As they passed between the empty rows of tables, Damiot saw that only two distant tables were occupied. An old man at one, engrossed with his dinner, and a middle-aged couple in a far corner who were drinking wine and engrossed with each other. He realized that Andrea was looking from side to side at the attractive room with its heavy stone columns and beamed ceiling. Rows of framed pictures on the walls, Lautrec reproductions alternating with oil paintings showing scenes of Languedoc. They passed a long table with a display of fruit, cheeses, and desserts. Shaded candles cast pools of light on each table. A trio of young waiters stood near the kitchen doors, observing their progress through the room.

Madame Gisquet led them to a table away from the other diners. "This will be satisfactory, M'sieur Damiot?"

"Perfect, Madame. As always." He pulled out a chair for Andrea then sat across from her.

"Maintenant! If you'll excuse me, I must tell my husband you've arrived." Madame bowed and headed toward the kitchen, snapping her fingers at the waiters, who sprang to instant life.

"This is charming," Andrea murmured. "Even more attractive than the Relais Touraine the other night."

"And Haute-Garonne food is very unlike that of the Loire Valley."

"As good or even better?"

"You must decide that for yourself."

"Most Americans never find an out-of-the-way restaurant like this. Or see Paris restaurants in the winter when they're half empty."

While they talked, one smiling waiter brought menus and another filled their glasses with Perrier. The third waiter, slightly older, bowed. "An apéritif, M'sieur Damiot?"

"By all means." He turned toward Andrea. "Dry vermouth again?"

"Please."

"Two vermouths. Au citron."

"Plaisir." The waiter bowed and went toward the bar.

Damiot drank some Perrier to clear his palate for dinner.

"You seem in a good mood tonight, Monsieur." Andrea smiled, her blue eyes brightening. "You were quiet driving here, but now you're like another person."

"Anticipating dinner. In the car I was preoccupied with thoughts of what had happened today."

"You mean the Scott investigation?"

"Yes."

"Bad things or good things?"

"Too soon to say. There have been several developments. Two additional murders."

Her eyes widened with surprise. "By the same murderer?"

"So it would seem. Two other men have died in Paris streets with a single stab wound in the back."

"This week? Since Scott was killed?"

"Oh, no! Both these men died last year. One in February and the other in July."

"Were their murderers found?"

"Not a trace. Their dossiers were marked uncompleted. That's an open file, in case new evidence turns up. Usually it doesn't." He looked up as the waiter served their apéritifs. "Merci." Waited until he had gone, then raised his glass. "À nous, Mademoiselle!"

She smiled and held up her glass. "À nous."

As they drank, Damiot was aware of le patron coming from the kitchen ahead of his wife.

"M'sieur Damiot!" His tall toque blanche bowed as he shook hands. "How good to see you again." Turning to Andrea. "And to welcome you, Mademoiselle."

"Merci." She noticed that Gisquet was as young and plump as his wife, who had returned to her desk.

"Everything is in readiness, M'sieur Inspecteur! Exactly as you ordered."

"And we are hungry! Mademoiselle Brandon has never enjoyed the cuisine of Languedoc before. I've told her that, after my native Provence, yours is one of the best!"

"Every province of France has its special cuisine, but one always thinks his own is the finest." He smiled. "Maintenant! There is much work still to be done. Bon appétit, Mademoiselle, Monsieur." He turned and hurried toward his kitchen.

"Our first course will be a pâté," Damiot said, finishing his apéritif.

"Eel again?"

"Something very different. A pâté of pheasant. Slightly coarser in texture than eel. With a white wine from Languedoc, called Gaillac. Which we will also drink with our fish. I did not order soup because the main course is a stew."

"I love stews! You were saying a moment ago that two other men had been stabbed. How did you learn about them?"

"Through a new computer system they've installed at the Préfecture. First time I've used the contraption. I resent all mechanical things. They're changing the world and may one day destroy us. But I wondered if there might've been any earlier killings—a knife wound in the back without cuts in the victim's clothing—so I had one of my assistants contact the inspector in charge of the computers. Asked him to check through the past several years to see if his machines could turn up any similar murders. To my surprise, they came up with two!"

"You think there's some connection with Alex Scott's death?"

"I've no idea. Now I must dig into both those old cases. Find out if those two men were in any way connected to each other and to Scott. I realize, of course, the only link between any of them may have been their murderer."

"Then you do suspect they were all killed by the same person?"

"That is certainly more than probable."

"And you still think it was a prostitute who killed Scott?"

"We've found one who could be the killer. She was reported to us by other prostitutes as one who was known to carry a knife on her person. Frequently worn in her hair."

"You've actually found her?"

"I questioned her today."

"You are making progress!"

"She lives in Montparnasse—rue Vavin—and her name is Lolo Yeung. Spelled, as she told me, Y-e-u-n-g. She's a Vietnamese—a refugee—and, I'm afraid, our only suspect at the moment. But I've a feeling she may not be the right one."

"Why do you think that?"

"Because Lolo answered my questions with such apparent honesty."

"How can you be certain?"

"I can't! And for good reason. Lolo had two knives in her possession, which I've turned over to our forensic lab. They should complete their tests tomorrow. If one of those knives turns out to be the weapon used to kill Scott, I will know that Lolo was an excellent actress."

Their conversation was interrupted by the first course, served by one waiter while another opened their wine and, after showing the label, poured it carefully.

Damiot sipped it and nodded.

The wine was golden in the candlelight, chilled but not too cold, and the flavors of the pheasant pâté were unlike anything Andrea had ever tasted.

"This is even better than that eel!" she exclaimed.

"It is different. I like both."

"So do I! And this wine . . ."

"It's sparkling, but not champagne."

"It's liquid sunshine!" She set her glass down and spread more pâté on a morsel of warm bread. "Tell me, why do all chefs wear the same kind of trousers? I noticed the other night and again this evening. Black and white checks."

"Most chefs do. But nobody seems to know why. The French call the pattern of that cloth chicken-foot."

"I think we call the same pattern houndstooth in America, but I'd always supposed the material was English."

"Nobody's ever been able to tell me why chefs wear such trousers, Mademoiselle Brandon. Or who invented the toque blanche—their white bonnet. I've asked many chefs."

"Wouldn't it be possible for you to call me Andrea?"

"Avec plaisir. It has a good sound. Andrea."

"And I shall call you Guy!"

"Mais certainement! How did you know my name is Guy?"

"It's been in the newspapers. Many times. Chief Inspector Guy Damiot."

"Those ridiculous stories they print!"

"I've found them fascinating. All of them."

As Andrea talked, he remembered Serena and her file of clippings in California. Wondered where she was dining tonight.

"I felt I knew you long before we met at the Café de la Paix! Guy also has a good sound—the way you French pronounce it. In English, however, Guy sounds hard. Like a gangster."

Their next course was grilled filets of sole with caviar butter and a second glass of Gaillac.

Followed by the lapereau à la chasseur.

When one waiter lifted the lid from the copper cocotte, Damiot sniffed the mouth-watering fragrance rising from the stew. As the other waiter served, the third waiter opened another bottle of white wine—a blanquette from Limoux—and filled fresh glasses.

The aroma from the lapereau filled the restaurant.

Damiot observed the old man at the far table sniffing the air appreciatively, but the couple in the corner were interested only in each other and whatever it was they were now eating.

Andrea gazed at her plate as the waiter set it in front of her.

"This is a famous Languedoc dish," Damiot explained. "Young rabbit with mushrooms."

"I love rabbit and adore mushrooms! French mushrooms taste like a dark and enchanted forest. I've never had any back in the States that compared to them."

"I'm delighted that my choice pleases you." He waited as she sampled her first morsel of meat with a slice of mushroom.

"I've never tasted rabbit or mushrooms like these."

"Bien!"

"This rabbit must've scampered in the fields of heaven!"

"Les champs élysées?" He laughed, picturing a rabbit hopping up the busy avenue, as he separated the tender flesh from a delicate ivory bone, added a plump mushroom, and raised the fork to his mouth. The combination of flavors was sublime. "I agree. This is excellent." Analyzing each ingredient as he ate. Sliced carrots, shallots, tomatoes, and a faint trace of bay leaf. Garlic and onion, both very subtle. All simmered in white wine, the mushrooms added shortly before serving.

Their next course was a fresh endive salad, the dressing made with walnut oil.

He realized, as they enjoyed the food, that their conversation had become more intimate. After dessert he would, as casually as possible, suggest that they make love. How did one say this to an American girl without shocking her?

They finished the bottle of Limoux with a ripe Roquefort, served in a small wheel from which Damiot cut generous wedges.

Dessert was a warm flognarde—a prune pudding fragrant with Armagnac—followed by black coffee and a glass of Armagnac.

"Such a lovely dinner!" Andrea warmed the brandy glass between her hands. "Even more delicious than our first together."

"And there will be two more next week."

"Each better than the last?"

"At least as good. I hope, chérie, that you are enjoying our dinners together."

"Completely! You've introduced me to a world no American can ever discover without a Frenchman to serve as guide."

"It's been my pleasure. I look forward to next Tuesday."

"Are we going to make love tonight?"

Her question surprised him. "What did you say?"

"Tonight. Will we make love?"

"I was hoping we might."

"Bien!" She finished the last of her Armagnac. "I had hoped we would, after our first dinner." Looking up at him mischievously. "But you didn't say anything."

"I had every intention of saying something before we left here tonight. In fact, I've engaged a room in a nearby hotel."

She laughed. "You were very sure of yourself!"

"Yes."

CHAPTER 16

THE NIGHT MANAGER OF THE SMALL HOTEL AROUND THE corner greeted Damiot like an old friend without glancing at his companion.

Damiot took the room key and followed Andrea upstairs, amused by her lack of embarrassment. He had brought other women here in the past and was aware that many of his fellow detectives patronized this hotel because of its discretion and the fact that it was not used by whores, but mostly businessmen with other men's wives and middle-aged wives and young lovers. One of the reasons he had selected the Café Toulouse tonight was because, even in the rain, they could walk here.

Their room was small but immaculately clean.

"Kempt, couth, and sheveled!" Andrea exclaimed, giggling.

"I don't understand."

"That's an American pun, I suppose."

"Oh."

"Sounds like a firm of lawyers—avocats."

"Oh, yes!" He laughed, but he still didn't comprehend.

They made love, tentatively at first, then with joy and abandon.

Andrea's body was plump but firm, and he discovered that her mouth was even more sensuous than he had suspected.

Finally, exhausted, they sank back onto the bolster, clasping each other, their mouths still joined.

Then, reluctantly, they separated and stretched out, Damiot's left arm under Andrea, the fingers of her right hand continuing to explore flesh.

She was first to speak. "Eh bien, chéri! Nothing frivial about that."

"D'accord!" He laughed. "Nothing the least frivial."

Andrea giggled again.

He glanced down at her compact body. She seemed so tiny beside him, almost like a child.

The small room was comfortably warm, and they remained uncovered as they relaxed.

"Are you happy?" Andrea whispered.

"Of course! And you?"

"For the moment."

"Only for the moment?"

"No one can ever be really happy for more than a moment. Only a fool."

"Would you care for something to drink?"

"Nothing, merci."

"They'll send up anything we want from the bar. Champagne?"

"After all that wine for dinner! I don't usually drink so much."

They lay looking at the ceiling, the hotel silent around them.

Andrea sighed. "The famous Chief Inspector Damiot has made love to me! And I can't tell anybody."

"Why not?"

"No one would believe me." Her fingers found his hand and clutched it. "When I am very old and write my autobiography, I will describe our gourmet tour of Paris."

"You plan to write an autobiography?"

"I don't even like to write letters! But one never knows. I suppose there are other women who could write about this room in their autobiographies. Where Chief Inspector Damiot made love to them."

"Fortunately, none of them will ever write a book."

He remembered again that Scott's wife was keeping a file on him and wanted to write a screenplay about a Paris detective. Nobody would guess it was about him.

The wail of a police van, up and down, reached them muffled by distance. Probably from Avenue de Clichy.

"You must have many friends in Paris." He said this only to make conversation.

"A few."

"Do you miss your family?"

"My mother's dead. I told you that when we first met."

"You said your father's alive."

"I hate my father."

"Shouldn't hate your father."

"He's a murderer."

He felt her body stiffen against his arm, as she slipped her hand away from his. "What did you say?"

"He killed my mother."

"You're joking, of course."

"It's the God's truth!"

"You want to tell me about it?"

"Well, yes. I suppose I do."

Could this be why she had sought him out Monday night in the Café de la Paix? To talk about murder?

"I was fifteen. My family had a small estate on the edge of Germantown. A high wall around it and an entrance gate with a drive winding between oak trees up to the front of the house. My parents had been quarreling for weeks, and I was aware that things were reaching a crisis. I went to a private school during the day but came home every night. I heard them arguing after I went upstairs to bed."

"Why were they arguing?"

"My mother had found out somehow that he was having an affair with another woman in Philadelphia. Walt was always involved with other women, but for some reason this latest one was too much. Apparently he had been seen with her at some party. Carla had been invited, but refused to go. So Walt went with Nina, his latest mistress, and some of Carla's friends reported to her on the phone next morning. I guess my parents' marriage had never been really happy. When I was younger I didn't realize it. Maybe because they didn't argue in front of me. In that last year, before Carla was killed, I became more and more aware that they were heading for an explosion."

"Why didn't your parents get a divorce?"

"Walt begged her to divorce him, but she wouldn't even discuss it."

"You called your father Walt?"

"They both liked me to call them by their first names. Carla and Walt. Even when I was a child. Looking back, I think that must've been Carla's doing. I suppose she hoped it would bring the three of us closer together, but of course it didn't. I was always much closer to Carla. Loved her more than I did Walt. She was a warm and loving person. Walt was so involved with business that he never had time for me. He'd wanted a son, not a daughter. Carla named me Andrea, but Walt always called me Andy!"

"How did your mother die?"

"They had been battling because Walt didn't approve of her spending the weekend in New York with friends. Younger people he didn't like. She refused to listen to him. I remember the maid bringing luggage downstairs after breakfast and Carla telling her to phone for a taxi to take her to the railroad station. Walt told her he would drive her. They argued, but he finally snatched up her bags and carried them out to the car. Carla kissed me good-bye. Said she would see me Monday evening. I walked outside with her and watched them get into the Mercedes. Walt didn't even open the door for her. She slammed it shut and waved to me as they went down the drive. I turned back into the house and was crossing the entrance hall when I heard the crash. I knew right away what it was. I ran from the house and down the drive. Followed by the maid. Saw the car smashed against one of the big trees. Walt came to meet us. I saw blood on his head and realized that he was stumbling. He waved us back. Ordered the maid to phone the police and tell then there'd been an accident. I remember his words. 'Tell them Mrs. Brandon is dead.' He tried to take me in his arms, but I ran past him to the car. It was horrible! I could see Carla's body hanging through the broken windshield. Walt finally pulled me back, but I pushed him away and ran into the house. Went upstairs to my room and locked the door."

"Your mother wasn't murdered. That was an accident."

"Walt drove the car into that tree to kill her. It was her side of the car that was destroyed, not the driver's. Walt's forehead was cut by flying glass, but he wasn't badly hurt. He killed my mother. Smashed that car purposely."

"What did the police say?"

"Exactly what Walt wanted them to say. He's an important citizen of Germantown. Walter Brandon the Second! Like royalty. He told them he lost control when one of our dogs ran in front of the car and caused him to swerve. Everyone knew he loved dogs. So nobody suspected it was murder. Except me! I knew it was."

"Didn't the police question you?"

"No. I stayed in my room until after they'd gone. Walt told them I didn't witness the accident."

"Actually you didn't. You say you were in the house." He realized that she was sobbing quietly, as though she didn't want him to hear. "You loved your mother?"

"I adored Carla!"

"What did your father say to you, privately, later on?"

"Exactly what he'd told the police. That it was an accident. But I knew he was lying! I could see it in his eyes. That he was covering up the truth."

"Did you ever accuse him of murder?"

"I didn't dare! Anyway, what good would that have done? It wouldn't bring Carla back, and my own life would've been even more intolerable! I couldn't tell him I knew he'd killed Carla. If I had, he might have killed me. He'd never loved me."

"Why do you say that?"

"Walt never wanted a daughter. He told Carla that, again and again, when he thought I couldn't hear. How he'd married her to have a son, but she'd only given him a daughter. After I was born Carla had two miscarriages. You see, Walt was still hoping she would produce Walter Brandon the Third! That's what he wanted. Like a vintage wine! A son to carry on the family business in Philadelphia, which had been founded by his father. Originally they made huge dynamos, but now they're into electronics."

"Didn't you become closer to your father after your mother's death?"

"I saw him even less than before. In fact, he rarely came home at all, but stayed in the family apartment in Philadelphia. I realized he must be seeing his mistress and wasn't surprised when he told me he was going to marry again. I was seventeen then and still in the same stuffy private school. After their marriage he brought Nina to live in the Germantown house, and I realized at once that she resented my being there. I stuck it out for a year, but then I told Walt I was going to take an apartment in Philadelphia. I had some money of my own that Grandfather Brandon had left me. So I moved into the city and enrolled at the Academy—that's the oldest art school in the United States—to study painting. Did that for a year, then decided I had no talent and moved on to New York, where I took ballet lessons."

"And your father?"

"His second wife, Nina, had a baby—a son—so Walt got what he wanted. Walter Brandon the Third! That was about the time I realized I'd never be a ballet dancer, so I found a job in New York with a television network."

"You didn't see your father again?"

"Not once. I knew he was in New York from time to time—I would read about him in the newspapers—but I never tried to contact him. I didn't want to see him. Not after he murdered my mother. And got away with it!"

"You have no proof that he killed your mother intentionally."

"I don't need proof. I'm as sure that he murdered her as if I'd been in the car with them. As if I'd actually heard him tell Carla he was going to kill her. I'm certain that's what he did. Just before he crashed into the tree." She pushed the long blonde hair away from her face. "I never want to see Walt again. Of course, he'd do anything to keep me away. He'd be afraid I'd tell his present wife that he's a murderer."

"What brought you to Paris?"

"Who knows?" She wiped the tears away with her fingers. "My jobs in television got to be terribly boring. Doing the same things over and over, week after week, seeing the same frantic people. I decided finally I'd had enough. So I took off for London. Stayed there a year, then came over to Paris. Liked it here best of all and decided to stay. Rented a small apartment at first, but then I ran out of money and had to look for a job. Tried several different things before I got into apartment-sitting."

"Does your father know where you are?"

"I doubt that. Although I've run into friends from Germantown during the tourist season, and they may have told him they'd seen me here. He's never tried to contact me. And I hope he never does. To me he will always be a murderer."

"I wonder if he did kill your mother purposely."

"You don't think so? From what I've told you?"

"What you say is not based upon evidence discovered by the police."

"They said it was an accident!"

"You base your guilty verdict on your knowledge that your parents had been quarreling. On your immediate feeling, when you saw your father coming toward you from the wrecked car, that he had killed your mother. That he was capable of murder."

"Yes!"

"Most of us are capable of murder. Your reaction, unfortunately, was hysterical. You were disturbed by what had happened. It was normal that a fifteen-year-old girl would be deeply shocked and would think a murder had been committed."

"You don't think so?"

Damiot hesitated. "I don't know." He realized that she was weeping again, silently now, her body shaken by the repressed sobs.

"At least you didn't say it couldn't have been murder."

"I wouldn't say anything one way or the other without positive evidence."

"Then you agree?" She faced him again. "It could've been murder?"

"It could've been. Yes."

She rested her head on his shoulder. "I've never told anyone about any of this before. About my father. You're the first person I've felt I could tell what I thought."

He kissed the top of her head, inhaling the delicate scent from her hair. "It is good to talk. Pour out the things you've tried to suppress."

She kissed his shoulder. "I do feel much better, telling you."

"I'm glad you did."

She pulled herself up on an elbow. "But you won't do anything?"

"I don't understand."

"Report what I've said to anyone else!"

"Certainly not."

"To the police? Here or in the United States."

"Why would I do a think like that? Your mother's dead. It's been several years, and it would be difficult to reopen the case, if not impossible."

"Why do you say that?"

"People forget, and the policemen who handled the investigation move on. Get promoted or die." He stroked her hair. "You would have to go back to this German Town and testify."

"I'm never going back there. Not ever!"

He kissed her on the forehead.

"It's been so good to talk to you. I suppose all these years I've needed to tell someone." She sighed. "But there's never been anybody I could trust." She kissed him on his chin, and her lips moved slowly to his mouth.

Damiot held her tight, protectively, as their bodies came together again.

CHAPTER 17

RAINING AGAIN.

Graudin jockeyed the police car up the Champs-Élysées as Damiot, beside him, scowled at the late-morning traffic.

A report from the forensic lab had been waiting on his desk when he arrived at the Préfecture. He had snatched it up, hopefully, but the two knives belonging to that Vietnamese girl were too small to have killed Scott. The murder weapon was longer, its blade a fraction wider. Neither of these knives could have penetrated deep enough to cause death.

He had spent an hour studying the dossiers on those earlier stabbings and sent Graudin upstairs to ask the inspector in charge of computers to check back on stabbings during three earlier years, in case more such unsolved deaths might turn up.

The details in the two dossiers were now filed in his head. Every fact they contained on Victor Montal and Luc Darbois. He had checked each detail of the autopsy and forensic reports. Read the typed pages and printed forms filled out by the detectives who had been involved with each case. Hadn't contacted them because he knew that everything they had learned was contained in those two dossiers.

Today he wanted to question the two women who would know most about those two dead men. Montal's wife and Darbois's girl.

The girl—she called herself Zita Vianne—was a featured dancer at the Lido de Paris, which they'd driven past a moment ago, but she wouldn't be free until noon. Madame Montal, fortunately, was available this morning.

They circled the Arc de Triomphe, edging toward the right, and turned down Avenue Carnot.

"What do you plan to do," Graudin asked, "about that Vietnamese girl?"

"Let her simmer a while longer."

"You think she killed Scott?"

"I'm not convinced. We'll see her tomorrow or Monday. Question her again and go over the apartment more thoroughly. Meanwhile, this afternoon, we'll talk to more prostitutes, ask if they know any girls who carry knives on their person. I'll walk around Place de la Madeleine and rue de Lorette. You cover Montparnasse this time, and Merval can take Montmartre. Cover all the same places again!"

"Maybe the rain will stop."

"The radio said it should continue through the weekend."

Graudin groaned. "Won't be many whores on the streets."

"We'll find them in the bars and cafés. Nursing a drink and hoping for a customer."

Graudin slowed the car into a parking space. "Am I going in with you?"

"Better stay here. You can come in next stop, at the Lido."

Graudin grinned. "Is that dancer working today?"

"Rehearsing. She'll be free during their lunch break."

"I've never been to the Lido de Paris. Not with kids to feed. In fact, the wife and I have never been to any nightclub."

"Lucky guy!"

"There's the address." Graudin nodded toward an apartment building across the avenue.

Damiot buttoned his raincoat and pulled down the brim of his hat before getting out. "See you in half an hour." He slammed the door and, lowering his head against the rain, hurried across to the other side.

Looking up at the gray stone building, he saw that at one time it must have been an elegant address. An old mansion that had been turned into apartments years ago when France was prosperous and many of the wealthy, who lived in the suburbs, wanted a comfortable pied-à-terre in central Paris.

He ran up the puddled marble steps and pushed against one of the tall doors with bronze grilles over gleaming glass. Found himself in a spacious octagonal lobby with a black and white tiled floor. There were no chairs—nobody was supposed to make himself comfortable here—only a gilded elevator cage in the curving sweep of an impressive marble staircase.

Pausing before a framed list of occupants, he saw that Madame Victor Montal was on the second floor. He climbed the two flights, peering up through the open well of the staircase, to a round skylight floating like a gray moon high above.

Each floor was lighted by clusters of shaded bulbs in bronze wall candelabra.

The second-floor corridor was silent. There were four closed doors, each with a name printed on a card in a small metal frame.

He pressed the button beside Montal and heard a buzzer sound inside.

As he waited, he wondered if Madame Montal would be younger than her husband. He had been thirty-five last year when his body was found on rue Tronchet behind the Madeleine. Not far from rue de Caumartin.

Damiot turned as he heard the door open and saw a pretty maid in an immaculate uniform.

"Chief Inspector Damiot?"

"That's right."

"Come in, please. Madame Montal expects you."

Damiot removed his hat as he entered.

She closed the door and went ahead through a small foyer. "Let me have your hat."

He gave it to her and watched her place it on a marble-topped console table. Followed her down an inner corridor.

This was a large apartment. The unlighted corridor extended out of sight beyond double doors, opposite each other, the pair to his right standing open, with light coming from what must be a salon.

The maid hesitated in the open doorway, looking into the room. "Chief Inspector Damiot, Madame." Stepping aside for him to enter.

He moved into the light and saw that it was an intimate, handsomely furnished salon. The woman seated on a small sofa was much younger than he had anticipated.

"Please come in, Monsieur Inspecteur." She gestured

toward a fauteuil. "Such wretched weather. Would you care for coffee?"

"Coffee would be very welcome, Madame." He unbuttoned his raincoat as he approached her and saw that she had been reading her morning mail and drinking coffee. There was a silver coffee service on a silver tray with an extra cup and saucer.

"Make yourself comfortable, Monsieur."

He sank into the fauteuil and watched her fill the extra cup with steaming coffee.

"Cream and sugar?"

"Black, no sugar."

"That's the only way to enjoy coffee in the morning."

He saw that she was extremely beautiful, perhaps in her early thirties, sleek black hair carefully arranged, wearing a pale yellow satin robe with a froth of lace around her throat and wrists. Nearly everything in the salon was a soft yellow color. Aubusson rugs, on the polished floor, had designs of mustard and faded yellow. Chairs and sofas upholstered in dull yellow satin or velvet. Curtains covered the windows, shutting out the gray morning, but several shaded lamps were lighted, and the variations of yellow in the room gave an illusion of sunlight.

"Here you are, Monsieur." She was holding out the delicate Sèvres saucer with its matching cup.

"Merci, Madame." He took it, along with the smallest napkin he had ever seen, which he rested awkwardly on his knee.

"I hope that's hot enough."

He saw the steam rising from the cup with its garlands of yellow roses. "Smells strong." Tasting it, cautiously. "Hot and strong."

"Bien!" She picked up her own cup and sipped the black coffee. "You told me on the phone that you wished to discuss something about my late husband."

"That's correct."

"Have there been new developments in regard to his death?"

"There's been another murder—very similar to your husband's."

"Oh?" She studied him across the coffee table, her dark

brown eyes showing more interest. "I've never understood why the police couldn't find who killed Victor. They didn't come up with a single clue! Then I was informed the investigation had been closed."

"Which happens more frequently than the public suspects."

"So they told me. What is this new murder? Is it someone my husband knew?"

"Perhaps you can tell me that. Have you read in the papers this week about an American actor who was found in rue de Caumartin last Sunday night?"

"I've read everything that's been printed! Alex Scott was one of my favorites. Not that he could be called a great actor. But he was so attractive." She hesitated, setting her cup and saucer down. "He always reminded me of my husband."

"Did he? That's interesting."

"You think Scott was killed by the same person who stabbed Victor?"

"This is a possibility. Did your husband ever know Alex Scott?"

"I couldn't say. Victor was part owner of a company on the Champs-Élysées that sold racing cars. So he met many Americans who were visiting Paris. Frequently he would tell me at dinner of some celebrity who had been in the showroom that day. There were several stars from Hollywood. They would look at the latest models, and sometimes they even bought one! But he never mentioned Alex Scott. I think he would have told me if he'd met him." She shrugged. "Then again, perhaps he might not."

As she talked, Damiot noticed two curious articles on the low coffee table. A toy racing car and a small doll. The doll had sleek black hair like Madame Montal, and its costume was Spanish.

"Does the doll belong to your daughter? The dossier concerning your husband's death said you had a child."

"Yes. That's Rosine's doll." She glanced at it with obvious affection. "She must've left it here this morning as she went off to school."

"That dossier didn't mention you have a son."

"Son?"

"Or does your daughter also like model cars?"

"Oh, no! That model belonged to my husband. It's a copy of the car he was driving that night he was killed."

Damiot saw that the model was an expensive miniature, bright scarlet lacquer and shiny chromium.

"Victor's car was sold because I never wanted to see it again, but I have kept the model. He is dead, but this model remains. It exists, Victor does not. If there is a God, he is cruel. I am Spanish as well as French, Monsieur, and I used to be very religious. But not anymore! Not since my dear husband's death."

"You loved each other? You and your husband."

"He and our daughter were my life. Now I have only Rosine. She is six, and my life is devoted to her. I go out only to take her somewhere. I've eliminated all casual friends from my life and devote every hour to Rosine. My husband's death showed how fragile is this life we are given. Each of us has such a brief time."

"What can you tell me, Madame, about your husband's friends?"

"I didn't know most of them. Especially his business associates. Only the married couples we entertained, whose homes we visited." She sighed. "I don't even see them anymore."

Damiot hesitated. "What about his women friends?"

"Women?" She studied his face. "To my knowledge, Victor never had a mistress."

"We believe Alex Scott was stabbed by a woman. A single wound in the back. Exactly like your husband, who also died in the street. The police didn't see any importance at the time in the fact that there was no cut in any of your husband's clothing."

"No cut?" She set her coffee cup down. "I don't understand."

"The only way he and Scott could've been stabbed like that would be if they were not wearing their clothes."

"Are you telling me Victor was undressed, Monsieur Inspecteur? With some woman?"

"That seems the most logical explanation."

"A prostitute?"

He put his empty cup down. "Yes."

"The papers are suggesting that Alex Scott may have been killed by a prostitute."

"Not only Scott and your husband, but another man. Luc Darbois."

"The name is not familiar."

"His body was found in rue Monsigny last July. Five months after your husband died in rue Taitbout. Both those streets are near rue de Caumartin, where Scott died."

"Then you believe the same person killed all three?"

"That would appear to be a possibility. We're checking through out files on the chance other men may have died in the same circumstances."

"This is incredible!"

"Did your husband . . ." He hesitated.

"Pick up prostitutes? I'm sure he did. Many times, when he came home for dinner and evenings—after some business meeting—I would notice cheap perfume when I kissed him. So I was aware that Victor was seeing other women. The perfume was never the same. I suspected he was seeing prostitutes, but of course I never said anything."

"Never questioned him?"

"Why should I? Our marriage was happier than most of our friends'. I had no wish to harm it in any way because of our daughter. Also, Monsieur, I loved Victor."

"What was there about the American—Scott—that reminded you of your husband?"

"I suppose it was something physical. The way he held himself. His swagger when he walked, as though, like Victor, he enjoyed sports."

"Scott had been a boxer before he got into films."

"My husband drove racing cars when he was younger. But most of all, I think, it was the dark look of the American. His tanned skin and curly black hair. So very like Victor. . . . What else can I tell you?"

"Nothing more, at the moment, Madame." He rose from the fauteuil. "I may need to see you again."

"Mais certainement. Although your visit has distressed me. Reminded me all over again of my husband's miserable death. In a Paris street I've never seen and never want to see! Talking about him has revived my loss. Brought back the past and angered me."

"I understand, Madame."

"You've been extremely tactful with your questions, Monsieur. And I've answered them to the best of my knowledge."

"One final question, if I may. Did your husband speak English?"

"Oh, yes! He went to some language school in his spare time."

"Au 'voir, Madame."

"Monsieur."

Damiot buttoned his raincoat as he headed across the salon toward the corridor. Glancing back from the doorway, he saw that Madame Montal was staring at the replica of her husband's car.

She frowned as she picked up the scarlet model and examined it more closely.

Continuing on, toward the foyer, he heard a crash from the salon.

Madame Montal had smashed the miniature motorcar.

"Zita Vianne? Over there, M'sieur." The little blonde, drying her perspiring face on a filthy towel, looked up at Damiot with the eyes of a mischievous child as she gestured across the noisy rehearsal studio. "The redhead in pink leotards."

"Merci, Mademoiselle." He headed for the girl in pink, followed by Graudin, aware that their muddy shoes were marking the waxed floor.

"You're Damiot, aren't you?" the blonde called after him.

"That's right."

"Recognized you from your pictures!"

"Merde," Damiot muttered under his breath, as Graudin grinned. "Better let me talk to this girl alone. You can find yourself a chair and watch the others. I'll never tell your wife."

Graudin flushed and went toward a row of empty folding chairs.

Damiot glanced at the chattering dancers, in rehearsal

clothes, scattered around the mirrored studio. A squat bald man in black tights was talking to one group and waving his arms. The place stank of sweat and perfumes.

He saw that the Vianne girl was relaxing on one chair, legs stretched out, feet resting on another. She looked slim in faded pink tights, her feet in worn white ballet slippers over heavy white socks. Holding some kind of drink in one hand. And she was watching him cross the dance floor.

"Chief Inspector Damiot?"

"That's right, Mademoiselle."

"Sit down. I don't have to rehearse again for several minutes. We're working later than usual because of the new girls."

He pulled up one of the folding chairs, removed his hat, and rested it upside down on the floor before he sat facing her. "You are, I believe, a British citizen?"

"That's right. The French, fortunately, like English dancers. Hire us for our long legs! Then they gave me an Austrian name! Zita Vianne." She smiled again. "You said on the phone that you're reopening the investigation of Luc Darbois's murder."

"I said we're considering it."

"I'd thought that was finished last year. The flics told me the case was closed. Although they hadn't solved it!"

"Unsolved cases are never closed, Mademoiselle. Only filed away to be reopened if new evidence turns up."

"What's happened to reopen Luc's case?"

"You may have read in the newspapers about that American actor."

"Every word!"

"Did you or Luc Darbois know Alex Scott?"

"I never did. And I doubt that Luc knew him, unless Scott stayed at the Hôtel Cambon, where Luc worked."

"Scott stayed at the Hôtel du Pont on the Left Bank."

"Then I doubt very much their paths ever crossed."

He saw that her bright red hair was natural and she was wearing no makeup. She was extremely beautiful, even this close. He noticed, with disgust, that the glass she was holding contained milk.

"What about a car salesman—Victor Montal—part owner of a sales room on the Champs-Élysées? Down the street from here. Did either you or Darbois know him?"

"I certainly never heard of him. Can't say about Luc. He always wanted a fancy new car but had to make do with an old Honda." She took a sip of the milk. "Won't offer you any of this foul stuff! Supposed to be warm, but it's cold. This weather's giving all of us the flu." She set her glass on the floor. "What about those two guys? Scott and the other one you mentioned."

"Both of them died in the street, like your friend Darbois, stabbed in the back."

"Such a filthy way to die."

"There's a chance that they were murdered by the same person."

"Who could've killed all three of them?"

"A woman."

"You mean a whore? Like the newspapers have been hinting about Scott's death?"

"We've traced one girl who's known to carry knives on her person."

"Luvly lass! So Luc was done in by a bloody whore, was he? Should've never turned his back on her. I suppose when he was taking money from his wallet."

"When Darbois was found, according to the dossier, his wallet was missing."

"That's right."

"Which made everyone think he'd been robbed and stabbed on the street. Nobody, at the time, seems to have noticed there weren't any cuts in his clothes, or if they did, they were unaware of its importance. I believe he was nude when he was attacked."

"I'll be damned!" She stared at him, wide-eyed. "The newspapers always say how clever you are. I'm beginning to see why."

"Did your friend Darbois make a habit of picking up prostitutes?"

"You make it sound like an addiction. And I suppose it was. Luc was terribly oversexed. Simple as that! He needed a woman every night after he finished work. Many times he didn't get home until dawn."

"You lived together on rue de Ponthieu."

"You do know everything! Luc shared my flat."

"His dossier says he was an upstairs floor waiter at the new Hôtel Cambon."

"Fanciest hotel you ever saw! Full of rich Arabs and Japanese."

"I dislike those enormous new hotels. They all look alike."

"Luc met lots of attractive women where he worked. He liked Swedish and American girls best. Always telling me I'm too thin!"

"Did he speak their language?"

"Only a little Swedish—the sort any bright waiter picks up—but he'd started to study English. Wanted to speak it fluently, and he was doing rather well, I must say."

"Where did he study?"

"Privately. With some English girl he picked up in a café."

"Didn't you object to his sleeping with other women?"

"We had an understanding. Let me get this clear! Are you saying Luc and these two other guys were not knifed in the street but in a hotel room with a prostitute?"

"That's right. We've found the room where Scott was stabbed. He managed to dress and leave the hotel. Hoping to reach his car, which he'd left around the corner in rue de Caumartin."

"Luc's car was found in rue des Petits-Champs."

"That's in his dossier. Which means he must've been in some hotel north of rue Monsigny, where his body was found. Did Darbois take money from these women he met at the Hôtel Cambon?"

"He boasted about the gifts they gave him. Must've been generous, because he always had cash in his wallet. Dollars, pounds, and francs!"

"You've been very helpful, Mademoiselle." He got to his feet.

She started to laugh.

"What is it?"

"I've only just realized! Luc took money from those rich

broads at the hotel and gave it to prostitutes! Isn't that a laugh?"

"Au 'voir, Mademoiselle." He retrieved his hat and motioned for Graudin to follow him across the dance floor. Aware of Zita Vianne's laughter above the noise in the studio.

CHAPTER 18

THE SEINE WAS INVISIBLE BEHIND A THICK MASS OF GRAY FOG that, moments ago, had seemed to be following the river through the city but had started to spread across Quai des Orfèvres until Damiot was unable to see the parapet beneath his window.

Swiveling his chair, he faced the three dossiers spread open in a circle of harsh light from his desk lamp.

Three men dead from single stab wounds.

Scott, Montal, and Darbois.

Their bodies found in rue de Caumartin, rue Taitbout, and rue Dalayrac.

He squinted at the big wall map of Paris tht he had marked with crayon. The crimson circles were within a few streets of each other. Only seven or eight blocks apart. Two in the 9th arrondissement and one in the 2d. He had drawn a red triangle connecting them with rue de Caumartin at the peak, the other two forming its base.

Did the murderer live somewhere within that triangle?

He knew that Scott had been stabbed while he was in the Hôtel Amadeus, but where had the others been when the knife entered their backs? In nearby hotels?

This morning the lab had reported that the width and depth of the three wounds matched precisely.

He had reported that fact immediately to his cheif and to the examining magistrate, who agreed that this information should not be released to the press before next week.

Three murders now! All done with the same knife.

And all three men had left their cars parked in nearby streets.

A rented red Peugeot, a scarlet Fiat, and an old black Honda.

He had found the hotel where Scott was stabbed by checking the direction the actor had taken back to his Peugeot. The same procedure must now be repeated with those other two cars.

He glanced through the dossiers, checking for other similarities.

Madame Montal had said that Scott resembled her husband.

He placed the photographs of the three men in a row with the glossy color shot of Scott between the pictures, taken in the morgue, of Montal and Darbois. Even in death there was a surprising likeness between the three faces. Curly black hair and rather cruel sardonic mouth. Straight nose, strong jawline. All three faces were handsomer than average. No wonder they had been so attractive to women. Actor, car salesman, and waiter.

All three were muscular and enjoyed sports. Scott was an amateur boxer, Montal drove racing cars, and, according to his dossier, Darbois had played soccer.

The telephone rang once, but Damiot didn't pick it up.

All three had been studying languages. Scott with a private teacher who came to his hotel, Darbois with an English girl he'd picked up in a café, and Montal at some school on Avenue de l'Opéra.

The buzzer sounded under his desk.

Damiot snatched up the phone. "Yes, Graudin?"

"Madame Scott calling. Says she has some information for you."

"I wish she'd give up trying to solve her husband's murder! After I talk to her, come in here and we'll go over several ideas for today."

"Madame Scott's on line two."

Damiot punched the button. "Bonjour, Madame."

"I wasn't certain you'd be in your office on Saturday."

"Usually when I'm in the middle of an important investigation. But I plan to sleep all day tomorrow."

"Any new developments?"

He hesitated, deciding it would be best not to tell her about the two additional murders. "I'm afraid we're at a point where nothing appears to be happening."

"Eh bien! It's not yet a week. I certainly didn't expect the case would be finished this quickly. I've called because I have a morsel of information for you."

"Oh?"

"You wanted to know if Alex had received letters from any woman in Paris after he returned from those earlier visits."

"That's right."

"I talked with our secretary this morning, and she tells me he had several communications. From two different women!"

"Did she recall their names?"

"Oh, yes! Greta's extremely efficient. Said she couldn't forget the names because one was unusual and the other was familiar. The unusual one was handwritten. Mademoiselle Linette Murzeau."

"Murzeau's daughter."

"So I assumed. Greta had never heard the name Linette before."

"And the familiar one?"

"Miss Jenny Carstairs. We have friends in La Jolla named Carstairs."

"Miss, not Mademoiselle?"

"Exactement! I asked Greta the same question. She said it was typed on each envelope. Miss Jenny Carstairs."

"Is that American?"

"Somehow it sounds more British to me. Our friends in La Jolla are English, but the wife's name is Madge."

"Did this Miss Jenny Carstairs put a return address on her envelopes?"

"Oh, yes! American Express Company, rue Scribe, Paris. That's where lots of British and American visitors have their mail sent."

"You think Miss Carstairs is a tourist?"

"She might be. Although many visitors settle down in Paris and keep American Express as their mailing address the whole time they're here."

"I will try to locate Miss Carstairs. You've no idea who she is?"

"None."

"Your husband never mentioned her name?"

"Never. I'm seeing Tristan Murzeau this morning. He's coming here to the hotel to discuss my working on that screenplay. I read the book last night and rather like it. Terribly cliché, but I think I might do something interesting. Suppose I shouldn't mention that his daughter had been writing Alex."

"Murzeau told me he'd ordered her not to see your husband."

"Then I shan't say a word! I've decided to fly over to London tomorrow. No point in staying here after I have this talk with Murzeau. He's taking me somewhere fabulous for lunch. By the way! You never gave me the names of your favorite restaurants. Perhaps another time?"

"Of course."

"Don't suppose you're free for dinner this evening?"

"Afraid that's out of the question, Madame." He was getting to bed early tonight. "I shall be having no social life until I find your husband's murderer."

"Nothing more about the Vietnamese girl with a knife?"

"That, at the moment, has become a dead end. The two knives found in her possession did not match the wound in your husband's back."

"Can't win 'em all! Oh! Meant to tell you. His body was returned to Los Angeles yesterday. The consulate found some nice American girl who didn't have the money for a plane ticket. Alex is still attracting the women! The young man at the consulate said he thought she would faint when he told her it was Alex she was taking home with her."

"I hope you have a pleasant flight, Madame. We'll be in touch, through the office of your consul, the moment we have new developments."

"Sounds terribly official! I'll let you know when I'll be returning to Paris. If I do this screenplay for Murzeau, it will mean several trips back and forth. There's so much I'd like to discuss with you! Including my idea for a film about Vidocq."

Damiot glanced at the lithograph of Vidocq hanging on the wall.

"Did you know that Vidocq wrote books on crime in Paris?"

"I have several of them."

"And he was a friend of Balzac. I read somewhere that the character of Vautrin in *Le Père Goriot* was based on Vidocq."

"I didn't know that."

"We'll discuss Vidocq another time. When you're not so busy. Au 'voir, Monsieur Inspecteur!"

"Au 'voir, Madame. Bon voyage." He put the phone down, scowling at Vidocq who, as usual, smiled back. That arrogant smile . . .

Before he could swivel his chair toward the window, the door opened and Graudin appeared with an interoffice memo.

"This just arrived from upstairs. That inspector in charge of the computers."

"Bien! Has he come up with something more?"

"His machines sifted through every unsolved stabbing in the past five years. Found no others with a knife in the back but no cuts in the victim's clothing." Dropping the memo on Daimot's desk. "So much for that!"

"At least his damn machines came up with two. We now have three unsolved murders instead of one!" He waved toward the other chair, and Graudin sat facing him. "I'm going to Montparnasse again. Have another talk with that Vietnamese girl and return her daggers." Glancing at the small manila envelope on his desk. "Ask her more questions."

"Am I coming with you?"

"I've other plans for you and Rispol."

"You'll want a car in this weather."

"No. I'll walk. The air may clear my head and help me to puzzle several things out. All these bits and pieces we've turned up in the Scott case."

"Learn anything from Madame Scott?"

"She tells me her husband had been receiving letters from two women in Paris. One was Murzeau's daughter, which isn't surprising, and the others came from a Miss Jenny Carstairs."

"American?"

"Madame Scott thought the name sounded British."

"Was there an address?"

"American Express, rue Scribe."

"That's where tourists pick up their mail."

"They should have a Paris address on file for this Carstairs woman. You'd better see whoever's in charge."

"Right."

"I want you and Merval to check on where those two bodies were found—Montal and Darbois—in relation to where their cars had been parked. Montal's body in rue Taitbout, his car in rue Provence, and Darbois in rue Dalayrac, his car in rue des Petits-Champs. Both of these men, like Scott, must've been going to pick up their cars when they died. So work back from where the bodies were found. Check small hotels on the side streets. Show people a photograph of the victim. There are copies in each of these dossiers. Show them to anyone who might've seen them. Manager, concierge, porter."

The telephone rang on his desk.

Graudin reached for it. "Chief Inspector Damiot's office. . . . One moment please." Holding his hand over the mouthpiece. "It's your hotel. Madame Lambord."

Daimot took the phone from his hand. "Bonjour, Madame! This is a surprise."

"Ah, Monsieur Damiot! We never see each other, even though we live under the same roof."

"My hours are uncivilized. Day and night."

"I've been reading about you again! This American actor who was murdered."

"The newspapers are giving it too much publicity."

"But he's a celebrity! And so are you, cher ami!"

"Nonsense!"

"You are much too modest! I'm calling you at the Préfecture because there was a phone call just now, which I suspect may be important."

"Yes?"

"Madame Damiot."

"Madame. . . . Oh! My wife?"

"She phoned to say she would like to see you tomorrow."

"Was she calling from Cannes?"

"Madame didn't say. Only that she never liked to phone you at the Préfecture. Asked me to tell you she would contact you here at the hotel in the morning."

"Did she say what time?"

"No. She didn't."

"I'll wait in my room tomorrow morning until she calls. Thank you, Madame."

"Plaisir, Monsieur. À bientôt."

"À bientôt, Madame." He handed the phone back to Graudin. "Merde!"

"Your wife?"

"In Paris. Which can only mean trouble."

Damiot knocked on the door of number ten and was answered by the screeching of the bird. Today it was even harsher than last time.

He waited, but there was no other sound.

Peering up and down the long hall, he observed—as he hadn't done before—that it was clean, the white walls recently painted.

The faint light came from small unshaded bulbs in the ceiling.

He knocked again.

This time the bird remained silent.

His hat was soggy with rain, and his trouser legs felt moist against his ankles. The fog had lifted as he walked across Pont Saint-Michel, but the rain had started again.

After he left there he would take a taxi back to his office.

He leaned close to the wooden door but heard nothing inside the apartment.

"Who is it?"

He moved away, startled by the proximity of Lolo's voice. "Inspector Damiot."

"One moment."

He heard the bolt pulled and watched the door open.

"Monsieur l'Inspecteur." Lolo smiled, bowing slightly, as she motioned him inside.

He noticed that the curtains still covered the windows and the only light came from the hanging lanterns. Lolo was wearing a soft green robe with another pattern of white birds. As she went ahead of him, he saw that her bare feet were in white sandals with green thongs. Her long black hair hung loose below her shoulders. Glossy and straight. Like the girl who had been with Scott at Chez Pavy.

She sank onto the divan, which was now covered by a black and gray striped spread piled with brilliant silk-embroidered pillows.

Damiot sat on the same chair and dropped his damp hat onto the table, glancing up at the white cage. "Your bird is quiet today."

"I think he is sick. Paris winters are difficult for birds—and people—accustomed to warmer climates."

He pulled out the small brown manila envelope from a pocket of his raincoat. "I came to return these two knives, Mademoiselle."

Her eyes brightened. "They were not—either of them—used to kill that American actor?"

"No. They are too small." He handed the envelope to her and watched as she opened it, removing the knives in their plastic folder.

"Then I may keep them?"

"Of course."

"Merci, Monsieur."

Damiot watched her shake the daggers onto the divan and quickly twist her hair into thick strands, which she deftly arranged around her head, jabbing both knives through a loose knot to hold it in place.

'You have no others, Mademoiselle?"

She looked startled. "There are several in the kitchen."

"May I see them?"

"Certainly." She rose and led him to a closed door, opened it, and snapped a wall switch.

Damiot saw that it was a tiny brightly painted kitchen with a one-burner gas stove. Dishes and bowls arranged on open shelves above a wooden work counter. More shelves underneath holding cooking utensils. He recognized a wok and a steamer for vegetables, but the others were unfamiliar.

Lolo pulled out a shallow drawer beneath the work counter. "Here are all my other knives."

He moved closer and peered into the drawer where a number of eating and cooking implements were arranged in a neat row.

"These are the only knives I have." She motioned with her delicate fingers to three wooden-handled knives.

He saw a large one for chopping, a chef's knife for carving, and a blunt paring knife. "None of these could've killed Monsieur Scott. Two are much too large, and the other one's not long enough."

"I am very glad." She gestured gracefully with both hands. "Look wherever you wish."

"That won't be necessary, Mademoiselle."

"Bien!" She went ahead of him into the other room.

The bird squawked as they returned.

Lolo sank onto the divan as Damiot walked toward the curtained windows and looked into the white pagoda cage.

"You have a bird, Monsieur?"

"No, Mademoiselle." He turned to face her. "I do not like to see any living creature in a cage. Human, animal, or bird."

"But you send criminals to prison."

"They deserve to be behind bars, but I get no pleasure seeing them there. I have a dog, but she is not caged. At least no more than any humans are caged by four walls." He sat down again. "Do you have any friends who . . . collect knives?"

"You mean other prostitutes?"

"Yes."

"No, Monsieur l'Inspecteur. But then I do not seek their company, their friendship. I would suspect that many must have knives for their own protection. But I do now know this for a fact."

As he studied her face, he was aware once again of her open countenance—as well as her beauty—and wondered what he was doing here, except that someone had to return those daggers.

He was here, he realized, because he had wanted to see Lolo again. In order to confirm what he had guessed at their first meeting—that she was innocent. And now he was convinced.

"What are you thinking, Monsieur?"

Her question startled him. He got to his feet and picked up his hat. "I am glad it wasn't your knife that killed the American actor."

"So! You are a kind man, as well as a policeman."

"Au 'voir, Mademoiselle." He turned abruptly and went toward the door.

"Au 'voir, Monsieur l'Inspecteur."

Damiot opened the door without looking back.

The bird didn't make a sound.

CHAPTER 19

As DAMIOT WALKED FRIC-FRAC ALONG QUAI DES Orfèvres he could hear the bells of Nôtre-Dame, although it was impossible to see the cathedral through the rain.

Only a few people hurrying to Mass, and the great bells sounded muffled and far away.

If he were not walking Fric-Frac, he would join the stragglers and cross Place du Parvis, into the incense-perfumed womb of the church. No jeweled beams of sunlight would slant through the rose windows today, but he would like to sit there for half an hour, relaxing under the hypnotic spell of the organ and the soaring voices, recalling his childhood and his parents.

Some other Sunday.

He hadn't been inside the cathedral since Fric-Frac had come into his life. Dogs weren't permitted inside churches.

Looking directly overhead, he had the sensation of an enormous dirty gray canopy pressing down over the entire city.

The rain had continued throughout the night, and his radio this morning said there was no end in sight. England was even worse, with floods in many areas.

He hoped these weeks of rain were not harming the grapevines of France. This year's crop, of course, had been harvested weeks ago, and the gnarled vines were bare for the winter. Would this constant rain damage their roots? Probably not. They must have survived much worse storms in the past.

Following their daily route, Fric-Frac performing her customary duties in spite of the weather, Damiot wondered again why Sophie had come to Paris. His wife's presence could only mean trouble. Probably some new plan she and her miserable mother had cooked up to get more money out of him. Eh bien! He wouldn't pay her another franc!

Sophie had told Madame Lambord that she would contact him this morning. Why the devil couldn't she mention a specific time? She'd always been like this. Vague about appointments, unwilling to pin herself down to a definite time when they were meeting for a Saturday-afternoon shopping expedition or a tour of galleries on the Left Bank. Her casual attitude toward time had annoyed him and led to many arguments.

That was finished! Grâce à Dieu.

He would listen to what she had to say and send her back to Cannes without taking her to lunch.

Between the imminent arrival of his wife and this endless rain, he felt even more depressed than yesterday.

Most of all he was frustrated by the lack of developments in the Scott case.

That little Vietnamese whore had nothing to do with the death of Alex Scott.

Lolo! There was an enchanting face. He had suspected from the first that she was innocent. Perhaps, after this investigation was finished, he would look her up again.

Graudin and Rispol had returned to the Préfecture yesterday afternoon without turning up any information about other prostitutes known to carry knives. They would start out again, Monday morning, through Montmartre and Montparnasse. Asking questions. Searching for a clue—any clue—to Scott's killer.

It must be a prostitute! No other way the actor could have been undressed when he was stabbed in the back.

And it had to be that girl Scott took to the Hôtel Amadeus after they had drinks in Chez Pavy. Long black hair and sunglasses. He'd been convinced those sunglasses were worn to hide the fact she was Oriental.

He saw that Fric-Frac was soaked, black curls clinging to her small body. "All right, Madame la Duchesse! We'll have a good rubdown when we get back to the hotel."

She wagged her tail, scattering drops of rain like a windshield wiper, as they turned up rue de Harlay toward Place Dauphine.

There was another piece of depressing news yesterday when, late in the afternoon, Dr. Bretty had phoned from the Institut Médico-Légal. At first he'd thought there was some additional finding from the Scott autopsy, until Bretty told him the hospital had reported that Dr. Allanic's condition was critical. Pneumonia at his age was a serious matter.

Poor Allanic! If the old man died, it would be a great loss to the Préfecture.

Must remember to phone Madame Allanic. Tomorrow.

The Scott investigation was getting nowhere.

Maybe he should see that film producer Murzeau again. Question him more thoroughly about Scott's quarrel with that actor Dario Maurin. Have another talk with Murzeau's daughter. Scott had received letters from her in California. Find out what she had written.

He hadn't gone back to the Murzeaus or to Maurin when it looked as though the killer was a prostitute.

Could that girl with Scott, at Chez Pavy, have been Linette Murzeau in a black wig?

Was it possible that Murzeau's daughter had known those two other men, Victor Montal and Luc Darbois?

Or were the three similar knifings only a coincidence? Each man could have been murdered by a different person. Three prostitutes?

But the knife, according to the lab, was the same in each of the three murders.

Three prostitutes with one knife? Ridiculous!

It had to be one prostitute who knew all three men.

And who was that other girl who wrote letters to Scott? Miss Jenny Carstairs! Whose address was the American Express.

Graudin would be looking into that tomorrow.

As Damiot followed Fric-Frac into the hotel, he realized that more lights had been turned on since they went out, but the empty lobby still looked dim and uninviting.

He would get out of his damp clothes after he toweled Fric-Frac, shave, and relax in a hot tub for half an hour. Maybe order a second breakfast. He would need another pot of hot coffee before he faced Sophie.

Passing the closed door to the manager's office, he saw that Pierauld was seated behind the desk reading a newspaper.

Madame Lambord paid him extra to handle the switchboard Sunday mornings.

The old man looked up from his paper and motioned with his head toward the lounge behind the partition of wood and etched glass.

Damiot realized that all the lamps in the lounge had been lighted. It wasn't possible that his wife . . .

Fric-Frac pulled on her leash, urging him toward the elevator.

He turned the corner and peered into the lounge.

A woman was seated on one of the brown plush sofas.

"Sophie?"

"The old man said you were walking your dog."

"Why didn't you tell Madame Lambord what time you'd be here?"

"Well, I . . ."

"Never mind!" He yanked on Fric-Frac's leash. "No, Madame. We're not going upstairs. Come!"

Fric-Frac turned reluctantly and allowed herself to be pulled into the lounge. She stared at the intruder.

"So this is that dog somebody gave you."

"This is Madame Fric-Frac."

"She looks like a drowned rat!"

Fric-Frac growled.

"Let me leave her with the porter." He turned back to the desk, Fric-Frac following reluctantly. "Pierauld, would you take care of her for a moment?"

"Certainly, M'sieur l'Inspecteur." He folded his newspaper and put it aside.

"Do you have something you could use to dry her?"

"There's an old towel here somewhere." He pushed himself to his feet and came from behind the registration desk. "Bonjour, Madame Fric-Frac! Wet again?"

She wagged her tail and followed him behind the desk.

Damiot removed his hat and raincoat as he returned to the lounge, tossing them over one of the squat chairs.

"I never thought the dog would last!" his wife observed. "It's been two years or more."

"She's become an important part of my life."

"So she's replaced your wife!"

"I wouldn't say that." He sat on the other end of the sofa, facing her, after discarding the idea of sitting in a chair. "You're the one who didn't like dogs."

"I still don't."

"I always had a dog when I was a boy." He saw, to his surprise, that she was more attractively dressed than usual. A small feathered hat revealed enough of her hair to show that it had been arranged by a professional, its color lighter than he remembered. An expensive dark gray coat, simple and elegant, with a luxurious brown fur collar. She had removed her gloves and placed them on top of a large leather handbag with a gold clasp that rested beside her on the sofa.

Sophie stared at him, aware of his inspection. "This hotel is depressing."

"It suits my needs. For the present." He realized that she was wearing more makeup than she had used in the past. "You're looking well."

"You look tired."

"I am. There's an important case at the moment, with no sign of a solution."

"That American actor?"

"So you know!"

"It's been in the papers. Even in Cannes. When I open the newspaper at breakfast, there's your name facing me every morning."

"I am sorry." Was this leading to an argument?

"All my friends question me about you. The famous Chief Inspector Damiot."

"I regret that being Madame Damiot causes you inconvenience."

She shrugged. "Even my customers at the boutique where I work ask what news I have about you."

"That's a handsome coat you're wearing."

"Oh?" She glanced down at the fur collar. "Bought this yesterday. After I arrived in Paris."

"You were here yesterday? Madame Lambord didn't say."

"I didn't tell her. I had shopping to do and a dinner engagement. Thought it would be better to see you this morning. I remember how you always used to sleep late on Sunday."

"That's not so easy anymore. With a dog."

"Anyway, I thought it might be better to see you after you'd had a good night's rest. In the old days you always got to bed early Saturday night. Especially when you were working on a case."

"I haven't changed." He realized that for some reason she seemed ill at ease. Her fingers were twisting together in her lap. "You're looking thinner."

"I'm on my feet all day at the boutique. You've put on some weight."

"A few pounds. I'm always planning to start a diet."

"I've been wanting for some time to have a serious talk with you, but the telephone seems too impersonal for an important conversation."

He tensed, preparing for what was coming.

"Maman said I should come to Paris to see you. That you had always been a considerate man. Logical."

"That's not what she used to say!"

"Maman has changed. In fact, you wouldn't recognize her these days. I suppose it's because she's getting older. She frequently talks about you. What a charming man you were when I married you."

"I certainly wouldn't recognize her if she talks like that!" Sophie was working up to whatever it was she wanted, but he wouldn't give her an extra centime in her monthly check. He must be firm.

"I want a divorce."

"What?"

"I've fallen in love."

"Congratulations."

"That's all you have to say!"

"What did you think I would say?"

"I was afraid you might be difficult."

"Why should I be?"

"I thought perhaps you might try to stop me."

"Certainly not! Who's the fortunate man?"

"Raymonde owns the boutique where I work. Raymonde Vernier. He's not as famous as you, but he has more money. We've known for six months that we're in love."

"Which means you've been sleeping with him."

"I didn't think you'd care. After all this time."

"I don't."

"Then you won't make any trouble? Try to stop the divorce?"

"Go right ahead!"

"Raymonde will pay for everything."

"I'll pay my share."

"Bien! Since you're not going to make trouble, it shouldn't cost too much. Raymonde has a lawyer friend who'll handle everything. He says, if you don't contest the action . . ."

"You have my word."

". . . it will be quite simple. He will file the necessary papers in Cannes, and there should be no publicity."

"I would insist on that."

"It would be more difficult, of course, if we were Catholic. My family never was, and you haven't been inside a church in years!"

"How soon will this happen?"

"Immediately! Raymonde hopes to get things started right away."

"You'll keep me informed?"

"Of course." She smiled for the first time. "I suppose you wouldn't be this agreeable if there wasn't another woman in your life."

"No special one."

"Then there must be several!"

"One or two. But I've no plans for another marriage." Since this was going so well, maybe he should ask her to have lunch with him.

"I used to think you were in love with your murderers."

"So you said. Several times."

"Certainly you spent more time with them than you did with me!"

"What about lunch somewhere?"

"I am sorry." She reached for her gloves and handbag. "Raymonde is waiting. You probably noticed his taxi as you came in."

"No. I didn't." He'd been too busy with Fric-Frac.

"We're lunching with some of Raymonde's friends." She rose from the sofa.

Damiot jumped up. "Eh bien! This has been pleasant."

"Maman was right. She said you'd be charming. As always."

"Give my best to your mother." He walked beside her out of the lounge. "I suppose we won't be seeing each other again."

"I'll read about you in the newspapers." She raised her face suddenly and kissed him lightly on the cheek. "I used to love you, Guy. Long ago." She turned and hurried through the entrance passage, swung the glass door back, and ran out into the rain.

Damiot didn't follow. He saw her go left, so the waiting taxi must be parked around the corner in rue de Harlay. They had passed it, he and Fric-Frac, without noticing the man seated inside.

He started back to get his hat and raincoat. "Where's Madame la Duchesse? Where is Fric-Frac?"

Her small black head peeped around the bottom of the reception desk.

"There's my girl! There's Fric-Frac."

CHAPTER 20

THE MORNING HAD BEEN A COMPLETE BLANK. NOTHING achieved.

Damiot stared at the rain beating against the windowpanes. It was like peering into a gray vacuum.

This weather was getting monotonous. Ten days of heavy rain.

His office was so damp, in spite of the hissing radiator, that he expected to see drops of moisture collecting on the ceiling and dropping onto his desk.

He had hurried from his hotel to the Préfecture, even earlier than was his custom, but Graudin had been ahead of him, waiting with a report on his Saturday-afternoon activity. He had gone first to the American Express office. None of the staff had seen Miss Jenny Carstairs in more than a week, but their files produced an address for her on rue Saint-Roch. She was a British citizen—occupation teacher—and Graudin had gotten her passport number from the form she had filled out at the American Express. The concierge of the apartment building on rue Saint-Roch, behind the church, had never heard of Miss Jenny Carstairs.

After that Graudin had spent several hours checking hotels near rue Dalayrac, where the body of Darbois had been found, while Merval went to rue Taitbout and checked hotels near the spot where Montal was killed. They had turned up nothing.

Damiot's phone hadn't rung in the past half hour. The last call was a reporter on one of the international news syndicates. Damiot hadn't talked to him, but told Graudin to explain there was nothing new on the Scott case.

If the press got wind of the fact that they had uncovered two similar murders, his outer office would be crowded with reporters.

Graudin and Merval were returning to Montmartre and Montparnasse, along with three younger sergeants, to continue their search for any prostitute known to carry a knife.

His chief had suggested assigning the additional men to the investigation during a lengthy meeting upstairs. They had jointly agreed it would be wise to postpone giving out the fact that two other men had died from similar stab wounds in the past year. They would withhold that from the press until the killer was found. And announce at the same time that three murders had been solved.

He hadn't mentioned Miss Jenny Carstairs to the old man or anyone else upstairs.

Damiot sighed, squinting at the drops of rain running down his window.

This afternoon he would pay a second visit to Tristan Murzeau. Question him about Scott's relationship with his daughter and Dario Maurin.

He should see both of them again. Daughter and actor.

Had Linette Murzeau done any acting? Possibly in her father's films? Find out, casually, whether she was in the habit of wearing wigs. Women did that now, more often than in the past. Shop windows were filled with wigs of every color.

Find out from Maurin exactly what Scott had talked about at the Murzeau party.

Continuing to star at the window, he wondered if his wife was flying back to the Riviera in this weather. Sophie and her lover. What was his name? Raymonde something.

After he paid his share of the divorce proceedings, he wouldn't have to give Sophie another centime! He could keep all his salary for himself. The way it was before his marriage.

This extra money wouldn't change anything. He would continue to live at the Hôtel Dauphin. Nothing wrong with his room. In fact, he'd gotten to like it. For one thing, it was convenient to the Préfecture.

And Fric-Frac was happy. The staff spoiled her. Even Madame Lambord fed her special treats from the hotel kitchen.

Madame Lambord! Mustn't get involved there. He would

tell the hotel staff nothing about getting a divorce. Sophie would be discreet and keep it out of the papers.

Even Andrea thought he was married and separated from his wife.

Better keep it that way.

Tomorrow evening he would dine with Andrea again. Their third dinner together! No matter what happened on the Scott investigation or how busy he was during the day. He had to take time out for dinner.

Must find the time, today or tomorrow, to decide on another restaurant. Which cuisine should it be this time? Normandie, Savoie, Côte d'Azur? There were restaurants in Paris for each cuisine.

It would relax him, take his mind from the Scott case, to select a restaurant, then phone tomorrow and order their dinner.

A restaurant with a small hotel nearby.

Tonight he should join Graudin in a tour of the bars where whores were known to hang out. They would work late again.

Perhaps he would have a good lunch before seeing Murzeau, then get a late supper in some Montmartre café before starting on a round of the night spots.

He hadn't taken time for lunch since the start of this case.

Better cash another check tomorrow.

Both those dinners with Andrea had cost more than he had spent since his mistress departed for Mexico. More than two years ago.

Olympe had always enjoyed dining at restaurants where she could meet friends from the world of opera.

Was she still touring with that provincial company?

Chère Olympe! She'd been his mistress for almost five years. Slightly mad, never dull. Always acting! Even in bed. And she had given some great performances. He missed Olympe, more than he had ever missed his wife. Sophie had been satisfying in bed but never exciting.

Andrea was even more interesting. There was something slightly perverse about her, which, as yet, he didn't completely understand. He had a suspicion she might have felt some sexual attraction for her father. Even though she claimed to hate him.

The phone rang on his desk, but Graudin would answer it, as usual, in the outer office.

There had been something in Andrea's voice, when she'd told him about her father wrecking that car and killing her mother, that had caught his attention. Was it really murder?

He looked forward to meeting her again. Tomorrow evening at Café de la Paix. They would go on from there.

The door banged open behind him.

Damiot swiveled his chair as Graudin hurried in, eyes dancing with excitement. "Yes?"

"Report just came in! Montparnasse police headquarters. That Vietnamese girl, Lolo Yeung."

"What about her?"

"Dead."

Damiot rose from his chair. "Cause of death?"

"Suicide. With a knife."

The uniformed policeman guarding the door recognized Damiot as he came down the silent hall with Graudin, saluted, and opened the door onto a scene of hushed activity.

Both lanterns were lighted, and somebody had removed the shade from a lamp. The bare bulb glared.

The first thing Damiot saw was the small body crumpled on the floor. At the same time he smelled the familiar sweet odor of blood. Moving closer, he realized that young Bretty, instead of Dr. Allanic, was kneeling beside the body with a leather satchel spread open beside him.

Damiot was aware of two men from the forensic lab working at a table. Several unfamiliar faces, watching and frowning, probably detectives from Montparnasse headquarters. Sauger, from the public prosecutor's office, nodded. Paupardin, the examining magistrate's sad-faced clerk, was talking to a police photographer who had finished taking shots of the body. He was aware of all this as he approached the dead girl.

Lolo's face was calm in death. Her long black hair was spread across the floor, and she was in the same blue robe, with its pattern of flying white birds, that she had worn at their first meeting.

He looked up quickly, toward the hanging cage and saw that

it had been covered with a scarf. That was why the bird was silent.

"Monsieur Inspecteur?"

Turning back, he saw Bretty straightening from the body.

"I had them send for you before I came upstairs, when the concierge said you'd been here last week."

"This young woman may have been involved with the Scott murder." As Damiot stood beside Bretty, looking down at Lolo's body, he noticed a dark stain of blood on the rug. It had been there for some time, because a skin had formed over its surface. "How long has she been dead?"

"At least twenty-four hours. Looks like suicide. Can't be sure of that or time of death until I've done the autopsy."

Damiot's eyes were darting. "What can you tell me?"

"She was apparently seated on this divan and thrust the knife into her abdomen. From the bloodstain on the blade, it went in deep."

"Where's the knife?"

"The forensic boys have it." Motioning toward the men working at the distant table.

"Did you find her body on the floor?"

"There where you see it. She must've slipped from the divan as she became unconscious. There's blood on the divan where she'd been sitting."

"The knife was still in the wound?"

"No. On the rug near her head. You can see a small bloodstain."

"Suicides don't usually remove knives after they've had the guts to thrust them into their bodies. Or so I've observed in the past."

"The knife could've been dislodged when she toppled off the divan. That might easily have happened."

Damiot stared at the small body curled on the rug. Lolo's face was an ivory mask, her lips a red smear of lipstick. The red seemed to have run down the side of her cheek. Then he realized it was a thin line of dried blood from her mouth. Just like Scott!

Lolo's troubles were over now. Her loneliness would no longer send her out into the Paris streets looking for kindness.

The accumulation of incense and perfumes in the closed

room, along with the sickening stench of blood, was overpowering. As many times as he had encountered the smell of blood, this combination caused the muscles of his stomach to knot.

"Any sign of a disturbance when you arrived?"

"No. Everything's exactly as we found it."

"Was the door locked?"

"The concierge had opened it. She became suspicious when she hadn't seen the victim since Saturday. Remembering that you'd been here last week."

They looked around as the corridor door opened and two burly young men in hooded white raincoats came in, the smaller one carrying a rolled stretcher.

"Will you want to examine the body?" Bretty asked.

"I leave that entirely to you."

"Then I'll let them remove it."

"Send me your report as soon as possible."

"Should finish it this afternoon."

"Call me when you do."

"Right." He started toward the attendants, who were unrolling their stretcher, but turned back to Damiot. "Had you heard? They don't expect the old man to live?"

"Dr. Allanic!"

"I called Bicêtre this morning. He hasn't responded to treatment."

"Merde. I'm sorry to hear that." He watched as Bretty joined the attendants to supervise removal of the body.

Another death. The little prostitute, and now Allanic. He stood there scowling, in the center of the room with Graudin, surrounded by all these men whose daily lives were constantly touched by death, and yet he for one found himself deeply moved. The pathetic Vietnamese girl and his old friend Allanic.

He turned away abruptly as the dead girl's body was covered and joined the two men from the lab, followed by Graudin, at the table where they were studying a small knife resting on a white sheet of paper in a glare of light from the unshaded lamp. "This is the knife?"

"We were waiting for you, Monsieur l'Inspecteur." One of the men touched the pointed steel blade with a rubber-gloved finger. "We think this is very likely the weapon that killed that American actor and those other two men last year."

"Can't be positive," his associate added, "until we get it to the lab and measure it precisely. But it looks right. Length and width of the blade."

Damiot stared at it, remembering the two knives Lolo had given him. The blade of this one was slightly longer and wider. It was a small stiletto with a leather-covered handle. "Did you find two other knives? The ones I gave you last week?"

"In the chest of drawers. Under some folded scarves with her passport."

"Were there any sunglasses?"

"No. But we found this." He picked up a leather shoulder bag from the table and held it open in his gloved hands.

Damiot saw the money inside. "American money?"

"Two new hundred-dollar bills. Like the ones we tested last week."

Damiot leaned closer. "From Scott's attaché case."

"I'll compare the sequence of numbers from our list when we get back to the lab."

"Anything else?"

"That's all. So far."

"Go over everything. Looks as though this girl is our killer." He moved away from them and, Graudin following, crossed to the hanging birdcage.

"You think she killed all three of those men?" Graudin whispered.

"So it would seem." He lifted a corner of the scarf with one finger.

The bird was gone.

Then he saw its body on the bottom of the cage. Head twisted as though its neck had been broken. Beads of blood on the white feathers.

CHAPTER 21

IN SPITE OF THE HOT COFFEE GRAUDIN HAD BROUGHT HIM, Damiot was shivering. He knew that he hadn't picked up some kind of virus, but was chilled by the unexpected news that had just come from upstairs.

Joffo had called from the lab to say that the knife from Lolo's apartment matched the wound in Scott's body and checked with the measurements of both those earlier stabbings. Montal and Darbois.

And the serial numbers on those two hundred-dollar bills contained the sequence of numbers on the list made from the money in Scott's attaché case.

So the little Vietnamese prostitute was the murderer. Motive, without doubt, had been money. She had taken a thousand dollars from Scott in the Hôtel Amadeus. Stolen it from his wallet. He missed it and threatened her with the police. When he turned his back to reach for his clothes, she had stabbed him.

Damiot studied the color photograph of Lolo that he had placed on top of the three dossiers. Lolo smiling into the camera. Looking childlike and innocent, against a mass of tropical foliage. He had found the picture under a pad of pale blue writing paper. There were no letters or papers of any sort. Only this one photograph.

When he came back to his office, he had sent Merval to have copies made.

Then he had gone to report to his chief, who was delighted that the murderer had been found but agreed that nothing should be released to the press until the forensic lab and the autopsy report had confirmed everything.

Damiot rubbed his hands together trying to warm his freezing fingers. He had drunk two cups of hot coffee, but they hadn't helped.

It was the excitement of knowing that the Scott investigation was finished that was making him shiver.

He swiveled his chair to gaze at the window, covered with rain, and smiled. No more walking in the rain today. This afternoon he would stay at his desk.

Turning back to stare at the photograph again, under the glare from his desk lamp, he wondered what had brought this Vietnamese girl to her death. He would question her family and friends as soon as the weather cleared, find out what they knew about her. Before he was finished he would learn everything about Lolo. Things even her family didn't know.

He would have much to tell Andrea tonight when they met at Café de la Paix. Must decide where to eat their third dinner together.

The telephone rang once, but he didn't reach to pick it up.

He wondered what had become of those sunglasses Lolo was wearing when she met Scott at Chez Pavy. They hadn't showed up in her apartment.

Why had she killed her pet bird? Was it because she didn't want anyone else to have it? People who kept caged birds were strange.

The buzzer rasped under his desk.

Damiot snatched up the phone. "Yes?"

"Dr. Bretty calling," Graudin answered. "On line three."

He punched the button. "Yes, Doctor? What have you found?"

"Several things, Monsieur Inspecteur. Not what I was expecting."

"What do you mean?"

"It's not suicide."

"What!"

"The knife entered the body at the wrong angle. Slanted slightly down."

"Yes?"

"Suicides usually make themselves comfortable before they take their lives."

"I observed that."

"This young woman appeared to have been seated on that divan. The wound—if self-inflicted—would probably be at an angle slanting upward, but this wound slants down. As though she was stabbed by someone else. Of course, she may have been standing and collapsed onto the divan, then to the floor. The person with the knife would've been slightly taller—if he or she was standing."

"Then you think it was murder?"

"I do."

Damiot shivered as another chill swept through his body.

"We're not finished with the autopsy yet. Wanted you to know what we've found. We're stopping for lunch, but I'll have a report for you this afternoon."

"What about the bird?"

"Neck broken. Somebody strangled it."

"Thanks, Doctor." He set the phone down and stared at the smiling photograph of Lolo.

Scott's killer had murdered her and probably killed the bird to make it look as though Lolo had done that before taking her own life.

Four murders now! Lolo, Scott, and those two others last year.

Four murders.

Was it one killer? Or two?

There was a brisk knock on the door.

He looked up as Graudin hurried in.

"What did they find?"

"She was murdered. Order a car. We're going out again. Merval can drive." Damiot got up from his desk and picked up Lolo's photograph. "Bring copies of this."

"She came in, middle of the afternoon, but I didn't see who was with her." The old woman's eyes were faded and wary. "There's a curtain over the glass."

Damiot and Graudin turned in unison to glance at the window in the door. Saw that it was covered with a clean lace curtain. They could see Merval's shadow outside but were unable to make out his face, only the dark figure of a man. They faced the concierge again as she continued her explanation.

"That's so people can't stare in here. I saw two people, but I couldn't tell if it was a man or woman with her."

"How'd you know it was Lolo?"

"The door was ajar. I was cooking dinner. Gets hot in here with no windows. So I heard Lolo's voice."

"You didn't hear the other person talking?"

"Not a word. Lolo was laughing, so I knew it must be a friend with her. I'd know her laugh anywhere. Used to tell her she sounded like a bird. Of course that might be because she kept that pet bird in a cage. People get to be like their pets. Strange she killed it. She loved that bird! She said she always had one, since she was a child."

"Did you hear this other person leave?"

"Not a sound."

"Thank you, Madame. We won't keep you from your cooking. Smells like chicken today."

"Stewing it for dinner. We have a little garden in the back. My husband's in charge of the chickens and rabbits. I grow the vegetables."

Damiot followed Graudin outside.

Merval waited expectantly in the dim passage that echoed with the sound of rain from the inner courtyard.

"There was someone with the Vietnamese girl," Damiot explained, his voice low, "when she came in yesterday, but the old woman doesn't know whether it was a man or woman."

"You think it was the killer?" Merval asked.

"Until I learn otherwise." Damiot went ahead of them, toward the street, pausing under the entrance arch to stare through the twilight at the rain. "You both have a copy of Lolo's picture. Show it in every café, bar, and restaurant. Someone's certain to recognize her. Ask in each place if she was there yesterday with another person. Find out if it was a man. Get his description and anything else you can learn about him and Lolo. We'll spead out. I'll check rue Nôtre-Dame-des-Champs. You take Boulevard Raspail. Leave the car here. See you later!" He pulled his hat down and headed toward the corner as Graudin and Merval went in the other direction.

The rain thudded against his damp hat and on the shoulders of his raincoat. His shoes felt heavy. They weren't leaking, but his feet were cold and damp.

He hurried up rue Vavin and turned right on the side street. Rue Nôtre-Dame-des-Champs was flooded with rain, the university buildings an anonymous mass in the distance. A few students, looking bedraggled in the early twilight, hurrying from classes. Several packed into an ancient car and one rain-soaked boy on a motorcycle with a girl perched on the pillion, behind him, clutching his wet raincoat.

The light was a pearly silver gray with violet shadows that made the street look like an Impressionist painting.

He went into a small restaurant where the staff was preparing for dinner and showed the photograph of Lolo to le patron, who had been reading a newspaper at the cashier's desk. The old man recognized Lolo and said that she had eaten dinner there many times before. Always alone. He hadn't seen her in months. She wasn't in the restaurant yesterday. They were closed on Sunday.

Damiot slipped the photograph back into his pocket and returned to the rainy street, aware that le patron had recognized him.

Two cafés in the next block were empty except for a man behind each *zinc*. One was polishing glasses, the other eating a bowl of onion soup that smelled so appetizing that it gave Damiot a twinge in his gut. Neither man recognized Lolo.

The next restaurant had an awning along the front, which in warm weather would shade a terrace with several tables. A small sign in the window said it was closed on Mondays.

He stood there, reluctant to continue through the rain, remembering how pleased he'd been earlier with the idea of spending the afternoon in his office. With Scott's murderer a suicide—the puzzle solved—he could have relaxed for the moment. Making a few telephone calls. Releasing the news to the reporters. Answering their questions.

Instead he was standing here, out of the rain, and cursing.

His attention was caught by a police car slowing beyond the cars parked along the curb. Saw Merval opening the door and waving for him to get in.

Damiot edged between two cars and collapsed onto the cold

leather seat, slamming the door. "What is it?" He was aware that the car was already moving.

"Graudin found a café where they knew the Vietnamese girl. She was in there yesterday afternoon."

"Alone?"

"With another woman."

They sped, siren sounding, going in the wrong direction down a one-way street, and turned into Boulevard Raspail, where, with a screech of brakes, they double-parked in front of a brightly lighted café.

Damiot opened the door and eased himself up from the seat into the rain. Slammed the door and, followed by Merval, hurried into the warm restaurant.

Here there were no aromas of cooking—they probably only served sandwiches—but there was an inviting smell of wine and beer.

As Damiot crossed toward the *zinc* he saw that Graudin was talking to la patronne. An aging dragon in black with an elaborate arrangement of black hair piled on top of her head, obviously a wig.

"Chief Inspector Damiot? A great honor."

"You identified the girl in that photograph?"

"Lolo? She comes in here all the time." She smiled ferociously, showing false teeth. "Such a nice little thing!"

"She was in here yesterday? With a woman?"

"That's correct."

"Had you ever seen this other other woman before?"

"Never. Usually Mademoiselle Lolo comes in alone. Although, from time to time, a young man has been with her."

"The same young man?"

"Always a different one."

"What did this other woman look like? Was she young? Tall or short?"

"She appeared to be young. Slightly taller than Lolo, but I couldn't say what she looked like because she was bundled up for the rain. Scarf around her throat and some kind of plastic thing over her head."

"Did they speak French?"

"Oh, yes! I heard them chattering like young girls when they came in. Laughing and giggling. Both of them."

"Could you see the color of the other girl's hair?"

"Her hair was covered, but some strands were sticking out. Long and black. Like Lolo's! In fact, they looked very much alike. She could've been Lolo's sister."

"You mean she was Vietnamese?"

She shrugged. "I couldn't say."

"What color were her eyes?"

"I didn't see them. She wore sunglasses."

CHAPTER 22

ANOTHER MISERABLE MORNING.

Damiot was silent as Graudin turned the car off Avenue de l'Opéra into rue Gomboust, slowing to a stop in front of the Saigon-Paris restaurant.

Young Merval and two other sergeants were going from bar to café again, in Montparnasse, searching for that other girl. Lolo's friend with sunglasses. He had joined them last night, visiting every bistro and restaurant near Lolo's apartment, but finding no trace of her friend.

"Wait here." Opening the door and and stepping out into the rain, glancing up at the unlighted sign above the entrance. The neon tubes looked limp and dead in the gray morning light.

Hurrying across the sidewalk, he saw that the windows on either side of the double doors were curtained with some sort of Oriental fabric. Reaching the scanty protection of a striped awning, he noticed a hand-printed closed sign leaning against the glass in both windows.

He grasped the knob and turned it, but the door was locked. Rapped on it, then tapped sharply on the curtained glass pane in the center.

"They won't be open today, M'sieur."

He looked around to face an old woman, broom in hand, peering from a dark side passage.

"There's been a death in their family. The people who run that restaurant. Probably be closed several days."

"You know where they live?"

"Somebody told me they have a little farm outside the city.

They don't talk much to their neighbors, although they speak good French. Keep to themselves."

"Merci, Madame." He ran back through the icy rain and got into the waiting police car again.

"What next?" Graudin asked.

'Hôtel du Pont." He touched his hat to the old woman, whose eyes were following their car. "When we get back to headquarters you can find out where the Yeung family lives. That concierge said they have a farm outside Paris?"

"I'll check."

"They've been notified of their daughter's death. For the moment, we needn't tell them she was murdered. Only that we're investigating her death. Find out if Lolo had a sister—or any other female relative who looks like her."

"Right."

Damiot hunched down in his damp raincoat, shivering again, as the car splashed through empty side streets toward the Pont Royal.

Would this weather never clear!

He had reached a point in the Scott case—it happened in every investigation—where he had several leads that would take him nowhere, but each of them had to be pursued to its end.

That girl with Lolo in the café Sunday afternoon, with the long black hair and sunglasses. Was she the one who had been with Scott the previous Sunday night at Chez Pavy? Was she another prostitute? Or some relative of Lolo's? Whoever she was, she had killed Lolo hoping to make it look like suicide. Planted that knife and the American money to make him think Lolo had murdered Scott. Of course, she didn't know that he knew about her other two victims.

Too many women involved in this Scott case! More than he could recall in any previous investigation.

Linette Murzeau, Serena Scott, Madame Montal who smashed her husband's model car, Zita Vianne—the English dancer with long legs at Lido de Paris—Lolo, and her friend who looked like a sister.

Then there was that other English girl, Jenny Carstairs, who had written to Scott in California! He'd forgotten about her.

And who was that girl who came to the Hôtel du Pont and taught Scott, privately, to speak French?

Too damn many women!

He left Graudin in the car again and hurried into the warm hotel lobby, where the assistant manager was sorting a pile of mail behind the desk. "Monsieur Renant."

Renant put the mail aside. "Bonjour, Monsieur l'Inspecteur!"

"I've stopped by rather than telephone, because I'll be away from my office all morning."

"Let me call Monsieur Valentin. He went upstairs with a party of guests that just arrived from Vienna."

"I'm sure you can tell me what I need to know. The name of the person who came here to instruct Monsieur Scott in the French language. Madame Scott told me the hotel arranged it."

"I handled that myself! And I believe I kept the young woman's name." He turned to a shelf, picked up a leather-bound address book, and flipped the pages. "Arranged for her to teach Monsieur Scott on his second visit, I believe, but after that he contacted her himself."

"Was she American?"

"I've no idea. Matter of fact, I only saw her once, and we spoke French. Her French, by the way, was excellent." He found the page and ran his finger down the listed names. "I remember contacting the École Suisse, and they sent her over. . . . Here we are! École Suisse—it's a branch of the famous Zurich school of languages—on Avenue de l'Opéra. Here's her name. Miss Jenny Carstairs."

Damiot smiled. Two leads had become one.

The attractive young woman behind the reception desk, at École Suisse, stared at Damiot's badge. "Police? But . . ."

"Chief Inspector Damiot."

"Damiot!" She raised her eyes to his face.

"I'm making inquiries about one of your instructors. Miss Jenny Carstairs."

"Such a lovely person! I hope nothing's happened to Miss Carstairs!"

"I wish to contact her on a police matter. You have an address where she can be reached?"

"One moment." She flipped the cards in one of several revolving white plastic wheels deployed across her desk.

"I must ask you, of course, not to inform Miss Carstairs that I'll be contacting her."

"Certainly not, Monsieur l'Inspecteur. I quite understand."

"Can you describe Miss Carstairs?"

"I've not seen her in several months." She kept revolving the wheel of cards. "She's one of our part-time teachers who prefers to teach privately. So she rarely comes in here. She's young and quite attractive."

"Color of hair?"

"Black. Long and rather straight. Last time I saw her was more than a year ago when she used one of the classrooms to teach a private pupil. Never more than one at a time. She wouldn't take a class, but there are many people who will pay a higher fee for private lessons. Mostly businessmen and celebrities." She detached a card from the plastic wheel and handed it to him. "This is her card."

He ran his eyes down the typed words.

NAME	Miss Jenny Carstairs
ADDRESS	c/o American Express Co., 11 rue Scribe
NATIONALITY	Grande-Bretagne
REFERENCE	Consulate de Grande-Bretagne
AGE	possibly early thirties
PROFESSION	teacher, governess
NOTES	Carstairs hightly recommended by her consulate. Prefers not to give an address. Has no phone. Can be reached by writing, care American Express. Picks up mail three times each week. Miss Carstairs's pupils have been highly complimentary of her teaching ability. Never any complaints.

Damiot continued to stare at the typed words. So Miss Jenny Carstairs had given her consulate as reference, and whoever interviewed her thought she was in her early thirties. She had no phone but went to the American Express office three times a week for her mail. He already knew she had given a false address to the American Express office. Maybe he should pay another visit there. Talk to the people who worked behind the mail window instead of their superior.

"I do remember one thing about Miss Carstairs."

He looked up from the card. "What's that?"

"She always wore sunglasses. Each time I saw her! I suspected she probably had weak eyes. Many teachers do, of course. If you wish the names of her pupils, you'll find them on the other side of that card."

Damiot reversed the card and read the list. Two names were familiar. Alex Scott and Victor Montal. "Could I have a copy of this?"

"Certainly, Monsieur l'Inspecteur." She pressed a button on her desk. "One of our secretaries will duplicate it for you. Does this have anything to do with Monsieur Scott's murder? I've been reading about that in the papers and remembered he was one of Miss Carstairs's pupils."

He handed the card back without replying. "Did you ever meet Monsieur Scott?"

"Unfortunately, I didn't. Miss Carstairs always went to his hotel, so he never came here."

"And where did Miss Carstairs teach Monsieur Montal?"

"In one of our private classrooms. He must've had five or six sessions with her." She looked around as a sour-faced young woman appeared from a many-doored inner corridor. "Would you have this duplicated right away?" She handed the card to her and turned back to Damiot. "Was Monsieur Montal involved with the death of Monsieur Scott?"

"That would be impossible, Mademoiselle. Monsieur Montal was murdered last year."

The apartment house on rue Edmond-Valentin was a handsome building that had recently been modernized.

There was no sound as the chromium capsule rose from the lobby.

Damiot felt trapped in the small space. He preferred the elegant old French elevators like the one that had taken him upstairs at the École Suisse.

When they left there he had Graudin drive him to the American Express office, where he had talked to a man on duty at the mail window who had seen Miss Carstairs many times.

She was, he said, young, with long black hair, she spoke with a British accent and always wore sunglasses. He hadn't seen her in the past week. So her description was confirmed, but nothing new was learned.

He had driven from there to the nearby British consulate, where he discovered that Miss Jenny Carstairs lived on rue Edmond-Valentin.

Graudin was waiting downstairs in the car. Damiot didn't want his assistant present when he questioned Miss Carstairs. Most people were less intimidated if no witness heard what they said.

The elevator slowed to a stop, almost imperceptibly, and a section of the gleaming capsule slid open.

He stepped out into a corridor, simply but attractively decorated, with doors at opposite ends, facing each other, numbered four and five.

According to the lobby directory, number five was Miss Carstairs.

He pressed the bell button.

No bell or buzzer responded, but a sound of dogs barking came from far away in the apartment.

When Damiot returned to his office he must decide immediately where he would take Andrea tonight for their third dinner together. Which cuisine this time? A restaurant with a nearby hotel where he was known. Although, in this weather, there should be no difficulty getting a room.

He pushed the button again, and the dogs resumed their barking.

If Miss Carstairs wasn't home, he would have to return later. He wanted to question this English girl himself. If he left Graudin to wait for her, she might become frightened. That would give her time to decide what she was going to tell him before he could return from the Préfecture.

The door was opened by the tallest and thinnest woman he'd ever seen. She had white hair, and she was smiling.

"Yes, Monsieur?"

Without realizing what he was doing, he glanced at her feet and saw that she was wearing black satin slippers like a ballet dancer.

"I know! I'm rather a bit taller than you, aren't I, even in slippers. Isn't it ridiculous? I think so."

"Forgive me, Madame. I didn't mean—"

"Everybody does this when we meet for the first time. Who the devil might you be?"

"Chief Inspector Damiot from—"

"Damiot? I'm a tremendous fan of yours! Do come in." She turned back into the apartment, motioning for him to follow.

"But I—"

"I've read about you so often, but the newspapers never said you spoke English."

He closed the door and, removing his damp hat again, followed her through a spacious foyer toward open double doors, aware of the barking dogs in the distance.

"I should've realized that you would, because so many of your cases involve foreigners. Speak English, that is. Like this current business of the American film star who got himself stabbed in rue de Caumartin. Have you managed to find his murderer?"

"No, Madame, I . . ." He followed her into a salon where several lamps were lighted.

"Of course you will! At any moment. Do you really think it was a prostitute? I know for a fact that a woman can quite easily stab a man in the back. Saw it happen years ago in Cairo. It doesn't require all that much strength. One careful jab—you must know, of course, what you're doing—a sharp knife penetrates human flesh like butter. If you avoid the ribs, it's quite easy to reach a vital organ." Motioning toward a sofa. "Do sit there!"

He sank onto the comfortable sofa—awkwardly because of his raincoat—aware of a comfortably furnished but cluttered salon, uncertain what to do with his hat.

"Toss your hat on that table. I adore antiques, but I believe in using them. That's because I'm British! You French hang cards on everything so people can't sit down."

He dropped his hat on the sturdy oak table.

"What do you drink, Monsieur Inspecteur? Sherry, gin, or perhaps a cognac?"

"Nothing, Madame. Merci."

"I suppose you're on duty and you're not permitted to

indulge. What in God's name are you doing here? I'm exploding with curiosity and questions."

"I regret having to bother you, Madame, but I would like to see Miss Jenny Carstairs."

"Nobody calls me Jenny any more. I've been Jen for more years than I could possibly remember! Even my pupils call me Jen."

"You are Miss Carstairs?"

"Perhaps you were expecting someone shorter? Younger and more attractive?"

"Certainly not! I—"

"I was never much shorter than this since puberty, but I was somewhat more attractive, I'm told, when I was a girl. Although, I fear, in a rather coltish way."

As she rattled on, he studied her more closely. She had curled up on a facing sofa, her long legs in tailored black slacks tucked beneath her, wearing a dark gray turtleneck sweater with a golden medallion on a heavy gold chain around her neck. Deeply tanned skin made her blue eyes more striking. White hair brushed back into a knot revealed surprisingly small ears with gold earrings matching the medallion. One of the most completely feminine women he had ever encountered. Long bony fingers gesturing delicately to punctuate her words.

". . . although some of my dearest friends say I seem to become younger as I grow older. Which is utterly ridiculous! I suspect it's my attitude toward life that keeps me young and, of course, my being with young people for so many years. Then, too, I like to travel. Keep moving constantly! Climbing mountains and riding camels across endless deserts."

He was conscious of shelves filled with books. Oriental brocades and small statues that could be dogs or dragons. White roses in a gleaming copper pot. Windows curtained to shut out the unpleasant day.

"But you haven't as yet explained your coming to see me, have you?"

"There is a possibility, Miss Carstairs, that Monsieur Scott's murderer is a prostitute."

"Ah, yes! That's what the papers have been hinting."

"A young woman with long black hair who speaks French—

as well as English—fluent enough to give private lessons in both languages at the École Suisse."

"An excellent school! I know it by reputation."

"She wears sunglasses, apparently at all times, which made us suspect she might be Oriental."

"You mean she wears sunglasses to hide her eyes?"

"So we assumed. But when we located one prostitute—a Vietnamese who answers her description and was known to carry small knives on her person—she, too, was murdered."

"Good Lord!"

"Her murder was arranged to look like suicide, but the autopsy report shows that it was not."

"Angle of knife? That sort of thing, I suppose."

"In addition to Scott and this Vietnamese girl, we believe this same young woman has stabbed at least two other men. One of whom also studied with her at École Suisse."

"And the second man?"

"He apparently took English lessons from a girl he met in a café. Probably this same prostitute."

"So four people have been stabbed. Why do you come to me?"

"Because this young woman uses your name."

"My God!"

"When she arranged to receive her mail at the American Express office on rue Scribe, she showed them a British passport made out to Jenny Carstairs, whose profession was listed as teacher and governess."

"But I've never been to American Express! I always go to Thomas Cook and Sons. Been doing that since I began traveling—years ago—went to their London office to arrange my first trip to Paris."

"Someone else is obviously using your name."

"What about the age listed on my passport?"

"That would be changed easily when the false passport was made." He produced the card from his jacket and handed it to her. "This is a duplicate of the record, from École Suisse, which they keep in their file on Miss Jenny Carstairs."

"Oh?" Scowling as she ran her eyes down the card. "She gave the British consulate as her reference! Pupils 'highly complimentary.' At least she hasn't damaged my reputation."

Laughing as she handed the card back. "How could this person have heard of me?"

"Has your passport ever been stolen? Here in Paris or during your travels?"

"Never."

"Where is it now? At this moment."

"I suppose it's in a drawer of my dressing table. That's where I usually keep it when I'm in residence here."

"Would you see if it's there?"

"Of course, Monsieur Inspecteur." She rose quickly from the sofa.

Damiot jumped up. "Just to be sure you have it."

"This is terribly exciting! Someone impersonating me. Won't take a moment." As she went toward the open doors, the dogs resumed their barking. "Little devils! They want to go out." She looked back from the doorway. "I have two miniature sheepdogs. Toto and Bo-Peep—my dear companions. They go everywhere with me. And they don't like being shut in the kitchen. I stuck them there when you rang. That's what took me so long to answer the door."

As she disappeared through the hall, Damiot returned the card to his pocket and moved around the room, considering what he had learned.

Someone was certainly impersonating Miss Jenny Carstairs. Using her passport or a counterfeit. Which brought him no closer to finding the murderer.

Four people dead! Without a clue to their killer, except what he already knew. She was young, had long black hair, and wore sunglasses. Spoke French and English. And was probably a prostitute.

He had been careful not to give Miss Carstairs precise details. Hadn't told her that Lolo was stabbed with the same knife that had killed the other three and that money from Scott's attaché case was in her purse.

The dogs were barking again.

He turned as the Englishwoman appeared, passport in hand.

"Here we are! Found it in my dressing table. Exactly where I'd left it. I'm not one to lose or misplace inanimate objects." She handed the passport to him before sinking onto the sofa.

Damiot remained standing as he flipped through the pages.

"Could anyone have taken this for a few hours—perhaps overnight—without your being aware?"

"Can't see how! I don't even have a maid."

"Of course, this would have to be before February of last year. That's when the first man was killed." He returned the passport and watched her drop it carelessly on the sofa. "Among your acquaintances is there a young woman with long black hair who wears sunglasses?"

"I've been wondering about that as we talked, but I can't think of anyone. Since I've given up teaching I don't come in contact with many young people."

"You own this apartment?"

"Does that surprise you? I was governess with a wealthy British family—three charming children—traveled all over the world with them for years. The parents eventually divorced. I was unfortunately involved but the proceedings were handled with discretion and nothing appeared in the newspapers. After a brief period of time Wilfred and I were married in Nice and lived in a villa he owned above Antibes. Wilfred had suffered from a heart condition for years, which unfortunately worsened and caused his death. But we had four glorious years together, and he left me a tidy fortune. I've kept the villa near Antibes and several years ago bought this flat."

"Obviously you are not the Miss Jenny Carstairs who goes around Paris stabbing people."

"But I'm terribly thrilled to be involved in your investigation. Even remotely! If you look at those shelves, you'll notice I read only travel books and novels of detection."

He glanced at the crowded shelves but was unable to make out any of the titles.

"My favorite writer, I suppose, is British—Josephine Tey. And I reread her books—I've all of them—at least once a year. I adore detective novels because they're like puzzles. And teachers learn to solve puzzles. Just as you solve the puzzle of your murder investigations."

"Yes. I do sometimes think of my cases as puzzles. Try to find the missing pieces and fit them together."

"I've always preferred Josephine Tey because her characters are not black and white. Human beings are never completely innocent or evil."

"That's very true."

"I don't like, for instance, to hear races labeled by color. Black or white! If you study painting, you discover that black is made from every color and white is the absence of color. I suppose when I was a girl I might've been called pink—a color with such a dubious reputation—but for the past thirty years I've been brown. From the sun! Yet no one ever calls me brown." She paused suddenly. "I am sorry. I've kept you here with my chatter." Rising from the sofa. "All retired teachers talk too much!"

"Plaisir, Madame. Please! Call me any time, if you think of someone among your friends with long black hair who wears sunglasses. Who might have had access to your passport prior to February of last year. Call me at the Préfecture."

"I would be delighted to call you at the Préfecture, Monsieur Inspecteur!"

CHAPTER 23

"YOU'RE ENJOYING THIS?" DAMIOT ASKED.

"It's heaven! What is it?"

"They scoop out a brioche and fill it with foie gras, then bake it again. Briefly."

"Incredible!"

He smiled and took another swallow of wine, a Viognier he had ordered that afternoon when he phoned to discuss dinner with le patron.

Andrea was eating the brioche au foie gras with obvious pleasure.

They had been quiet tonight, both of them, since meeting at the Café de la Paix, as though the continuing bad weather had finally dampened their spirits.

Damiot was aware that he had been in a foul mood all afternoon, although he had looked forward to dinner.

The day had been a disaster.

His only positive accomplishment was finding Miss Carstairs and learning that someone had been impersonating her. Somebody had managed to get her passport and have a copy made, obviously changing the age listed, before arranging for American Express to hold her mail, including the letters she received from Alex Scott. And she had given the American Express office as her address when she was accepted as a part-time teacher at the École Suisse.

Who was this counterfeit Miss Carstairs? British apparently, according to that man at American Express.

Merval, this afternoon, questioned Zita Vianne at the apartment where she had lived with her waiter lover, Luc

Darbois, but the English dancer had never heard of Miss Jenny Carstairs, and Darbois hadn't mentioned the name of the young woman who was helping him with his English.

Graudin had driven out to the Yeung farm, which, he reported, was unlike any French farm he'd ever seen. Even the ducks looked Oriental! He found the family grieving for the dead girl, weeping and wailing, her parents overcome with shock. They had learned only that Lolo was dead and that her death was being investigated. The local police had been instructed not to inform them that she was murdered. Graudin talked to the dead girl's sister, who was older than Lolo, looked nothing like her, and could give him no information about her friends in Paris.

Damiot frowned as he washed down the last of his brioche with the excellent white wine.

Lolo's death was the result of information given by two whores—Picolette and Carine—one reporting that she carried a knife and the other confirming this.

From the first, when he questioned the unhappy Vietnamese girl, Damiot had felt she was innocent of Scott's murder. She had denied knowing him or ever seeing him in a film.

The murderer—the fake Miss Carstairs—had planted the two hundred dollars in Lolo's apartment and murdered her with the same knife that had killed Scott and those other two men. She hadn't left the sunglasses because she was wearing them to prevent identification if anyone saw her leaving Lolo's apartment.

The sunglasses and the missing eight hundred dollars must still be in the possession of the counterfeit Miss Carstairs. Or had she already exchanged those crisp new dollars for francs?

There were many places where that could be arranged, for a fee, in Paris. By the time those bills showed up again they would have passed through many hands and "Miss Carstairs's" fingerprints would have been smudged over by many others.

His chain of thought was interrupted by their waiter returning with a tray holding steaming brown earthen bowls of soup, which he served after the garçon removed their empty plates.

"Onion soup!" Andrea exclaimed, sniffing the rich aroma.

"One of the joys of the Lyonnaise cuisine." He nodded his approval to the young waiter who departed with the garçon. "In fact, the citizens of Lyon claim that onion soup was invented in their city."

"Is that true?"

He shrugged. "I've never heard of any other city boasting of its creation." He eased his soup spoon through the thick crust of Gruyère, releasing even more of its essence.

They remained silent briefly, enjoying the steaming soup.

Damiot glanced around the pleasant low-ceilinged restaurant as he ate, observing the other diners. In spite of the weather, a dozen tables were occupied. Mostly young couples, although there were a few middle-aged people. At both those other restaurants, where they had dined last week, there had been old men eating alone. This place somehow had a warmer and more comfortable look. Perhaps that was because it was owned by a young chef and his entire staff was much younger than usual in Paris.

He looked at Andrea as she ate her soup. Her mood, like his, was different tonight. She seemed more relaxed, and although she wasn't talking as much, she seemed to be enjoying the food, smiling and happy. He mustn't show his irritability or let her suspect that he was troubled and depressed. After all, what had happened today—rather what hadn't happened—with the Scott investigation had nothing to do with their dinner together.

Later, after dinner and a visit to that nearby hotel, he would take Andrea back to where she had parked her car near the Café de la Paix. Then he would drive on to rendezvous at midnight with Graudin and Merval in Montparnasse. They would make another round of the late-night spots, hoping to find some trace of the counterfeit Miss Carstairs.

"Most delicious onion soup I've ever eaten!" Andrea exclaimed.

"I'm glad." He realized that she was wearing a different dress tonight, some kind of soft green material. Hair brushed back from her face and coiled in a thick knot, low on her neck. She looked charming.

Feeling his inspection, Andrea raised her eyes. "You aren't eating?"

"I stopped for a moment, to look at you. Thinking how seductive you are."

"But everyone looks seductive when they're enjoying good food! They both satisfy a basic appetite. Eating and having sex."

"C'est vrai!" He continued to eat his soup. He'd been worried this afternoon, seated in his cold office and staring at the rain slashing against the window, preoccupied with his lack of progress on the Scott case. Afraid that, because of his concern, tonight's dinner would not be as pleasant as the previous ones. His fears had been groundless.

Going to his hotel and enjoying a hot tub before driving to the Café de la Paix had relaxed him, mind and body.

Damiot continued to be troubled about his unrewarding day, but Andrea, as before, was such a pleasant dinner companion that he was starting to unwind.

More than he had ever relaxed with his wife during dinner, when he was involved with an important investigation. Sophie asked endless questions but didn't really listen to his answers. She had never been interested in his work.

Tonight he mustn't tell Andrea too much about the Scott case—at least not as much as he had previously—although for the first time she wasn't asking questions.

The next course was served in individual casseroles, which they were warned not to touch.

"What is it?" Andrea whispered as the two waiters returned to the kitchen.

"Quenelles à la crème," Damiot explained, "with a coulis of crayfish." Refilling their wineglasses. "This dish is a favorite of mine. When I phoned this afternoon, le patron told me he had fresh crayfish."

"The things you're teaching me about French food!" She took a cautious taste and closed her eyes. "I shall remember this moment for the rest of my life! These quenelles are as light as angel wings!"

"Bien!" He returned the wine bottle to its bucket and began to eat. "Yes. Le patron has surpassed himself."

"This is not la nouvelle cuisine?"

"Certainly not! This chef is a master of the classic Lyonnaise cuisine."

"What do you think of la nouvelle cuisine?"

"From what I've read, that's only an extension and simplification of la grande cuisine. Much of it will be accepted and will no longer be called la nouvelle cuisine. Its best features will become part of the classic cuisine. Every good chef is an artist! And I don't mean only the famous chefs—I've never eaten in their restaurants—but every chef who uses fine ingredients and respects them creates a perfect dish. The simplest one can be a masterpiece."

"Like the one we're eating?"

"This young chef didn't invent quenelles à la crème, but he has produced a perfect example of a classic. Actually, what we're eating is the creation of many chefs. The original chef, perhaps a hundred years ago, invented the basic dish, and another, perhaps fifty years later, added the coulis of crayfish."

They finished the quenelles without further conversation, mopping the last drop of the coulis with a morsel of bread.

The young chef, who had greeted them when they arrived, hurried from his kitchen followed by two waiters and preceded by the garçon pushing a wheeled cart. He was tall and thin, and his white toque blanche made him appear even taller. He bowed as the procession reached their table. "Everything is satisfactory, M'sieur l'Inspecteur?"

"Everything is perfect."

"Perfectly delicious!" Andrea exclaimed.

He smiled and motioned for the garçon to remove their empty plates, whipped off the lid from an immense copper serving skillet as one of the waiters set fresh plates in front of them, then held the skillet down for Andrea to see its contents.

"How beautiful!" she murmured.

"This is a gros-double à la Lyonnaise," Damiot explained. "Tripe cooked in white wine."

"The wine is a Côte Rôtie." The chef served them as he talked. "I suggested to M'sieur Damiot on the phone that you should drink the same wine with the gros-double."

There was the sound of a drawn cork, and the second waiter leaned forward to pour a swallow into Damiot's fresh glass.

He tasted it, nodding.

The waiter filled their glasses as the chef served the tripe and the first waiter added galette lyonnaise to each dinner plate.

Andrea watched their performance with interest and after a moment asked the chef, "How did you happen to call your charming restaurant La Mère de Lyon?"

"My parents own a restaurant in Lyon called La Mère Yvette. For centuries many restaurants there have had such names. The first is said to have been La Mère Guy. So! When I opened my restaurant in Paris, I decided to name it La Mère de Lyon."

"The mother of them all?"

He laughed. "Oh, no, Mademoiselle! Nothing so immodest. It means simply the Mother from Lyon. So Parisians will realize they can find la vrai cuisine Lyonnaise here." Bowing again. "Plaisir, Mademoiselle, M'sieur." He motioned both waiters and the garçon, with his cart, ahead of him toward the kitchen.

Damiot raised his wineglass. "To good food!" Touching his glass to hers. "And a perfect companion."

They tasted the wine.

"Everything is perfection," she whispered. "Magnifique!"

Damiot picked up his fork. "Wait until you taste this."

Andrea closed her eyes as she took a first bite. "I didn't know anything could be this good. It melts on the tongue."

"Been cooking for hours."

They ate silently, savoring every morsel of tripe and enjoying the wine.

This was followed by a cheese that, Damiot explained, was called Saint-Marcellin and came from an area near Lyon.

Dessert was a génoise with myrtilles over which they spooned a purée of framboises.

"Unfortunately," he explained, "huckleberries and raspberries are out of season, so these were probably preserved by some farmer's wife not too far from Lyon."

"I wouldn't know the difference, I'm afraid. Fresh or preserved."

He smiled. "You'll learn."

They finished their wine with the génoise, and afterward, Damiot ordered black coffee and Calvados.

"What a lovely dinner!" Andrea sighed. "Je suis contente." She reached across the table and squeezed his hand. "Très contente."

"Moi aussi!"

"You haven't told me what happened to that girl you mentioned."

"Which girl?" He knew which girl she meant.

"You said last week you'd questioned some Vietnamese girl. A prostitute."

"Oh! That girl." Better not tell anyone just yet what had happened to Lolo. It would be in the newspapers soon enough. "I haven't been able to question her again. She seems to have disappeared."

"You still think that whoever killed that actor, Alex Scott, also killed those other two men?"

"That's one theory." He was in no mood to discuss the Scott case with anyone, even Andrea. He didn't want to think about it for at least another hour. It would be soon enough when he met Graudin and Merval.

"Then you have other theories?"

"One or two."

"But don't wish to talk about them?"

"They would only bore you." He was pleased to see one of the waiters bringing a bottle and two glasses on a silver tray. "After our coffee, shall we make love again?"

She laughed. "Our final course for the evening?"

"And the best!"

Her laughter made the young waiter grin as he sat his tray down.

CHAPTER 24

DAMIOT KISSED HER PASSIONATELY ON BOTH BREASTS. HER flesh was warm and sweet. "Our bodies are getting to know each other."

"Isn't it lovely?" Nibbling at his ear one final time.

"Soon they will be good friends. Every part familiar." He rolled over, away from her, stretching out on his back.

"I'm in love with you," she whispered.

"Never say that unless you mean it."

"I do mean it!" Snuggling her face against his shoulder. "Do you love me?"

"I'm fond of you. Very fond. But I'm always cautious, pursuing a criminal or a woman. We've only known each other a few days."

"Exactly one week, last night!"

"That's right." He slipped an arm under her shoulder and kissed her neck.

"It's been a glorious week. In spite of all the rain! At least these three evenings we've been together have been heaven."

"They've been the happiest I've had in a long time."

"Since your wife left you?"

"There've been one or two other happy evenings since then."

"Oh!" She pummeled his chest with her fists.

Damiot laughed. "My father and mother made no secret about making love. Our bedrooms were close. So I knew about men and women at a very young age."

"I'll bet you did!"

"My parents never called it sex. Always love. Papa once

told me bed was good for four things. When I asked what he meant, he said, 'Figure it out for yourself!' I was perhaps seven years of age. I thought about what he said for days, then I told him, 'I can only think of three things. Sleeping, eating, and reading.' He laughed and said, 'You'll find out about the fourth.' Then I heard them one night, laughing in their bedroom. I got out of bed, knocked on their door, and went in. 'I know the fourth thing you can do in bed,' I told them. 'You can have fun.' They laughed and had me sit on the foot of their bed while they explained to me about love."

"Only the French! You must've had wonderful parents."

"I did."

"You loved them?"

"Yes."

"Both of them?"

"Of course." He stared at the ceiling, remembering his parents, aware that Andrea was crying softly. "Do you realize that all third-class hotel rooms have identical ceilings?"

"Do they?"

"With one long crack wall to wall. They must order them from some company that sells cracked hotel ceilings." He turned toward her. "Why do you cry?" In the faint light coming from the bath he was unable to see her face, only a glaze of tears on one cheek. "Are you unhappy, chérie?"

"I'm crying because I've never been this happy in all my life!"

"Bien!" He kissed the damp flesh under her eye.

"I lied to you the other night."

"Everyone lies to me. I'm a flic."

"Told you my father had killed my mother."

"I didn't really believe you."

"It was a lie. I'm the murderer."

"Are you?"

"I was the one driving that car."

"I still don't believe you."

"It's the truth! I swear it. You're the first person I've ever told. Walt took all the blame—said he was driving—but he was covering up for me."

"You had an accident, and your mother was killed. Your father took the blame to protect you. He must be a fine man."

"I loved him! But I hated Carla. So I murdered her."

"Nonsense! You were a child."

"I was fifteen. And I knew exactly what I was doing when I drove the car into that tree. It was a big tree. I was sure she'd be killed. I'd planned the whole thing for months. So, you see, it was premeditated murder."

"For what possible reason would you do such a thing?"

"Carla knew about Walt's mistresses—that had been going on for years—and she did nothing about it, but she was furious when she found out that he was in love with me?"

"Your father?"

"She threatened to have me put in an institution!"

"Are you saying your father made physical love to you? Raped you?"

"It wasn't rape." She giggled. "I suppose I seduced him. A fifteen-year-old girl knows about seduction. Most of them are afraid to do anything. I wasn't."

"What happened after your mother's death? Did you stay in this German Town? In the same house with your father?"

"Of course! We were very happy. And I was careful not to get pregnant. It was wonderful not to have Carla bossing me all the time and arguing with Walt. Everything was fine until he married Nina. She'd been his mistress for years, but finally she decided to make him marry her. And he did! After the wedding she moved in with us."

"You lived with them?"

"Until they told me to get out. Nina was worse than Carla! Demanding and greedy—and jealous. She began to suspect there'd been something between us. Walt and me. I suppose we gave it away when we were together. The way Nina looked at me, I knew she suspected, but I didn't realize she was working on Walt to send me away. Finally, just before she was to have the baby, she demanded that I go. Didn't want me there when her child was born. Walt told me one morning that the maid had packed all my belongings. Nina never wanted to see me again. If I tried to return, he would have me put in an institution for killing Carla. Walt kissed me on the cheek, said he was sorry but I must leave. Gave me a thousand dollars to get started on my own. Said there wouldn't be any more."

"And you left?"

"That morning!"

"Ever see your father again?"

"No. I wrote him when he and Nina were divorced—after the death of her baby—but he didn't answer."

"Never?"

"I received a note from his attorneys saying he was in Bermuda and I shouldn't try to contact him in the future. So I didn't. Even when I would read in the newspapers that he was at some banquet in New York—where I was living—and later that he had married again. Eventually, when I saved enough from my various jobs, I moved to London, and, three years ago, came to Paris." She leaned her head against his shoulder. "Now you know! I'm a murderer."

"There are more murderers walking free, even in Paris, than there are behind bars."

"You aren't going to arrest me?"

"What happened in America is no concern of mine."

"What I've told you won't change anything? Between us."

"How could it?" He rolled onto her firmly fleshed body again, covering and embracing her as Walt must have done.

"Then you do love me? Oh, I'm so glad. So happy."

He silenced her, pressing his mouth against her lips, wondering if she was still thinking about her father.

What was the truth? Which was the murderer, father or daughter?

Or was it all a mass of lies?

No matter! She was fascinating.

HE WAS EXHAUSTED AND DEPRESSED.

He'd been sitting for more than an hour, back turned to his desk, facing the window. Impossible to see anything through the rain except faint pinpoints of light for each street-lamp on the Quai des Orfèvres directly below.

This was the twelfth day of continuous rain, and the gutters of Paris were overflowing tonight. There were rumors that rats were swarming up from the sewers to escape drowning and cellars were flooding on Île St.-Louis.

In spite of the sweater he was wearing under his jacket, he felt chilled. His shoes and the cloth of his trousers against both ankles were damp from the hours of walking he had done.

First thing that morning, he and the examining magistrate had been summoned to the office of their chief. They had talked for half an hour without reaching any decisions. He had reported every fact he had turned up—something he didn't usually do—explaining his search for Lolo, his theories about her death, and the two Miss Carstairs, the real one and the impersonator. Explained that Graudin and several other sergeants would be going from door to door in Montparnasse again today with photographs of Lolo. Asking if anyone had seen her with another girl who could be her twin sister.

The old man had agreed that news of Lolo's murder should continue to be held back from the press as long as possible.

Damiot had joined Graudin and the others in their search through the side streets of Montparnasse, but left them early in the afternoon to pay another visit to Tristan Murzeau.

The producer, who once again was eating hot chicken soup, confessed that his plans, without Alex Scott, had come to a halt. The Arab money men had arrived and were installed at the Ritz, but they would make no final decisions about the film until another American star was signed. He had been negotiating with several Hollywood agents, who, unfortunately, knew he was desperate for a replacement. Murzeau stared at the photograph of Lolo with no sign of recognition and denied ever having heard her name. "Is she an actress?" he asked.

From Murzeau's office, Damiot drove to the Murzeau apartment, where Linette Murzeau denied knowing Lolo Yeung, shaking her head as she studied the photograph. She acknowledged, in response to Damiot's questions, that she did at times wear wigs. They were always blond because they were old wigs her mother had worn, years ago, when she was an actress in Vienna. She revealed that her lover, Dario Maurin, had departed for Italy because there would now be a delay getting *Paris Pursuit* into production, and even then, there was no guarantee that her father would give Maurin a part in the film. He'd told Murzeau that he'd signed to do a film in Rome. Which wasn't true. Actually, he was half Italian and had decided to fly there and visit his family while he tried to find another job.

Damiot had returned to his office late in the afternoon and placed the four dossiers on his desk. Spread them open, left to right, in the sequence of their deaths, starting with Montal and ending with the Vietnamese girl.

Victor Montal, Luc Darbois, Alex Scott, Lolo Yeung.

Was it possible that one person—using Miss Carstairs's name—had killed all four of them? Eliminated Lolo, hoping to make her death appear to be a suicide, so the police would think Lolo had murdered the other three.

Why had "Miss Carstairs" killed these three men? What was the connection?

A car salesman, a waiter in a luxury hotel, an American actor.

The motive for Lolo's murder was obvious. All the prostitutes in Montparnasse and Montmartre must know the police were looking for an Oriental whore known to carry a knife. Many of them must've heard that Lolo had been questioned. Perhaps Lolo had known the murderer of those men—the counterfeit Miss Carstairs—without realizing she was the killer. An easy matter for "Miss Carstairs" to return from the café with Lolo to her apartment. One lurch with the knife before Lolo realized what was happening. Unfortunately for "Miss Carstairs," she didn't know that the angle of the knife would show it was murder. She had planted that American money in Lolo's apartment and killed the pet bird before she left. The lab had found Lolo's prints on the handle of the knife, indicating that she must have pulled it from the wound as she died.

Now, staring at the rain hitting his window, he decided there was nothing more he could do here today. No point in making another tour of Montparnasse tonight.

Graudin and the other sergeants had phoned in after six, reporting that they had found no trace of "Miss Carstairs." He had told them to call it a day and get a good night's rest. Start out again tomorrow.

Maybe the weather would clear before morning.

He had to decide where they would eat tomorrow night, he and Andrea, select which cuisine they would enjoy next. Make phone calls.

What would Andrea be doing tonight? Would she be out in this rain? More likely she was eating dinner in that fancy apartment she was taking care of for those rich people who had gone to Mexico for the winter.

Mexico. Warm sunshine. He had never eaten Mexican food.

And once again, he thought of what Andrea had told him last night. Which story was true? That her father had killed her mother or that she had crashed the car purposely, and he had taken the blame?

He suspected both stories were lies.

Nothing had happened today! He was depressed, and he had a strong feeling that he might be getting pneumonia.

Which reminded him of Dr. Allanic. Should've called his wife this afternoon. Do that tomorrow.

He would have a quiet dinner at a restaurant in Place Dauphine, on his way to the hotel.

Let old Pierauld walk Fric-Frac tonight.

And he would get to bed early, after relaxing in a steaming tub for at least half an hour.

CHAPTER 26

THURSDAY MORNING THE RAIN WAS HEAVIER THAN IT HAD been on Wednesday.

The thirteenth day of rain!

Damiot hunched at his desk again, studying the four dossiers in the bleak circle of light from his desk lamp.

He compared the faces in the four photographs for the hundredth time. The smiling actor with his too perfect teeth, and the three pictures that had been taken by police photographers. Scott in brilliant color, the others in a bluish light that accentuated the fact that they were dead.

The three men had several things in common. All were in their middle thirties. Better than average looking. In fact, all three were handsome enough to be extremely attractive to any woman.

Checking through their dossiers once more, he mentally listed other characteristics they possessed in common. All three were tall, approximately the same height, with curly black hair. Their dossiers listed the fact that Montal had driven racing cars, Darbois played soccer, and Scott, of course, was an amateur boxer.

And all three had studied languages. Scott and Montal had contacted the École Suisse for their instructor—"Miss Carstairs" and Darbois had studied with a girl he had picked up in a café—also probably "Miss Carstairs."

Damiot's eyes blurred with fatigue as he reread the typed words.

He hadn't slept last night. Whenever he dozed off, he would have a nightmare from which he would surface abruptly. One was about Lolo. She had been desperately trying to catch an enormous white bird that had escaped from a cage, but its huge wings slashed at her face in an attempt to remain free. Her lovely face was covered with blood.

From time to time, as he went over the pages of the dossiers, his eyes began to close, and he would have Graudin bring more hot coffee.

Then back to checking every word again.

He didn't go out for lunch because the rain hadn't slackened.

But he did put the dossiers aside briefly to phone several restaurants and, after lengthy conversations, finally decided on where he would take Andrea tonight and discussed with le patron what they would have for dinner.

Before meeting Andrea at the Café de la Paix he would go to his hotel, relax in another hot tub, and change his clothes. He was looking forward to their evening together.

He would take a car because—after dinner and a visit to a nearby hotel with Andrea—he would have to join Graudin for another tour of Montparnasse.

Still nothing in any of the newspapers about Lolo's death, but they were certain to find out at any moment. Someone always talked.

Graudin was taking calls in the outer office, but there had been nothing of importance, because, whenever the bell rang, he didn't bother to put the call through. He knew when his superior didn't wish to be disturbed, but late in the afternoon he came in to report that Dr. Allanic had died.

This news further distressed Damiot. He had meant to call Madame Allanic for the past two days.

The old man's death was a personal loss. Dr. Allanic had been an important influence during his early days at the Préfecture.

Returning to the dossiers, he studied each page over and over, checking every word, hoping to find something that might reveal the identity of the killer. One fact that would complete the puzzle.

He found nothing. There were no loose ends to be cleared up. Nothing left to be done but locate "Miss Carstairs." This young woman with long black hair and sunglasses who had taught French to Alex Scott and English to Victor Montal. And had very likely taught English to Luc Darbois.

She had been seen twice. First with Scott, at Chez Pavy, and later at that café in Montparnasse, with Lolo.

"Miss Carstairs" had to be found!

As he sat there, frowning at the four photographs, he remembered something. One small fact he'd been told, at the start of the Scott case, information that had been filed away in his memory until this moment.

He stepped on the button under his desk, snatching up the phone.

"Yes, M'sieur l'Inspecteur?" Graudin responded.

"Come in here!" He slammed the phone down.

Two things for Graudin to do and one question that he must ask.

The door opened, and Graudin hurried in.

"Several things to be done!" Damiot rose and reached for his raincoat. "Number one. You go to the École Suisse. Tell them to write a note to Miss Carstairs, care of American Express, saying they have a new student for her, an American who wishes to study French, and asking her to get in touch with them immediately."

"Right."

"Number two. Take a note to American Express and stay there until they close, in case she shows up this afternoon." Slipping into his raincoat. "I'll put another man there tomorrow morning."

"Yes, M'sieur l'Inspecteur."

"We'll take 'Miss Carstairs' into custody when she comes to pick up her mail." Buttoning his coat and putting his hat on. "Should've done this before!"

"But that man at American Express said he hadn't seen her since last week!"

"Which means, unless she's been scared away, she'll be stopping in for her mail at any moment." He went toward the door. "I'll meet you here. Half an hour. We'll take separate cars."

"Where will you be?"

"I'm going back to see Miss Carstairs. The real Miss Carstairs! I've one more question to ask her."

CHAPTER 27

DAMIOT REALIZED THAT HE WAS FINALLY BEGINNING TO relax, seated across the table from Andrea, both drinking a vin blanc Cassis.

"This is a lovely restaurant," she whispered.

"One of my favorites."

"Why is it called Le Carnac?"

"The original owner came from the town of Carnac in Brittany." He kept his voice low, aware that she seemed more subdued than usual tonight. "When he died, his wife sold the restaurant to their chef, who was born in Quimper, also in Brittany, but he kept the name to honor the original owner. The Breton cuisine is unlike any of the others we've had."

"I've enjoyed them all!"

"I hope you'll enjoy tonight's dinner as much or perhaps even more. I've taken the liberty again to order ahead, so that the chef could prepare everything at his leisure." He studied her face as she glanced around the attractive restaurant. That intriguing gamine face he'd seen for the first time only last week. Tonight she was wearing a dress made from some rough-textured dark violet cloth, her straight golden hair hanging to her shoulders again. "You're smiling."

"I was thinking about our chef. He's so huge!"

"I'm afraid le patron enjoys his own cooking. He honored us tonight by greeting us at the door. Usually he leaves that to his daughter or son. They all eat well." Glancing at the plump woman behind the cashier's desk and the overweight young man supervising two waiters who were serving people at a distant table. "He won't appear again until after we've finished our dinner. Always shows up promptly to accept any compliments. I've ordered a glass of the house Muscadet with our first course and a bottle of champagne with the lobster."

"Champagne and lobster! What're we celebrating?"

"Celebrating?" He hesitated. Mustn't tell her he had solved the Scott murder. "Not really celebrating. Other than the fact we're together again. Happy to be here, in this warm and comfortable place, when around us Paris is flooding, and the radio said more rain tomorrow."

"I, too, am glad I'm here. Happy to be with you."

"Santé!" Raising his glass, saluting her, and drinking the last of his apéritif as their waiter brought two glasses of Muscadet.

Damiot's eyes darted from the open fire blazing in a rough stone fireplace to the row of white-shuttered windows under tangerine awnings along one wall. There were no windows behind those shutters, but they gave a pleasant effect of a terrace with large pots of artificial white and purple hortensia arranged against the walls. Dark beams across the ceiling and antique Breton cupboards on either side of the swinging kitchen doors. White cloths, purple napkins, and cutlery with ceramic handles. Candles lighted in old copper lanterns on every table, larger lanterns suspended from overhead beams. At least half the tables were occupied, and there was a delicious aroma of cooking—a symphony of scent he wouldn't attempt to analyze—floating from the kitchen whenever the doors swung open.

Their first course was a slice of pâté from an oblong terrine, which they spread on hot bread, lightly buttered, and ate with gusto as they drank the Muscadet.

"Again I must ask you." Andrea giggled. "What is it?"

"Pâté de ris de veau."

"Sweetbreads? Each pâté has been so different."

This was followed by succulent Belons, the color of pearl gray satin, served with a wedge of lemon. The oysters tasted as though they had just been taken from the ocean.

They finished their Muscadet with the last oyster.

Steaming soup, served from an enormous white china tureen, came next. A creamy soupe de poissons with crisp croutons.

Damiot could feel warmth spreading to his extremities. Hands and feet were no longer cold, for the first time today.

The champagne was opened for a homard grillé with beurre blanc à l'estragon. The combination of lobster, tarragon, and champagne was subtle perfection.

They ate, savoring each morsel, in complete silence. Unwilling to break this moment with conversation.

Damiot, in spite of himself, thought of his afternoon visit to Miss Carstairs. La vraie Mademoiselle Carstairs! He had asked his question, and she had given him an immediate and direct answer. Many pieces of the Scott puzzle had clicked into place instantly. They had talked for half an hour, he and Miss Carstairs, before he drove on to the American Express office to join Graudin out of sight behind the mail windows, where they waited for "Miss Carstairs" to ask for her mail. The note from École Suisse was in her box, but she hadn't shown up before the closing hour.

After a stop at the Préfecture to make a report to his chief—withholding several facts for the moment—he had gone to his hotel for a hot shower followed by a nap with Fric-Frac curled beside him. He would have overslept if Pierauld hadn't phoned from downstairs, as directed, at seven.

The Scott case would be finished with the arrest of the false Miss Carstairs.

He was exhilarated and relieved, but he mustn't show his mood or say anything about the end of the Scott case to Andrea.

Their main course was a gigot rôti aux haricots blancs, which their waiter presented, then divided the lamb and beans between two dinner plates. The meat was succulent, pink and tender, the white beans fragrant with herbs and garlic.

"This is the most delicious food I've ever eaten!" Andrea exclaimed. "Brittany wins over those other three. At least for the moment."

"It's the chef who wins. Each cuisine is excellent, but the degree of excellence depends entirely upon the chef, his mood at the moment. Which can be ruined by anything! His relationship with wife or mistress. Even the weather."

"The weather didn't bother our chef tonight."

Damiot laughed. "He's from Brittany! He probably likes this miserable weather."

"I've never tasted such lamb."

"How's your lamb in the United States?"

"Not as good as this. I had delicious lamb in London but was told it came from New Zealand. I've noticed in most Paris restaurants there's no music playing while you eat."

"Music?"

"From invisible speakers. Very soft."

"Good food deserves complete attention. Nothing to distract. I've heard there are restaurants on the Champs-Élysées where they have music all the time. Their food must be terrible! Of course, those are tourist spots."

"I like it much better without music."

After the lamb, avoiding the plateau de fromage, Damiot watched as the waiter served crêpes to Andrea. "Ordered this especially for you when I phoned. No dessert for me tonight."

"I'll be embarrassed, eating alone."

"Not when you taste those!" He watched her eat the thin brown crêpes with their sauce of golden raisins and mandarins sautéed in cognac.

She sighed. "Nothing frivial about this!"

"Bien!" He smiled, sipping black coffee, observing her enjoyment as she ate. She was in so many ways, this young woman, like a perverse child. Spoiled, petulant, unpredictable.

She sighed again when she finished the last morsel. "That was heaven! Utter heaven."

"What about a Calvados with your coffee?"

"Yes, please."

He ordered two apple brandies as the waiter poured Andrea's coffee.

"Which cuisine do you have planned for Thursday night?" she asked after the waiter went toward the bar. "Nothing could top this dinner. The most delicious I've ever eaten in my entire life!"

"My next selection will require much thought."

"Tomorrow I shall eat nothing all day. Remembering tonight. . . ."

They became silent again as they drank their coffee, observing some of the other diners and what they were eating, until the enormously fat chef appeared—as Damiot had predicted—to accept their compliments.

His many chins, pink from the heat of the kitchen, quivered when he bowed, beaming with pleasure at their words of praise.

"I shall never forget this dinner," Andrea whispered as le patron moved on to another table. "Or the other three we've had together."

"I, too, like to recall great meals I've eaten. Especially ones I had as a child. Dinners my father cooked for the family, for my mother and me. Some of those were the best I've ever eaten. Not as elaborate as tonight but, in every way, just as perfect."

"I'm in a much better mood than I was earlier, when we met at Café de la Paix." She reached across the white tablecloth and touched his hand. "It is very good, always, to be with you. We will make love again tonight?"

"I've reserved a room."

She smiled, eyes dancing.

"This time it's not around the corner, but a short drive."

"You can drive fast. There'll be no traffic in the rain." She pulled her hand back as the waiter returned with their brandies.

Damiot glanced at his watch, checking the time, before he picked up his glass and warmed the brandy between his hands. Graudin would be waiting.

"You haven't mentioned the Scott investigation tonight."

"Very little I can talk about." Raising his glass. "Santé!"

"Santé."

As they drank, he wondered what he could tell her.

"There's been very little in the newspapers."

"I know."

"I've been told when nothing's printed in the papers, it means the police have found new evidence they don't wish the public to know about. That they're working on something important."

"That's frequently true. There's one thing I suppose I could tell you."

"Yes?"

"Which hasn't yet been given to the press."

"I won't say a word to anyone!"

"That Vietnamese girl I mentioned the other night."

"Lolo? You said you hadn't been able to question her again."

"I never did. Unfortunately, she committed suicide."

"How terrible!"

"We were hoping to question her, but she was dead."

"What does this mean?"

He shrugged.

"You still think she killed Alex Scott? Is that why she took her own life?"

"I've already told you too much." He was aware of the disappointment clouding her eyes.

"Suicide is so terribly final. I suppose she did that as a confession of guilt. That she had killed Scott."

"We found evidence in her apartment that seems to confirm that."

"Poor Lolo." Raising her glass. "To Lolo!"

They drank silently.

"I suppose she met Scott somewhere and fell in love with him. The handsome American film star . . ." Staring at the brandy glass. "It's very sad. He must've rejected her, said he wouldn't see her any more, and she killed him."

"Something like that. Yes."

CHAPTER 28

THEY LEFT THE CAR AT THE CURB AND HURRIED THROUGH the cold rain, across the puddled sidewalk and up the steps to the entrance of the hotel.

Damiot, holding Andrea's arm, felt her body tense under the white plastic raincoat as they passed the small sign—Hôtel Amadeus—near the entrance. He pushed the door open, and walked beside her down the narrow passage to the registration desk, where the concierge pushed a key across the marble counter.

The old woman barely glanced at Andrea.

"Merci, Madame." Damiot snatched up the key and, still holding Andrea's arm, led her toward the winding steps, up to the next floor and down the hall to the remembered middle door.

She remained silent as he unlocked the door and swung it open.

The bedside lamp was lighted, but the corners of the depressing room were in shadow and the air was chilly.

Andrea entered first and walked slowly toward the old-fashioned wooden bed with its faded cover, without removing the white plastic hood from her head.

He closed the door, dropping the key into a pocket of his raincoat, noticing that the bathroom door was closed. He didn't move toward her but remained with his back to the hall door.

There was a long moment of silence before she faced him.

Damiot spoke first. "You've been in this room before."

"How long have you known?"

"Since this afternoon. I talked to Miss Carstairs."

"Who's she?"

"Friend of yours. I didn't think, the first time I saw her, to ask if she knew an American girl named Andrea Brandon. There was nothing to connect you."

She stiffened, clutching her gloved hands together. "Why did you ask this Miss Carstairs—whoever she is—if she knew me?"

"I'd already discovered, from their police dossiers, that Alex Scott, Victor Montal, and Luc Darbois had studied languages. Scott and Montal with a teacher they found through the École Suisse. And I learned, through the school, that they had recommended an Englishwoman—Miss Jenny Carstairs—who gave Montal private instruction at the school but went to Scott's hotel for his lessons. Luc Darbois picked up a woman in some café who taught him English. That was you, wasn't it, taught all three of them?"

"How can you say that! What does any of this have to do with me?"

"I realized your connection this afternoon, as I went through those dossiers again. Remembered that you had told me when we first met that you'd taught English lessons to make money."

"I don't remember saying anything like that!"

"And I knew you spoke French well enough to teach Alex Scott. Which made me wonder if you could be the 'Miss Carstairs' I'd learned about at École Suisse. The real Miss Carstairs says you lived in her apartment several times while she was away from Paris. Once when she was traveling in Spain as governess to some wealthy French family, and again while she was with an American family on the Riviera. That time she left her passport behind, in the apartment, which gave you an opportunity to have a counterfeit made. Why did you do that?"

She shrugged. "The passport was there. Seemed a good idea to have another identity ready, in case I should ever need it. I thought Jen Carstairs wouldn't find out."

"She never did. Until today."

"I didn't use that passport for more than a year. Then, when I was utterly broke, I applied at École Suisse for a job teaching either French or English."

"Wearing a long black wig and sunglasses."

"In case I ran into anyone who might recognize me. I even developed a British accent, as Jenny Carstairs. It was wonderful having another identity! I could do things I'd never have done as Andrea Brandon. Terrific things!"

"Such as murder?"

"I didn't plan to commit murder." She smiled, innocently.

"No?"

"Please believe me! Victor—he was the first—turned his back while he was getting dressed. I've always had a knife in my handbag, since I left home and went to New York. For my own protection. I never intended to kill anyone, but Victor rejected me. Said he wouldn't be able to see me again because his stupid wife was getting suspicious and asking questions. He told me to keep away from him. After taking me to all those wretched hotel rooms! I was furious when he turned his back. I opened my handbag and took out the knife. . . . It was the same with those others. Luc and Alex. Both of them told me they wouldn't be able to see me again. Luc said he couldn't afford me. He had a mistress—some dancer—and Alex said he'd be too busy, making some new film. He gave me a thousand dollars! Said he was sorry we had to stop meeting. He was nicer than the others, but they all rejected me. And I can't accept rejection anymore. My father was the first. Told me to get out! He didn't love me anymore. Didn't want me! Drove me out of my own home!"

"You have killed five people?"

She frowned. "Five?"

"Victor Montal, Luc Darbois, Alex Scott, and Lolo."

"You said five." She continued to smile but her eyes were sly. "That's only four."

"You told me yourself. You killed your mother."

"No! Walt killed her! I swear he did!"

"I will make a call, tomorrow, to the police of German Town in Pennsylvania."

"You'll never be able to prove I've killed anyone!"

"I know why you killed Lolo. I'd told you I was looking for an Oriental girl. From your description, wearing a long black wig and sunglasses, when you were at Chez Pavy with Scott, I suspected you were Oriental and the dark glasses were worn to disguise your eyes. You killed Lolo with the knife that killed

Scott, making it appear to be suicide, planted some of the money Scott gave you in her apartment, so I would think she'd killed him. The forensic lab quickly discovered Lolo wasn't a suicide."

She suddenly pressed her gloved fingers across her mouth as though to prevent herself from saying anything more.

"The lab found that those two other men—Montal and Darbois—were stabbed with the same knife that killed Lolo and Scott."

A muffled choking sound came from her throat.

"Why did you come to my table last week, that first night at the Café de la Paix?"

She lowered her hands from her mouth. "I'd always wanted to meet you—the famous Inspector Damiot. I told you, I'd been reading about you ever since I came to Paris. How you often ate dinner there and liked to sit on the terrace, winter and summer, at the end of the day. I'd been there many times at that hour, hoping to see you. I did see you, two or three times last summer, but didn't dare speak to you. Then, after Alex Scott was killed, I decided to go every night, until you showed up. I would introduce myself and we would talk. It intrigued me that we might see each other from time to time, speak to each other, while you were looking for Scott's killer. I had no idea you would invite me to have dinner with you."

"You wished to meet me because you wanted to be caught."

"Caught?"

"Most murderers do."

"But you're not going to turn me in? No, Guy! You wouldn't do that to me!" Her eyes widened with apprehension. "We're friends! Much more than friends. Aren't we?"

"I'm sorry, Mademoiselle. I am a policeman."

"You can't prove anything! I'll deny every word I've said. There were no fingerprints on the knife! Only Lolo's. I saw to that. I'm not stupid, you know. You can prove nothing without witnesses. And you have none!"

"All right, Graudin!" Damiot called.

Andrea peered from side to side. "Graudin? Who is Graudin? There's no one else here! Nobody!"

The bathroom door opened and Graudin, wearing hat and raincoat, stepped out of the darkness.

She gasped.

"You got everything she said?" Damiot asked.

"It's all on the tape." He went into the bath again.

Damiot turned toward the hall door. "Merval!"

The door swung open and Merval hurried in.

"Take her in your car."

Andrea screamed as Merval approached her. The sound was high and shrill.

Merval placed his gloved hand across her mouth as he propelled her toward the open door. She continued to scream, but the sound was muffled now.

Damiot's body sagged with relief and fatigue.

Graudin returned from the bath with a compact recording device.

"Go with them. I'll follow in my car."

"Yes, M'sieur l'Inspecteur." He grinned. "It's finished."

"Still many questions she must answer." He followed Graudin into the hall, closing the door.

Andrea's voice rose from the stairwell as Merval guided her down the curving steps.

A door opened and a man looked out but closed the door again.

Damiot scowled as Andrea continued to scream.

He remembered when he was a boy, in Provence, his father killing a rabbit for dinner. It had sounded like this. The same shrill sound of terror.

CHAPTER 29

FRIC-FRAC WAS SOAKED.

Damiot hurried, pulled by her tugging leash, along Quai des Orfèvres.

The rain was much heavier, and the Left Bank had disappeared again.

Looking up at the towering dark mass of the Préfecture, he wondered if Andrea was asleep.

Not likely.

The admittance routine had taken more than an hour, and he was weary. Mentally and physically.

He would certainly sleep tonight.

Andrea had been escorted to a cell by two guards. In her white plastic raincoat and hood she had looked small and childlike as they led her away.

Had they given her enough blankets to keep her warm tonight?

He felt sorry for her, alone in that small cell.

She had told him during one of their first dinners that she suffered from claustrophobia, and a prison cell was the ultimate enclosed space. Bars on door and window. Cold weight of walls and ceiling pressing in and down. The sensation must be horrible.

Whenever he caught a murderer, he regretted having to put him behind bars and avoided seeing him in his cell. Had him brought down to an interrogation room when he needed to question him.

He wondered if his idol, Vidocq, had felt compassion for his murderers.

Certainly Vidocq would've had sympathy for any attractive female! He had frequently slept with prostitutes.

Fric-Frac jerked on her leash, pulled him across the street, and started back, past the Préfecture, toward their hotel.

The psychiatrists would swarm around Andrea. Could they ever learn the true facts from her? She was certainly a habitual liar. That story about her mother's death. First her father had killed her, then it was Andrea who crashed the car. Possibly neither story was completely accurate. Or was the whole thing a fabrication?

He would learn the facts tomorrow, from the police in that German Town.

Andrea could probably hold her own with the psychiatrists. She was sly and devious. He had suspected several times during the past week that she was lying.

The psychiatric boys would say she killed Alex Scott and those other two men to get back at her father. Her revenge for being rejected by him and by them. She had, perhaps unconsciously, wanted to be caught because of what the publicity would do to her father.

He'd known other murderers like that.

There would be headlines in every paper, and the news would flash from radio and television. Even in German Town they would learn about what Andrea Brandon had done in Paris.

He hoped his name would be omitted from those stories. When he was younger he hadn't minded publicity, but now it was less enjoyable. Maybe because he was getting older.

Forty-six! In his forty-seventh year.

Mustn't think about that or he wouldn't sleep tonight!

He would play one of his Offenbach discs. That always relaxed him.

What if Andrea told those psychiatrists she had slept with him?

They wouldn't believe her.

Her responses to their questions would reveal that she'd been promiscuous for years but had no real emotional involvement with any man. Their tests would show that she was immature and neurotic. That she had slept with many men in a hopeless search for her father . . .

He had read of similar cases in psychiatric reports, which indicated that such women could never be satisfied with any one man.

He glanced up before they turned the corner, Fric-Frac straining on her leash, and saw a patch of dark blue flashing with stars. This unexpected glimpse of clear sky was like a revelation. Then, as he watched, clouds moved together and the vision was gone.

"All right, Madame la Duchesse. Home to bed."

She jerked on her leash, up rue de Harlay, pulling him along.

As he followed, hurrying again, he remembered what his wife had said during one of their quarrels. "You think more of your murderers than you do of me! They're your children."

Sophie was wrong. Murderers were not children. But she had been close to the truth about one thing. He had respected most of them. Enjoyed matching his brain against that of a murderer and winning the game of wits that ended with the criminal behind bars.

Once they were there, he lost interest.

It was the pursuit of the criminal he enjoyed, not the capture.

He thought of Andrea again, and hoped she was asleep.

The rain was heavier as he followed Fric-Frac across the edge of Place Dauphine. She was heading straight for the entrance of their hotel. "You're wet, Madame!"

She wagged her bedraggled black tail.

He would towel her dry when they got to their room.

Glancing up, between the bare branches of the chestnut trees, he saw that more black clouds were churning overhead.

He knew now that there was a clear sky behind them. Filled with stars.

Tomorrow, perhaps, the rain would stop. The sun would shine.

Paris would sparkle again.

About the Author

Vincent McConnor is the author of *The French Doll*, *The Provence Puzzle*, and *The Riviera Puzzle*. He lives in Los Angeles, but he has spent years in both New York and Paris.

Vincent McConnor is currently writing a new mystery.